"DAMN! I'M HIT. . . ."

No kidding, boss. You're leaking.

"Get a patch on, it, Bogie, and let's get out of here."

As the sentience within his battle armor edged over to his shoulder, Jack felt a gentle warmth begin to drive away the icy pain. . . .

Bogie settled gingerly over Jack's torn flesh. He was cold, always cold now, and the power reserves of Jack's armor no longer fed him the energy he needed. Blood welled up around him. He tasted life. He knew the flavor. It sang in him, gave him heat.

He knew that Jack was dying, even as he sensed that he himself had begun to live again, for the first time in long, cold months. It was the blood. It had to be.

Jack's pulse thundered in his senses. He could heal Jack somewhat, and he could carry the human to safety within the shell of the battle armor, if there was safety to be found anywhere on this planet.

Or he could touch life himself and grow, taking what Jack had to offer until there was no life force left for Jack to give. . . .

ALIEN SALUTE

BOOK FOUR OF THE SAND WARS
CHARLES INGRID

DAW BOOKS, INC.
DONALD A. WOLLHEIM, PUBLISHER

1633 Broadway, New York, NY 10019

First Printing, March 1989

1 2 3 4 5 6 7 8 9

PRINTED IN THE U.S.A.

Prologue

Where in the hell was their transport? What had happened to recall? Jack fought the maddening impulse to scratch inside his armor, as sweat dripped down, and the contacts attached to his bare torso itched impossibly. To scratch now, the way he was hooked up, he'd blow himself away.

Damn. Where was that signal? They couldn't have been forgotten, could they? If the pullout had happened, they would have been picked up . . . wouldn't they?

As sweat trickled down his forehead, he looked around.

Sand. They had been dropped in a vast sea-gulf of sand. Everywhere beige and brown and pink dunes rose and fell with a life of their own. This was what the Thraks did to a living world. And the Knights, in their suits of battle armor, trained and honed to fight a "Pure" war destroying only the enemy, not the environment, were all that stood between Milos and his own home world lined up next in a crescent of destruction that led all the way back to the heart of the Thrakian League.

So far, they'd been lucky here on Milos. Only one of the continents had gone under . . . still, it was one too many as far as the lieutenant was concerned. The Dominion Forces were losing the Sand

Wars. And he was losing his own private struggle with his faith in his superior officers. They'd been dropped into nowhere five days ago and had been given the most succinct of orders, gotten a pithy confirmation that morning and nothing since. Routine, he'd been told. Strictly a routine mop-up. You don't treat Knights that way—not the elite of the infantrymen, the fastest, smartest and most honorable fighters ever trained to wage war.

Jack moved inside the battle suit. The Flexalinks meshed imperceptibly and the holograph that played over him sent the message to the suit and, in turn, the right arm flexed. Only that flex, transmitted and stepped up, could have turned over an armored car. He sucked a dry lip in dismay over the reflex, then turned his face inside the helmet to read the display.

The display bathed his face plate in a rosy color and his eyesight flickered briefly to the rearview camera display, just to see which of the troops were ranged at his back. The compass wasn't lying to him. "Five clicks. Sarge, have they got us walking in circles?" His suit crest winked in the sun as he looked to his next in command.

"No, sir." Sarge made a husky noise at the back of his throat. Sarge wore the Ivanhoe crest—a noncommittal comment on what he thought of his lineage and his home world, but it made no difference to Storm. The men who joined the Knights came from every walk of life and the only criterion was whether a soldier was good enough to use a suit. If he was, and if he survived basic training, his past became a sealed record, if that was the way the man wanted it.

The sand made Jack thirsty. He waved his arm. "All right, everybody spread out. Advance in a line. If the Thraks are here, that'll flush 'em. Keep alert. Watch your rear displays and your flanks."

The com line crackled as Bilosky's voice came

over in sheer panic. "Red field! Lieutenant, I'm showing a fracking red field!"

Storm swiveled his head toward the sound, cursed at the obstruction of the face plate, and re-turned a fraction more slowly so that his cameras could follow the motion. "Check your gauges again, Bilosky. It's a malfunction. And calm down." The last in a deadly quiet.

Bilosky's panic stammered to a halt. "Yes, sir." Then, "Goddammit, Storm—those Milots have pilfered my suit! Every one of my gauges is screwed. I'm showing a red field because I'm running on empty!"

Storm bit his tongue. He chinned the emergency lever at the bottom of the face plate, shutting down the holograph field. Then he pulled his arm out of the sleeve quickly and thumbed the com line switches on his chest patch so that he could talk to Bilosky privately. Without power or any action to translate, his suit stumbled to a halt. The Flexalinks shone opalescent in the sun.

"How far can you get?"

Not listening, Bilosky swore again. "Goddamn Milots. Here I am fighting their fracking war for them, and they're pirating my supplies—I ought to—"

"Bilosky!"

"Yes, sir. I've got . . . oh, three clicks to go, maybe. Then I'm just another pile of junk standing on the sand." He turned to look at his superior officer, the black hawk crest rampant.

Storm considered the dilemma. He had his orders, and knew what his orders told him. Clean out Sector Five, and then stand by to get picked up. The last of Sector Five ranged in front of him. They could ration out the most important refills for Bilosky once they got where they were going. "We'll be picked up by then."

"Or the Thraks will have us picked out."

Storm didn't answer for a moment. He was asking a man with little or no power reserves showing on his gauges to go on into battle, in a suit, in full battle mode. Red didn't come up on the gauges until the suit was down to the last ten percent of its resources. That ten percent would carry him less than an hour in full attack mode. Not that it made any difference to a Knight. Jack sighed. "We're on a wild goose chase, Bilosky. You'll make it."

"Right, sir." A grim noise. "Better than having my suit crack open like an egg and havin' a berserker pop out. Right, Lieutenant?"

That sent a cold chill down Storm's back. He didn't like his troopers repeating ghoulish rumors. "Bilosky, I don't want rumors like that bandied around. You hear?"

"Yes, sir." Then, reluctantly, "It ain't no rumor, lieutenant. I saw it happen once."

"Forget it!"

"Yes, sir."

"Going back on open air. And watch your mouth." He watched as the other lumbered back into position. Then, abruptly, Jack dialed in his command line and watched as the miniscule screen lit up, his only link with the warship orbiting far overhead. The watch at the console, alerted by the static of their long-range comm lines, swung around. The navy blue uniform strained over his bullish, compact figure. He looked into the lens, his nostrils flaring. The squared chin was cleft and its line deepened in anger. A laser burn along one side of his hairline gave him a lopsided widow's peak.

"Commander Winton here. You're violating radio silence, soldier. What's the meaning of this? Identify yourself."

"I'm Battalion First Lieutenant," he said. "Where's

our pullout? We were dropped in here five days ago."

"You're under orders, lieutenant. Get in there and fight. Any further communication and I'll have you up for court martial."

"Court martial? Is that the best you can do? We're dying down here, commander. And we're dying all alone."

The line and screen went dead with a hiss. Suddenly aware of his own vulnerability, Storm pushed his right arm back into his sleeve and chinned the field switch back on. His suit made an awkward swagger, then settled into a distance eating stride. Fighting wars would be a hell of a lot easier if you could be sure who the enemy was.

Bilosky and Sarge and who knows who else were talking about berserkers now. The unease it filled him with he could do without. He squinted through the tinted face plate at the alien sun. Strange worlds, strange people, and even stranger enemies. Right now he'd rather wade through a nest of Thraks then try to find his way through the rumors surrounding the Milots and their berserkers.

There was no denying the rumors though. The Milots, who had summoned Dominion forces to fight for them against the Thraks—those same low-tech Milots who ran the repair centers and provided the war backup—were as despicable and treacherous as the Thraks whom Storm had enlisted to wipe out. And there were too many stories about altered suits . . . suits that swallowed a man up and spawned instead some kind of lizard-beastman who was a fighting automaton, a berserker. Rumor had it the Milots were putting eggs into the suits, and the heat and sweat of the suit wearer hatched those eggs and then the parasitic creature devoured its host and burst *forth*—

He told himself that the Milots had a strange

sense of humor. What Bilosky thought he'd seen, whatever every trooper who repeated the gossip thought they were talking about, was probably a prank played at a local tavern. Knights always took a certain amount of ribbing from the locals, until they were seen in action, waging the "Pure" war.

Ahead of him, the dunes wavered, sending up a spray of sand. His intercom burst into sound.

"Thraks at two o'clock, lieutenant!"

Storm set his mouth in a grim smile. Now here was an enemy he could deal with. He eyed his gauges to make sure all his systems were ready, and swung about.

Thraks were insects, in the same way jackals were primates or ordinary sow bugs were crustaceans. They were equally at home upright or on all fours, due to the sloping of their backs. Jack took his stand and watched them boil up out of the sand from underground nests and launch themselves in a four-footed wave until they got close enough to stand up and take fire. Thraks were vicious and dedicated to a single purpose . . . at least, fighting Thraks were. Diplomatic Thraks, so he had heard, were as vicious in a far more insidious way.

He cocked his finger, setting off a burst of fire from his glove weapons that slowed the wave. The line of Thraks wavered and swung away, even as they stood up and slung their rifles around from their backs.

On Milot, they had the slight advantage, having gotten there first and having begun their despicable planet transforming. Even a slight advantage to the Thraks was disastrous to the Dominion. Milot was already as good as lost. Battalions had been wiped out, forced into the deserts, to make as graceful a retreat as possible. Inflict as many casualties as they could, then pull out. Jack's job, as he understood it, was to make the toll of taking Milos so heavy, so dear, that the Thraks would stop here.

Storm's grim smile never wavered, even as he strode forward, spewing death as he went, watching the gauge detailing how much power he had left. Bodies crunched under his armored boots.

They were mopping up. They were to distract the Thraks and the enemy cannon long enough to let most of the troop ships—almost all of them cold-ships—pull out, and then they would be picked up. That was the promise. . . .

He strides through the line, knowing the wings of his men will follow, and seeing that the front is not a front, but an unending wave of Thraks. What was reported as a minor outpost is a major staging area, and he's trapped in it, wading through broken bodies and seared flesh. He sweeps both gloves into action, firing as he walks, using the power boost to vault walls of fallen bodies and equipment.

Somewhere along the way, Bilosky lets out a cry and grinds to a halt, out of power. He screams as his suit is slit open with a diamond cutter and the Thraks pull him out. Jack ignores the screams and plows onward. He has no choice now. The pullout site is ahead of him. He has to go through the Thraks if he wants to be rescued. Ahead of him is the dream of cold sleep and the journey home. The dream. . . .

He lives long enough to fall into a pit, a pit ringed by Thraks, surrounded by what is left of his troop, and by stragglers from other battalions. They stand back to back for days, firing only when absolutely necessary, watching the unending waves of Thraks above them. And he sees a suit burst open, days after its wearer expired with a horrendous scream and the armor halted like a useless statue in the pit. He sees the seams pop and an incredible beast plow out, and charge the rim of the pit, taking fully a hundred armed Thraks with it, even as it bellows, striking fear in those beyond its reach. He knows he is dreaming that he has seen a berserker, and tries to ignore the empty shell-like suit with the crest of Ivanhoe left behind in shards and settling into the sand.

Even as he stands and fires, he thinks of what it is he wants to dream. He wants to dream getting out of there alive, with his men. That is what he wants most. Then he wants to be able to scratch. And he thinks he hears something inside the suit with him, something whispering at his shoulder, and he knows he's losing it. Aunt Min back home always said that when the Devil wanted you, he began by whispering to you over your shoulder. Storm is scared to turn around. All he wants to do is find his dream of going home. And when the recall comes, he doesn't know if he's hearing what he's hearing or not . . . or if he can even be found behind the wall of Thraks.

And then he realizes he is cold sleep dreaming, on an endless loop, dreaming without beginning or end until someone finds and awakens him.

But that was then. This is now. . . .

Chapter 1

The aged freighter hardly qualified as a transport ship, let alone a cold ship, but none of the nearly five hundred people crowded into it complained. They stood and shivered and talked quietly to each other in knotted groups, looking pale and shaken as they waited for processing.

Only one man had an expression of triumph seized out of the jaws of the defeat that had forced them into exodus. Tall, made massive by his opalescent battle armor, he looked the crowd over now, and his eyes flashed with eagerness even as he assessed the results of the evacuation.

"What if the emperor offers you the command?"

He made a noise of anger. "Kavin's hardly cold in the ground."

The woman with the questioning, gentle brown eyes remained composed under the wash of his anger, tilting her head slightly to one side as though to veer away from it. "But we have to consider it, don't we?" She kept her hand on the Flexalink sleeve he supported her with. Beneath her fingers, she felt the smoke and grime of battle, and her delicate nose still scented blood faintly though most of it had been washed away. They'd both witnessed the violent death of his commanding officer and friend. They stood intimately close in the immense hold of the transport ship that vibrated loudly under their feet. "And I need to talk to you . . . I need time to tell you what happened."

The man's helmet was off, hanging from an equipment hook at his waist. Sweat darkened his sandy blond hair and fatigue washed out his blue eyes. Even with his strong cheekbones, he was plain-faced, ordinary, but there was something commanding in his features. Tiny lines were etched at the corners of his eyes and into his forehead, for all he appeared at the prime of his twenties. His avid gaze deflected from his field command to her, and softened as he took her in. The reflection of her image in his eyes was as intimate as an embrace. "You don't owe me an explanation. I just thank god you came back."

A shiver swept over her, setting off the intricate blue patterning of the tattoos that covered her— that made her alien from her lover. These tattoos were only a small portion of what she had suffered when the religious wars had swept across Bythia and forced the Dominion settlers to flee. But she knew Jack was most concerned about facing Emperor Pepys. "You've got two months of chill time to think about it," Amber returned. "You'd better have an answer for the emperor by the time we get home."

"If he offers it to me, I'll think about it."

"Not good enough," she said, and streetwise savvy edged her tones. They were among the last of the evacuees to be processed. "You have to accept, if Pepys asks you. You're the only one left who knows how to fight a "Pure" war. Anyone can wear a suit— "

He looked down at her and his mouth twitched.

"—well, not anyone, but no one understands the warfare the way you do."

"I know," he said then, heavily.

The freighter seemed to groan around them as it picked up acceleration speed. It would take days to hit warp speed, weeks in transit, and then days of deceleration. Those days would pass as if in a dream to the vast bulk of its passengers.

Amber pressed her fingers into his armor. "And then we can talk."

Storm shifted his weight uneasily. He did not like the prospect of cold sleep, never had, never would. A nurse came by, still in sterile greens, and Jack stepped out to block his passage.

"I don't want any of these people on a debriefing loop."

The nurse came to a startled halt. His face was narrow and his chin pointed, giving him a feral look. "We take our orders from Emperor Pepys—"

"Not now you don't. I don't want any of those evacuees stressed out. They won't forget what happened." He felt Amber shudder at his side. As if any of them could forget the bloody civil uprising out of which they were being emergency lifted, compounded by the ever-present, ever-dangerous Thraks and the rumors of war.

The nurse sniffed. "Of course, commander." He hurried past then, skirting around the battle-armored man with caution.

Jack smiled. Too tired to do so, he couldn't hold it, and the expression faded rapidly from his face.

Amber relaxed a little. "Thanks, Jack," she said softly.

"Not just for you. I don't trust the debriefing loops." He looked out over the hold as another small group of evacuees pressed forward into the medical bay. Far ahead of them stood St. Colin of the Blue Wheel, watched over by his lumbering bodyguard and aide, Jonathan. The Walker prelate leaned on a cane, injured but hearty nonetheless. Fine gray and chestnut hairs strayed across a balding head, but his chin was square and his massive hands gestured as he talked to the group surrounding him. His preaching voice reached Jack. The man in battle armor shifted his weight, temporarily warmed by what Colin was saying. Nearby stood young Denaro, also a Walker, but looking sullen in his uniform, weapon belts crisscrossed over his chest, his militancy a kind of insult to his affiliation. Storm frowned as he watched Denaro a second longer. The Walker ministry had suffered a profound loss on Bythia. Denaro did not look as if he would tolerate it for long.

Amber must have sensed his thoughts. Her chin pointed in the militant's direction. "I hope Colin keeps an eye on that one."

"He'll have to," Jack answered. "I've done all I can. I've got the Thraks to worry about now." He'd escorted a wave of humanity aboard the shuttles to the transport. The Thrakian warship orbiting Bythian space was momentarily distracted by the necessity of getting its own personnel off-planet. He had time, but only a little, and he didn't like seeing it wasted. The column shuffled forward. He and Amber were at the rear and would be last. "Amber . . ." and he hesitated, because what he said next the young woman would not want to hear, and he knew it. "I don't intend to be chilled down."

She pulled back. "I have to go alone?"

"Yes."

"I don't—"

"You have to. Just as I have to stay up and alert."

Amber looked up at him. Her chin jutted defiantly, and then her jawline softened. "You don't think the Thraks will let us go?"

"Not if they don't have to. This transport is a

load of potential hostages. Colin, my command, almost everyone on here is of value to the League."

"It would be worth even more if you could have gotten that bushskimmer out alive."

Jack had no answer for that. He'd lost a valuable witness in the Sassinal riots, a man who could testify to the firestorming of Claron. But that was over now. At least he'd heard the testimony . . . words he'd never forget. He looked down at Amber. "It's over," he said.

She nodded. She grabbed up his gauntleted hand and held it tightly and even though he wore battle armor, he could almost feel the chill of her grasp through it. "What if they insist on cold sleep?"

Her question suggested that she knew instinctively what also worried him: the transport pilot was in command here now and not Jack. He shrugged. "It'll take a lot more men than Harkness has got to hold me down."

Now she knew why he hadn't removed his armor once they'd boarded.

Amber laughed briefly. "I hope I'm awake when they try."

"You run a sloppy ship."

The pilot twisted his head to peer at the tall man . . . seeming even taller now that he stood in the bulkhead framing. Sandy blond hair swept back from his brow and his faded eyes reflected disapproval. The ship shuddered with the vibration of engines thrusting the vehicle nearer and nearer warp velocity. Harkness grumped and slumped lower in his chair. "And if I do, it's my business," he said.

Around the chipped and battered plastic table, the navigator and enginoor got up quickly and left. They did not look the intruder in the face as he moved to let them shrug past the bulkhead.

Harkness' voice sounded thick and lumpy as if it

needed to be strained through a filter before issuing out of his mouth. He pointed at the interloper. "I'll chart no interference from you," he said. "Or you'll be chilled down yet and shipped like the rest of the stiffs. This is a cold ship transport and don't you forget it."

The intruder had eased a wide shoulder against the bulkhead. He smiled pleasantly. "You've already tried it once," he said. "You have other worries. We slipped out of Bythian space easily enough, but you're a sitting target coming out of decel, and there's a good chance the Thraks will be waiting for us. There's a war on now."

Harkness' eyes narrowed. He reached for his bag of whiskey and poured a level glassful. "I took out a contract to lift a shipload of evacuees and return 'em to Malthen. I did not take out a contract to listen to your mouth."

The man's smile did not vanish, but neither did it warm his clear blue eyes. "Not yet," he said. "But you will." The man lifted his shoulder, shifted his weight, and removed himself gracefully from Harkness' vision.

The pilot scowled before lifting his drink. Too full, it washed over his fingers before he got it to his mouth. With a curse at his shaking hand, he slogged the whiskey down.

Jack walked the cryogenic bays where his friends and fellow soldiers lay asleep yet not asleep, their pale bodies seemingly devoid of life under sterile white sheets. He stopped at the plastic shield of a privacy crèche and paused to look inside at Amber, lying there, her dark honey colored hair a-tumble about her face. The sheet covered her from ankle to neck, but it could not hide her beauty which was all the more exotic for the bizarre tattooing. She'd said she wanted it removed the minute she got to Malthen, if it could be done. Jack looked at the dialysis shunt in her ankle, preparatory to the stage when she would one day be awakened and, unable to help himself, he shuddered before looking away.

Only Amber knew if he was a really a hero or a coward for refusing to be chilled down with the rest of them.

He paused now and spread his hand out over the plastic shield as though he could touch her face and share her dreams with her. It had been another battle to keep psychological debriefing loops from being hooked up to her cold sleep dreams, but he'd won that one, too. The human mind should have some dignity in cold sleep, even if the body did not. He looked at his four-fingered hand, at the scar where the little finger had been sheared off. It had been amputated, a victim of frostbite from a cold sleep occupied too long. Seventeen years too long.

Two months of real time was not too much to be added to his years, Jack thought. He'd endure it, waiting for the end of the voyage and the beginning of the war, his war, with the Thrakian League. Endure it, hell, he'd welcome it.

His emperor, the traitor, was another matter.

Jack dropped his hand from the shielding, took a deep breath, and continued his journey through the frigid hold, not pausing to look at his men who lay like fallen soldiers. He did not stop until he reached the gym where he stripped off his shirt and began to exercise, chasing his thoughts like demons from his mind.

The gym was ill-used, but that hadn't surprised Jack after a look at Harkness' crew. The surprise was that the transport even carried a gym. He winced a little as he flexed. Deep, purpling bruises still covered his torso. He'd be healed by the time they pulled out of hyperdrive and began to decel though . . . one valid reason for not being chilled down.

His peculiar susceptibility to cold sleep fever was another.

The action on Bythia had not injured him badly, but it had cost him the life of his commander and friend. Jack would be long in forgetting Kavin. Besides their friendship, the two had shared the common background of being battle armor Knights, infantry soldiers who were mobile tanks, fighting ground warfare designed to annihilate the enemy and not the planet they fought upon. Virtually no one beyond the two of them was now trained in "Pure" warfare, although the art of wearing battle armor had recently been recommissioned by Emperor Pepys. Now Jack stood alone.

He would have to find a way to carry on.

Sweat tickled its way down his skin. He counted off his sets mercilessly, whipping his body back into shape, until he was too exhausted to move.

Jack woke, groggily, on his back on one of the exercise mats, his face still clammy with sweat. Jack looked up, his neck stiff and cramped, and stretched. Over him stood a white suit of battle armor, opalescent Flexalinks muted by the dimmed lights of a ship in downtime. The deadly gauntlet, powerful enough to crush his skull, each finger the firing barrel of a destructive weapon, was poised, curving over him as though in benediction.

Jack smiled, grasped the gauntlet and got to his feet.

Hi, boss.

"Hello, Bogie. Feeling better?"

The regenerating being that now occupied his battle armor paused. *I'm cold.*

Jack bent over to loosen the muscles in his legs preparatory to finding the refresher and cleaning up. He craned his neck to look back. "It's standard temp in here, buddy."

He returned to his standing position and frowned. He knew little about the creature in his armor except that it was as fierce in fighting nature as a Milot berserker, but hadn't, thank god, the cannibalistic, parasitic tendencies of the giant saurians. Jack had not been sure about that at first, and had been haunted by the growing sentience of his battle armor.

More than microscopic, regenerating out of a square of leather that ought to have been dead tissue, Bogie had been implanted in his suit on Milos during the Sand Wars, twenty-five years ago. It was hot in a suit. Jack had welcomed the adaptation by his Milot repair technician. The circuitry and gear inside occasionally poked and prodded at his back, and the weight of a field pack with a small-muzzle laser cannon could dig holes in his flesh. Many of the Knights hung a leather chamois. It had been the death of a lot of them. Their body heat and sweat could nurture a berserker into parasitic life. By the time a Knight knew what was happening, he was a consumed man, trapped inside his suit of armor like it was a meat locker.

Jack looked at his own suit of battle armor.

Bogie had a small towel draped across his left wrist. Jack took it and mopped his face, wondering briefly where the Milots had gotten the leather chamois they used for his infestation, thinking that they were implanting a berserker and giving him Bogie instead. He tossed the towel in the corner.

Unlike a Milot berserker, Bogie had soul. In fact, his mind and soul were forming far more quickly than his physical being. The chamois hanging inside the armor showed little change from when it had originally been placed there. It was a little thicker. If Jack held it between his fingers, he could sense a pulsing life. Bogie was like an embryo and neither

he nor the sentience knew what it was he had to
have to finish regeneration. Berserkers ate their
way through blood and flesh. Though there was no
denying that Jack's presence in the suit vitalized
Bogie, neither knew how. Because of that, and Bogie's hardwired-like psychic hookup with the suit
circuitry itself, he had not removed and incubated
the chamois. He feared killing the creature that
way.

From a liability, Bogie had become an asset. From
a parasite, he had evolved into a companion. Jack
didn't like the armor's coldness and considered the
fragility of life that was Bogie's present state. The
only way he knew to warm the suit was to wear it.
He looked about the massive ceiling of the gym. It
had once been part of the freight hold, he decided.
He had room.

"How about we suit up and go through some
basic exercises?"

I would like that.

Jack unsealed the seams and got in. He spent
some time clipping leads to his bare torso before
settling in and then sealing himself up.

The holo came up, a soft-tinted rosy glow that
read his muscular movement and relayed it to the
suit, through a step-up transformer. A blow meant
to swat a butterfly could conceivably crush a small
mammal. Such was the power of a man once inside
a suit.

There was more now. Jack felt the immediate
enveloping embrace of Bogie, close and intimate,
like a lover.

Only this being was born to fight, Jack knew. Just
as he had been sworn to.

Jack smiled tightly to himself as he finished suiting up. "Okay, Bogie. Let's pretend we're killing
Thraks."

Kick ass, boss, the armor responded.

He began to drill.

Neither man nor machine saw the twilight wrapped shadow that watched from the far recesses of the hold as, with a muffled burp, Harkness reeled out of sight and lumbered back down the corridors of his command.

The navigator frowned at his blipping screen. "I don't like it," he complained to his employer.

Harness hawked and swallowed it down. "Quit whining," he said. "What do you want me to do, pull out of hyperspace and make a fracking coordinate change? We might end up inside solid rock."

Alij stabbed a pointed nail at his screen. "Sir, we might anyway. Something's happening out there, and I don't like it."

The pilot straightened. He scrubbed a hand over his patchy head of grizzled hair. The slim brown navigator glared at him. That arrogant Dominion Knight son of a bitch had warned him it would come to this. The pilot shrugged. He reached for the com system and thumbed it onto page. "Captain Storm, your presence is requested on the bridge."

Alij sat back in his chair and hid his startled expression in the glow of his screen, but he was the first to jump in eagerness when the bridge doors *schussed* open minutes later to admit the soldier.

The was not a man in Harkness' crew who hadn't at one time or another spied on the Dominion Knight, particularly if he could be found drilling in the gym. Most of the Knights aboard had had their equipment destroyed before retreating. The crewmen had a morbid fascination in watching the battle armor at work after having faced it themselves when they'd tried to subdue Storm. It was a killing machine, no doubt about it. Now, Alij watched warily as the man entered the bridge.

"Problem, pilot?"

Harkness growled in this throat again, then said, "My navigator says he's getting feedback through his hyperspace readings. Any idea what could be going on?"

Jack looked at the pilot. He knew the grudging expression for what it was. Capitulation, fueled by worry. He looked to the navigator. "When are we due to pull out and decel?"

"Beginning of next watch. Say, twelve hours. We're two weeks out of Malthen, putting on the brakes all the way."

"Close." Without edging the pilot out of the way, Jack squeezed in as close as he could to the instrumentation board. He was no pilot. His skill was warfare, specifically, the infantry. But Harkness was a transport pilot, a man used to handling freight and the occasional cold ship. Jack could not read what he saw on the screen either, but he didn't like it.

He wondered if the Thraks could be waiting for them at the edge, having calculated their most likely reentry point from hyperspace. The Thraks knew they'd been at Bythia—hell, that was the incident that had started the war six weeks ago. It would take about that long to begin mustering forces.

Harkness' cold ship would be priceless to them because of its cargo locked in cold sleep. Jack frowned. He looked at Harkness and the copilot swiveled in his chair. To the copilot he said, "Bring up the subspace bulletin board."

"Sir, we haven't got time to put out a call and receive an answer—"

"I know, officer. I'm looking for bulletins, not placing a call."

"What?" Harkness practically gargled in his sputtering rage.

Jack ignored him until the monitor scrolled up the info he wanted. "There!"

The copilot froze the screen.

Some subspace ham had spread the word the best way he knew how, and Jack's face tightened in appreciation. He had no way of knowing yet if Thraks had attacked anywhere, but here at least were corridor coordinates of the latest warship placements. "Navigator—"

"Alij, sir."

"Order up a graphics overlay. I'll bet my armor you've got Thraks sitting there, waiting for us."

Alij moved to the computer and made his verbal requests.

"Damn." Harkness smacked a beefy fist on the back of his chair. The bridge quivered in response. "Any chance of collision?"

Jack said, "I doubt it, but they'll be firing as soon as they can track us."

"They'll never catch up with us."

"They won't need to. They'll catch you turning the corner for braking, and trap us on the right angle, during the vector changeover."

Harkness' expression flickered. Grudgingly, he said, "Thought you weren't a pilot."

"I'm not. But I've fought Thraks before and I know how they can attack vessels."

The pilot said nothing. He looked to Alij as the computer began to show graphic overlays of corridors and windows. Alij, without knowing what he was doing, began to nod vigorously as Jack's suspicions were confirmed. "Yes . . . yes . . . here they are . . . yes . . ."

The pilot squeezed his bulky body upward into a firm stance. He nodded at Jack. "Thank you, captain."

"You're welcome, Harkness. We're not out of this yet. A transport vehicle like this is most vulnerable when it pulls out of hyperspace and turns that corner to begin braking . . . and it's my bet the Thraks aren't going to blow us out of the sky."

"No?" A bushy eyebrow went up.

"No. I'm afraid what they'll have in mind this time is taking prisoners."

The copilot broke the silence with a hoarse whisper. "We'd be better off dead."

Chapter 2

"Giving up already, Leoni?" Harkness growled.

"No, sir." The sallow-faced man straightened hunched shoulders. "Have you ever seen a sand planet, sir? After the Thraks have come in and taken over?"

Jack stood quietly, listening to the exchange. He was very careful not to let emotion flicker across his face.

Harkness shook his head.

"Well, I have. About ten years ago. The crew I was on had to bring in a load of supplies under treaty. Not that the bugs need much on a sand planet, but trade is trade, right?" His brown eyes blinked guiltily. His employer did not respond. Leoni plunged ahead. "It's eerie. My guess is the planets don't survive long, with the whole ecosystem shot like that . . . the oceans are there, but most of the vegetation is gone. It's been eaten down into these coarse granules, beige and rust colored. I held some in my bare hand. It felt like bugs were in it, squirming around. My skin stung for weeks. The Thraks lay their eggs in the stuff, and the larvae eat the sand, sort of. I remember looking at it and thinking, this used to be grassland, once. Or maybe a forest or someone's farm. No more."

Leoni looked around the control room. "I could stand there. I could still breathe the air even though it had thinned out some. But I wouldn't want to live there. It's my idea of hell."

"You were lucky," Alij said. "I heard about a trader run that stayed—the bodies of its crew added to the supply list."

"That's an old story," Harkness countered. "I've never heard proof of it."

"What proof would there be? We know from the Sand Wars that the Thraks have little use for prisoners. Even if they wanted us, we wouldn't be kept in very good shape."

"Then we need to make sure it won't go that far."

Jack let his breath out slowly. He felt their gazes upon him. He looked about the control room. Harkness cleared his throat.

"What are you going to do?"

He took it in before responding, "What kind of weaponry do you have?"

"Four guns, two mounted on each fin aft. Not much."

"Is the firing circuitry mounted on a single board, or do you have to have a man at each gun?"

"They're tied in."

"That helps. Anything else? Mines?"

"No. My reputation is my best defense. Everybody knows I don't carry much of any worth," Harkness said.

"And this ship maneuvers like a garbage scow." Jack saw the pilot wince, but did not apologize. He looked over Alij's shoulder to the computer screen where the graphics overlay brilliantly detailed the window of their exit and the likely placement of the Thrakian warship waiting for them. "We have some time," he said. "I need to think." With that, he left a stunned silence behind him on the bridge.

*   *   *

He sought the gym and Bogie. The battle armor hung on its rack, quiet and yet deadly. Jack approached it and sat down cross-legged in front of it.

The battle which the transport crew and the Thraks were about to engage in was not in his line of expertise. He knew that and surely Harkness' crew comprehended it—but perhaps not. He fought on the surface, a man-shaped mobilized tank, a machine meant to slog through the lines of the enemy. He was, in so many words, a weeder.

The thought creased into a smile. Some weeds were tougher than others to pull.

He stood up and went to the suit. He needed to think and there was only way he could do it without interruption. Bogie blossomed open to him and, after kicking off his boots and stripping off his jacket, he stepped in. Inside, he kept himself occupied cliping leads to his torso and taking care of the other details of suiting up. He tried to ignore the chamois at his back as it settled about this shoulders like some bat-winged creature. He closed the seams and snugged the helmet on with a half-twist to seal it. The world immediately became muffled. Isolated. Refined to the visor and the target grid.

"Bogie," Jack said. "I need to remember."

The sense of welcoming surrounding him pulled back in surprise. Then, *Jack, do you not remember on your own?*

How could he explain what had been done to him in the name of the Dominion? The seventeen years he'd lain in cryogenic sleep, adrift on a lost transport, his mind locked into a military debriefing loop. Those years had stripped away most of his memory of his youth and his beginnings just as the Thraks had physically stripped away his family when they'd attacked Dorman's Stand and reduced it to a sand planet. The corner of Jack's mouth twisted bitterly.

Nor had he been well-treated when found. There had been ugly hints that perhaps his mind had undergone indoctrination when being brought out of cold sleep and treated for the side effects those seventeen years had wrought.

Jack had one recourse left to capture those years— Bogie. He had no way of knowing for sure if the creature had been alive enough while first incubated on Milos to absorb any of Jack's conscious or subconscious memories, but while on Bythia, there had been some indications of Bogie's ability to do so. It was Jack's only way to regain what being a soldier for the Dominion had stolen away from him.

He could feel the warm and comforting presence of the chamois across his shoulders and back, almost as though a fatherly figure had put an arm around him.

"Bogie," Jack said quietly. "Your memory is all I have left of Milos and before. If you can remember, if you can give it to me so that I can remember, then. . . ."

Then what?

"I'm not sure. Then I'll know why I fight. Why I hate. Why Amber is in danger just being a part of me. But today I have to remember all of what I know about how Thraks fight. I remember most of it . . . but it's overshadowed by the Milots and their damn berserkers." Jack plunged to a halt. "Dammit, I'm not a computer. I don't have access to old files."

Neither am I. I . . . cannot do what you wish of me.

"Bogie, you remember, I know you do—you kept me going on Bythia, and what you remember may be piecemeal but it's better than nothing! It's mine. *Give it back to me!*"

I have no control. I don't understand things well enough yet. I'm still new, Jack.

Jack stood inside his armor and suddenly felt alien to this piece of equipment that had been his second skin for as long as he could remember. *Could remember,* dammit, that was the problem. He stretched and felt the Flexalinks move with him. Because he had no solace other than in movement, he fell into a drill routine.

The armor moved with him supply, far more gracefully than most would suspect looking at its rigid links, but that was part of its effectiveness. The rest depended a great deal on the man wearing it, for the structure took care and maintenance and a man was only as good as his mechanical ability in the field.

Bogie said suddenly, in his undervoice which sounded like rocks tumbling over one another in a deep-running stream, *I can give you this.*

Jack had hit the power vault before hearing Bogie, and as the memory hit him, he doubled over and the suit slammed into the hold flooring, but Jack barely felt it, for he was burning inside his mind.

Fire swept across a verdant world. Peace and healing disrupted in the middle of the night. The skies vibrated as warships came down, and their weapons struck. A firestorm sweeping across Claron, charring all in its path—his breath caught in his throat. Fear again. The suit, his escape, his tumbling in freefall in deep space without hope of ever being caught . . . the horror of knowing this memory came courtesy of, not the Thraks, but warring factions within the Dominion itself where he should have had no enemy.

"Bogie!"
Jack.

"Stop it," Jack ground out, his body curled tightly in pain, his temples throbbing, his gut sucked to his backbone in the nauseating panic of endless freefall.

As abruptly, the memory left.

Jack caught his breath first. Sweat dripped off his forehead. He had no idea the memories he'd asked for would be vivid recreations of what he had gone through. Before he could say anything else, Bogie said, *Perhaps this will be better.*

He was swept away again. . . .

Dust motes swirled in the air, and he sneezed as he leaned over a row of greens, the sound of the automatic harvester droning in the background. The sky was the color of his mother's eyes, brilliant yet everchanging blue, even to the clouds which wisped across. The dirt gave up the smell of growing things, leafy greens hybridized from what had been collard greens on old Earth, Home World, but which Jack was just used to seeing heaped up in his mother's crockery, steaming under butter as greens. He liked them well enough. They were a staple product of his parents' farm. Jack preferred the orchard though he could not climb in any of the trees except for the windbreaks.

He pinched at a leaf now, examining the underside critically for sign of mites or fungus, frowning in an expression which he knew imitated that of his father. His father stood far away at the fields' end, carrying his keypad in the crook of his arm, varying the harvesting pattern of his machinery as he worked.

Jack stood up. He looked down the row of growth and saw, almost beyond his eyeshot, a nest resting under wavering, wilting leaves. The harvester loomed beyond, darkening the horizon with its presence.

He moved so quickly he almost lost his cap. His brother's cap, too, and not only would he catch hell for wearing it, he'd catch double hell for losing it, he thought as he bolted forward. He pitched forward, scampering down the irrigation trough, even as the nesting bird dove past his face, wings fluttering and beating at his eyes. Jack ducked away and tugged his hat on tighter.

He stopped a few meters from the nest and stood, his chest heaving from the run. His shirt clung wetly to his back. Dust swirled around him and then settled. The noise of the harvester battered against his ears and he looked up, watching it head straight at him.

His dad was beyond sight and hearing. Jack would have to save the nest on his own. He eyed the creamy black and white swirled shells. The mother would come back—she'd just been nipping at his ear—and if she perceived him as a real threat, she'd cover the nest, feign a broken wing, then try to lead him away.

It was the nest covering movement he waited for even as the harvester bore down on them, blocking out the sun's rays as it came.

Jack stopped squinting as the shadow fell across them. He reached up and took his brother's cap off as he waited.

The bird wheeled about him once, her gray and speckled body arrowing across the field. He caught a glimpse of white-ringed amber eyes, piercing and alarmed.

If only Dad hadn't taken the safety off the harvester, it would have perceived him and halted. It was a drain on the batteries, Dad said, and so he'd removed it. Who would be stupid enough to stand in front of the machine, anyway?

Salty sweat dripped into his eyes and he brushed the sting away with the back of his hand, wincing as his vision blurred. From the corner of his eye, he saw the mother bird drop frantically to earth and attempt to cover her nest with both her body and any stray twigs she could scratch up.

Jack pounced, cap in hand.

He could feel the heat reflecting off the harvester's grill, waffling off his face. He'd have freckles for sure after this!

The cap swooped down, locking over fowl and nest. Jack shoveled in his other hand underneath and plucked the nest from the ground, a mere meter from the harvester's whirling blade. He turned and ran.

He didn't stop running until he reached the windbreak. There, he found a tree with a comfortable fork that he could reach if he shinnied up high enough. It was tough going with the nest in hand, but he made it, locked his legs around the trunk and deposited the nest. He left the cap on it and fell back to earth.

The grass here was lean and stringy, half-browned by the sun, and it did little to cushion his fall. Jack leaned back on his spare hips and bruised elbows— always bruised, he remembered—and watched the nest. The cap joggled and dimpled as something under it moved.

He had to leave it alone now, leave it alone or risk chasing off the mother bird for good. He knew that. He knew almost as much about the local creatures as he did about his father's farm. So he watched as the mother bird emerged, fluffing her wings out indignantly, and knocking the cap off herself. It fell to one side and hung on a slender twig. He thought of what he'd tell his brother to get him to come out of the house and see what had happened to his cap.

The mother bird looked over her nest and appeared to be satisfied with conditions. Jack caught his breath. He, too, was satisfied. As he got ready to get to his feet and dust himself off, the twig broke and the cap slid down to land at his feet. Jack grinned and picked it up. All in all, a good day.

Jack sat up. The suit moved with him. Bogie said, *I cannot control it.*

"I understand," Jack answered. He drew in his breath. His brother. The farm. His father. He'd forgotten most of that. He leaned his head forward, touching the cool shield of the visor to his forehead. He had his nightmares of the Thraks. He'd encountered one or two as a free mercenary. He knew what he had to know to face them.

He got to his feet. The gauntlets flexed as he balled his hands. Nine fingers clenched. Ten in his memory of a boy scooping a nest out of the path of destruction. How close had that blade been? Perhaps it would have been only a matter of time until he'd had that finger sheared off, for he'd cheated the blades that day. The scar ached in response.

Again, Bogie said.

He wanted to tell her she was free, but he was afraid she'd smell the murders of two men on his hands, and so he decided to wait until morning to gift her with their deaths.

"Amber," he said, to capture her attention. "Look at me."

Her face turned. She used her hair to veil her thoughts from him, its strands sweeping down and covering half her face. One soft brown eye watched him warily.

He could think of nothing else to do and nothing that he wanted to do more. He crossed the room and knelt beside her on the pillows, and took her in his arms. Gently he swept back her hair.

The expression in her eyes shocked him. "You love me," he said quietly, and was surprised to hear his voice waver.

Amber shook her head. "Dammit, Jack. It took you long enough to see it."

"I haven't been looking."

"No." She reached up and traced the side of his face where a very faint scar swept into his dark

blond hair, all that was left of a laser burn she'd
doctored for him long ago. "And if I were looking,
what would I see?"

A heat rose in him and he found it difficult to
answer, "The same, I hope."

She hugged him tightly again, burying her face in
the curve of his neck where it met his shoulders.
That was all the answer he needed.

The pile of pillows shifted, covering the floor
near the Bythian courtyard window as they lay back.
Jack fought for control, trying to move slowly, his
hands seeking out, then holding the curves of her
body. She answered, biting his lower lip gently,
then moving away so that she could open his shirt.
She uncurled the hairs on his chest as though they
were buds and found his own nipples, and caressed,
then kissed them.

She took her robe off. Bare skin touched bare
skin. The port wine dark sky without sheltered them
in privacy. A house lizard skimmed the curtains as
Jack moved over her. She tangled her fingers in his
hair, drawing his face close to hers, gentle brown
eyes widening in the mystery of their first lovemaking.

Even as he moved to open her, lightning struck
his mind. Its blue fire silvered through and he stiffened, unable to move without pain. All desire was
seared from his flesh even as Amber moved to draw
him closer. Paralyzed, his senses darkening, he could
say nothing as he slipped from consciousness, knowing Amber's mind had struck to kill him.

He came to, sweat cascading down his torso, and
Bogie said, *I am sorry.*

Jack's throat had constricted and he could not
respond for a moment.

I don't understand these memories, Bogie added.
Then, *Again.*

"No!" Jack cried, as a crimson wash flooded his

eyesight, and his body froze in catatonic reaction as Bogie fed him one last memory. Thrakian forms rose before him.

Harkness leaned over Alij's shoulder. He straightened and looked out over the bridge. "Where the hell is he? Is he going to do something or not? We're out of frigging time."

Leoni said tersely, "He's still suited up in the gym. He's been motionless like that for hours."

"Maybe he's meditating or something before battle. I heard about those Knights," Alij added.

"Meditating." Harkness made a sound deep in his phlegmy throat. His response was cut short by the opening of the bridge portal, and then the opalescent glare of the whitish battle armor filled the bulkhead. The man could not move all the way inside; he was too large for the compartment.

Jack took his helmet off. Fresh air tickled across his face. Sweat plastered his hair to his head as he cautiously ran gauntleted fingers through it. He smiled briefly in memory of a bald sergeant who swore he'd lost his hair that way, lasering himself with his own gauntlet.

The three officers looked at him.

"Well," Harkness rumbled. "What are we going to do?" He stabbed a finger at the screen where the edge of subspace now defined the clear presence of a Thrakian warship waiting for them.

Jack said, "I suggest we surrender."

Chapter 3

"Surrender?" Harkness straightened his bulk, a half-growl smothering in his throat. "I knew it the minute you wouldn't go into cold sleep. I should have known it the minute I saw the lot of you straggling in, your butts whipped. You're a goddamn coward."

Alij had gotten to his feet, resting a slim but trembling brown hand on the back of his chair. "Pilot," he said to his employer, but Harkness was advancing on Jack, battle armor or not.

"You're afraid of the deep sleep and you're afraid of them, out there!" Harkness jerked his head. Spittle hung from the corner of his mouth that he did not bother to wipe away.

"You're a damn fool if you're not afraid of the Thraks," Jack said evenly. He carried his helmet under his left arm like a second head. Removed, but not inactivated, faint noises came from the gear.

"I won't lose my ship to Thraks!"

Jack arched an eyebrow. "I don't think you have much choice, pilot. This . . . ship . . . is not equipped to fight. Leoni, am I correct in my assessment of the cryo bay as a lifeboat unil that can be detached?"

"Yes, sir."

"How long is it equipped to maintain life support?"

"Four weeks."

"With its cargo awake?"

"No, sir," Leoni said, ignoring Harkness' look of spite and hatred at him. "Awake, a little less than ten days."

Jack looked back to Harkness who stood, his beefy frame shaking with ineffectual rage. "Ever docked with the lifeboat before?"

"What has this to do with anything, you ball-less wonder?"

"Everything." Jack pressed against the bulkhead, leaning in as far as he could, until his broad-shouldered armor stopped him. "You do have a pilot's license, do you not?"

"Yes. Yes, goddammit, I've got a license."

"Then, sometime in your career, you must have passed the exams to do so. Could you do it again?"

Harkness' face worked even as the veins went from red to purplish, mottling his expression. "I could," he said, finally, defeated by his inability to vent his anger adequately. "You damn son of a bitch."

Jack ignored him. "Alij, I need you to set up coords for some alternate windows."

Cat-quick, the navigator sat back down. Harkness spat and then said, "Belay that order."

"Do it, Alij."

The navigator looked from Jack's quiet insistence to his pilot. He stopped, unsure of what to do next.

"I need those coords now."

"No, goddammit! This is still my ship!"

"No," Jack said. "Not now it isn't. Now it is damn near the Thraks' ship and the longer we argue, the closer we are."

The pilot's ham hands folded into fists. "I won't let you do it!"

"Sir?" Alij looked from face to face.

"You stupid son of a bitch," Harkness threw at him. "He means to jettison the cold bay and let the Thraks scuttle after it."

The two subordinate officers stopped in their movements and looked to Jack, shock livid on their faces.

Jack shook his head. "No," he said. "I mean to set them free in subspace, before the Thraks know we've done it. It's their only chance. We'll still be the main target." He waved a gauntlet about the cabin. "The main lifeboat gone, we'll still have considerable left of this hulk. Most of it empty, isn't it, Harkness?"

"You're my only contract this run," the pilot grumbled reluctantly. His mottling began to fade and his small eyes showed a flicker of interest instead of rage. "I still think you're a son of a bitch, but I'm beginning to think you're up to something."

"Good," Jack answered. "I am. Set the crew to readying the lifeboat for detachment. As soon as Alij has coords to show me, I'll be picking out the release point."

"Where do you want them to be?" Alij asked as he swung around in his chair and prepared to manipulate the computer.

"Away from us and the Thraks. Preferably behind them, if they'll have the trajectory. Pilot, come with me."

Harkness' rage was gone now, replaced by wariness. "Why?"

"I need you to give some orders, and a tour." Jack smiled, but it was not an altogether pleasant expression. "I want to see what's left of this shell with the main lifeboat gone."

Jack doubted if Harkness had ever heard of a Trojan Horse or would appreciate the strategy if told of it. The pilot gave orders to cast off the lifeboat without further question, but was uncharacteristically silent as he waddled along beside Jack's armor. Most of the transport was dimly lit, if at all.

Jack paused a moment and waited for their foot-steps to stop echoing inside a corridor.

He looked down at the pilot. "No wonder you're a poor man, Harkness . . . all this space and only one contract for the run."

The man flushed again, red bursting all the way into the wattle of his neckline. He spat to one side. "What do you want from me?"

"I want to know where you keep the contraband. The corridors and holds." Jack rapped sharply on a metal plate. "Like behind here."

With a noise that was more growl than hawk, Harkness reached for a bolt and twisted it. The panel slid open. Jack aimed the sensor-tripped lightbeam from his helmet into the area. It was empty. He looked at the pilot.

Harkness shrugged. "Figure it out," he said. "I had to make the run empty this time. Pepys didn't give me a chance to pick up any other cargo."

Jack pursed his lips in thought a moment as he examined the interior of the hidden hold. He stopped his inspection long enough to reply, "And that just might save your life, Harkness. Now show me the rest of the tunnels."

The pilot shook his head, not in denial but in puzzlement. He looked up at Jack, one eye nar-rowed as if trying to focus on him better. The pilot's intense gaze swept across Jack's face. "Where the hell does Pepys get his Knights from?"

Jack smiled tightly. "You'd be surprised, pilot. You'd be surprised."

"I already am. Follow me," Harkness returned and then continued waddling down the corridor. He did not seem to notice that his gripper boots made far more noise than those of Jack's heavy armor. "It occurs to me that I might owe you an apology."

"For thinking I'm afraid of Thraks? I have a healthy respect for them, and the damage they can do. If I didn't, I wouldn't even consider casting the cryo bay off."

"Then what do you have in mind?" Harkness stumbled to a halt, and his eyes narrowed. "You're going to let them board us."

"Yes."

"And we'll hide like smugglers."

"No," Jack corrected. "You'll hide like smugglers. I'll be hunting."

"Jay-sus," Harkness blurted. He rubbed his hand over his face.

"Now," Jack finished. "Show me the whereabouts of the backup lifeboat."

This request the pilot didn't even try to figure out. He just turned and led Jack to it without another word.

Jack sat in the gym, the only place really large enough to accommodate him when he was equipped, and he studied the information Alij and Leoni had brought him. The copy lay across his lap. The shortness of time niggled at him when a buzz of static came across the intercom and Leoni intoned, "The cryo bay's ready for cast off."

Jack stood. The copy sloughed off his lap and drifted to the floor, but Jack did not pick it up. The information was branded in his mind and it was not likely that he could close his eyes for the next few weeks and not see it emblazoned across his vision. He traversed the corridors to the bridge where harkness and the other two awaited him. They were standing double-watch, and the stress of the command showed in their bloodshot eyes as they watched him fill the doorway.

He told Alij which coords he wanted used, and the navigator repeated them to the computer.

Harkness had his head tilted, listening. "That doesn't give us much time," the pilot remarked.

"No. Nor them." Jack cleared his throat. "Before it goes, I want you to tell the nursing staff to start waking the sleepers."

"What? What in the hell are you thinking of? They've got four weeks' supply with sleepers. Less than ten days awake, or maybe you didn't hear Leoni earlier. And that's just an estimate. If any of those Knights are as big as you are, the demand's stronger."

"I heard," Jack said. He felt the pain etching itself into furrows across his forehead. "But I won't condemn anyone to drift into death asleep."

"If the Thraks take us," Harkness persisted, "it'll take two weeks to get Dominion needlers out here to pick them up. They can't make it awake, you've got to leave them chilled down."

"Then," Jack said, "I'll just have to make sure the Thraks don't take us." He turned and left the bridge, but he could feel the fear and hatred in their eyes washing after him.

Jack felt the lurch and plunge of the transport as the cryo bay left it. He moved to the portal screen and watched it drop away suddenly, its inertia carrying it on a different voyage from that of the mother ship as Harkness fired retros to change the course of the transport. He felt Amber's and Colin's nearness torn away from him as if, even in sleep, they had been close in their dreams and thoughts. *Don't let this be a mistake,* he thought. Then he straightened. Ten days and counting. Amber had ten days of life left for him to defeat the Thraks and relocate the cryo bay.

As painful as it was, he did not stop watching the tracking blip until the screen lost it. Instead of ordering it to fine tune on the blip and follow it, Jack let it go.

* * *

He hooked up the suit in a way it hadn't been since the Sand Wars. He paused as he reached the dead man circuit. That little device was to prevent the armor being taken from him by enemies on the battlefield. Remove a dead or wounded Knight from his armor without knowing how to disarm the circuit, and the suit self-destructed. He would be facing the enemy now. He looped the circuit in. He was nine days and counting when the freighter erupted out of subspace and began braking for Malthen, and the Thrakian warship flared into being beside them, tractor beams on full, and the two ships shuddered as they made contact.

Then he smiled.

Chapter 4

Amber wore her thermal sheet about her like a cape. It kept her warm. Her clothes weren't enough; cold sleep permeated the entire atmosphere of the bay, and her skin was peaked with goosebumps that refused to go away, even when Colin dropped his arm about her shoulders. His presence was enough to light a fire normally and she gratefully shrugged into the added heat although nothing would help the emptiness of waking up and finding Jack gone.

"Your hands are ice cold, child," the older man scolded after reaching for and cupping one. "You came off dialysis too quickly!" His handsomeness had softened into aged good looks, but his square chin jutted in concern.

"No! No, it's not that." Amber cut him off from summoning the nurse. She darted out from under his embrace with a quickness born of the streets. Colin watched her impassively as, now facing him, she remembered their shared past together, how the two of them had met, and knew he also remembered. She had the grace to flush. She'd been stranded on a very wintery and inhospitable frontier post and she'd tried to roll the Walker prelate. His aide had caught her—her punishment had been that Colin took her in and helped her in her quest. That time, after basic survival, it had been to find Jack.

A cold tremor swept through her. Colin put his hand out to her again. "Come on," he said. "You'll feel better when we find Jack. We'll both feel better."

Amber shook her head even as they moved off together. "Jack's not here," she said.

"Nonsense. Maybe he's not up yet, but we'll find him."

Amber stopped in her tracks, forcing Colin to a halt also. "Colin, Jack didn't go into cold sleep. *He's not here.*" She added softly, "I think we're detached. That's why the nursing staff isn't letting us disperse to transport quarters. This bay and the three rooms—that's all there is."

"Detached? You mean we're floating free?"

"I think so. Jack thought this whole bay looked like a lifeboat. Something's gone wrong and they won't tell us until everyone is awake." Suddenly, the thermal sheeting had done its work. She felt warm, burning, and she let the sheet fall to the deck. The shame of being left behind by Jack flushed through her being. He didn't trust her—how could he? Somehow he must have learned that her mission on Bythia had been to kill him. And although the snakeskin Hussiah had taught her well, had peeled away her subliminal training to kill, he had also brought her psychic assassination abilities to the surface. Her rescue by Jack had saved his life as well as her own. But . . . had he known? Did he doubt her still? She rubbed at her blue-dyed arms as if she could chafe away her past and her fears.

Before she could say more, a young man detached himself from the group forming at the interior bay doors and strode their way. He wore the rich dark blue uniform of a Dominion Knight. Its color set off the white-blondness of his looks, silken hair in a defiant brush, eyes that were blue without compromise of gray or green, fair skin that had acquired a sprinkling of freckles from exposure to the Bythian sun. He drew near them, a wrinkle across his young forehead from his earnest expression. A look passed between the Walker saint and this young soldier. He paused as if he'd intended to speak to Colin first, then turned and looked at her.

"Are you all right?"

Amber looked at him. She tried to quell her rapidly growing anger, but Rawlins evidently felt it. His blue eyes showed his pain. She shook her head. "I'm sorry, Rawlins. Jack isn't here."

"I know that, ma'am. The commander told me he was staying awake."

"He *told* you?" Amber thought he'd told no one but her.

"Yes, ma'am. He's been anticipating action from the Thrakian League. I'd say from our present situation that we've been cut loose from transport and as we lose momentum, we'll be coming out of subspace shortly. I'd also say he's had some of the trouble he's been looking for." Rawlins flushed across the cheekbones as though he'd relish sharing that trouble.

Colin frowned. His wrinkles, unlike Rawlins', were permanent. "What's our situation here?"

"Air and rations for about ten days. Maybe more if we stay relatively dormant. We're on a kind of autopilot but without the navigational equipment we need to redirect our course." Rawlins' gaze flickered and he looked toward Amber. "I came by to ask if I can help. I'd like to . . . look out for you."

Amber was hugging herself and staring off at a plated wall of the bay as though her gaze could burn a porthole through it. She brought herself back long enough to meet Rawlins' gaze. "I'm all right."

"Are you sure?" He bent quickly and picked up the thermal sheeting. "Cold sleep fever can be awfully hard on some people."

"I don't get it," Amber said tightly, as though her throat had closed up.

Rawlins looked back to the older man. "St. Colin?"

"I'm fine, thank you, lieutenant."

"I never had a chance to thank you, sir, but I'm told you saved my life."

There was a strange faraway look on the older man's face, but he gave only a short nod and said, "I was pleased to do it. You came to my aid in a difficult situation."

"Yes, sir. I don't remember much. I guess I just acted in a rush . . . but I'm glad I could be of help." Rawlins straightened but stopped short of snapping off a salute. "I'll be back if you need me."

Colin waited until Rawlins was out of earshot, then chuckled. Amber broke away from her inner thoughts long enough to glare at the Walker saint. "What's so funny?"

"Ah, my dear. It's you. You're breaking hearts again."

"I am? Oh." She stared off after Rawlins who'd disappeared into the ranks of now awakened Knights. She said nothing further, but folded herself up and sat down cross-legged on the cold floor. Jonathan detached himself from the medical quarters and, lumbering bearlike through the crowd, came in search of his minister. Colin sighed as he saw his body-guard approach and looked down at her. "What are you going to do?"

"Meditate," Amber said.

"That sounds like an excellent idea. I could do with a bit of prayer myself." Unceremoniously, Colin joined her on the floor.

The old ship creaked and groaned as it was invaded. Jack leaned back inside his suit and listened through his mikes, picking up movement despite

infamous Thrakian stealth. The short hairs along
the back of his neck prickled. A rivulet of sweat
started down his bare back between his shoulder
blades, but the chamois that was Bogie's regener-
ated life soaked it up greedily.

The waiting would be the hardest. He had no
qualms about that. Killing them would be difficult,
but waiting for them to penetrate the various traps
and deceptions he'd planted throughout the ship's
hulk would be the hardest. That, and wondering if
the Thraks would simply kill off Harkness and the
crew once Jack's work began.

It was the little glitch in Jack's Trojan Horse plan
which he'd forgotten to mention to the pilot. The
Thraks might forget they were looking for Dominion Knights and simply take out their anger on the
nearest human captives. Harkness and the crew
would be easy for the Thraks to pick up, if they
hadn't already. In a ship riddled with hideyholes,
Jack had left them no place to hide. Jack had had to
categorize the ship's crew as expendable. He'd had
no choice. But that didn't mean he liked having
done it. He wanted surety he'd be able to retrieve
the cryogenic bay and Amber safely.

A hair thin thread of noise reached him. Jack's
palms began to sweat. The gauntlets tingled at his
wrists, indicating power up. He set his teeth.

He could hear them now. Their measured tread
along the corridor flooring. The occasional metal
clank as they probed the plates. Soon. Very soon
now the two of them exploring this corridor would
discover a hollowness where there should be none.
They would, of course, investigate. Thraks might be
alien, but they were not lacking in curiosity.

Metal and plastic sounded as the plating was drawn
back. Jack braced himself as his target grids suddenly registered two blips. He was hidden. He wanted
the Thraks within this hold before he killed them.

And he wanted to kill them as quietly as he could.

A blinding white beam Jack's visor could not screen out quickly enough swept his face plate. Vision seared, Jack swore and fired automatically, trusting his targeting grid. With a high keen, two forms thumped to the decking. He could hear their muffled death throes.

Blinking until he could see through his watering eyes, Jack stumbled out of the back of the hold. Both Thraks lay still, their chest plates punctured by his glove lasers. Lucky shots.

No. Not lucky. Instinctual.

He stared down at their huge bodies. Not quite insects. Supple, within their own dark brown and sable body plates. In death, their face plates had gone slack, exposing leathery skin and gaping mandibles. He supposed that would count for an expression of surprise. He'd never seen a Thrakian face without its face plates carefully held in a masklike position. Each mask indicated an emotional nuance, very formalized in its positioning. Diplomatic Thraks were more theatrical than the warriors, but even warriors used their masks as if they were shields.

Jack kicked the forms aside and left the contraband hold, making his way to the next trap.

He encountered his next victim in the corridor. As the creature seemed to sense him and turned, Jack hit the power vault and kicked. His foot connected with a sickening crunch. The armored boot knocked its head bouncing down the dim aisleway where it rolled into a crevice. Jack caught up the spasming body and carried it with him to the next hold where he threw it as far as he could into an empty corner. Ichor splashed as he did. Jack stepped into a shadowed far corner.

They sent another trio after him six hours later.

Jack jerked awake from his doze as Bogie said, *They're here, boss.*

"Where?"

Three meters down the corridor, according to the sound grid.

Jack blinked hard. He had grit in the corners of his eyes. Carefully, he rolled his shoulders to ease the tension in his back. "Thanks, Bogie."

Don't mention it. The warrior spirit's voice carried an edge of irony. *If you'd done it my way, we'd have been out of here a long time ago.*

"If I'd done it your way," Jack retorted, looking over his screens, "we'd have the whole Thrakian League on our necks, you bloodthirsty old pirate." He had time enough to wonder how many more his booby traps had picked off before the cubbyhole's plate was wedged aside.

No lights this time. The corner of Jack's mouth twitched. They knew he was stalking them now. The Thraks were aware enough of human composition to know that lighting might give Jack something of an advantage. What they were unaware of was that the power of their beams could blind him.

He could hear their clicking and chuckling beyond the opening. They seemed to be discussing who would penetrate the hold first. His twitch stretched into a half smile.

He watched as the first Thraks eased into the hold, slope-backed, on all fours, supple and quick, as cautious as a canine with its back up. It could not see him, Jack realized, and watched as its deathmask gaze swept his shadowy corner several times. Feathery antennae erected at cheekbone height from behind the mask.

Jack had never seen antennae on Thraks before. Adjunct sensory equipment? He watched the creature as it reared up into a fighting stance.

A second Thraks moved in, clacking angrily. It

shadowed the first. Jack looked over their shoulders to the third, hovering in the background. He'd bring that one down first—its body would block the exit. As soon as it leaned in closer to its fellows. . . .

There was an immediate reaction when the first Thraks discovered the shell of a companion in the corner. Jack had a split second as the third Thraks reared in the doorway.

He shot, rolled, and stood up, fingers pointed, and blasted the other two even as they pulled their weapons into position.

A fiery beam glanced off the side of the helmet as the last Thraks went down, its mandibles white with froth.

From fear or anger?

Jack stepped over the bodies as he left the hold and shut it behind him. He could have walked through them to relish the crackle and crunch, but he had no way to clean the stain off his armor just yet.

He made his way deeper into the bowels of the freighter to yet another contraband hold, and closer to his ultimate objective, and waited for the next to the last time.

If his plan held.

The wait gave him time to think, and remember, and compare. He could not ever remember having seen antennae before, but then, he'd never stalked Thraks before. And he'd never before had the sensation he hadn't even been *seen*.

What was different this time?

Nothing. Not a damn thing that he could think of.

Perspiration beaded his upper lip. Bogie had flooded his mind with memories of the Sand Wars. If he had enough time to sort them out, perhaps. . . .

But his time was not his own. There was Amber to think of, and Colin, and his command of Knights, and his obligation to the evacuees.

They sent a whole damn company after him this time.

Bogie spoke just as the target and sound screens lit up.

"I see it," Jack told him.

You'd better be quick.

"Or I'll be dead. I know."

He had only a split second in which to notice that the antennae had gone out again, quivering after him as eagerly as dogs sniffing after a scent. Were they sniffing him out?

He did not have time to know if they'd succeeded, for his plan called for him to make himself a living target.

"Here I am," Jack called, and stepped out into the open.

Now you've done it.

Jack was too busy to retort.

He hit the power vault, spraying fire down below as he soared toward the cavernous roof of the cargo hold. He caught the hatch doorway above, and was through, in a wash of laser fire that turned the suit red-hot. He broke out in a sweat as he slammed the hatch lid down and secured the bulkhead, sealing the bay. The outer door below closed automatically as he set off the sensors, sending the last remaining lifeboat into launch sequence. The armor cooled as he waited for the inevitable.

The stripped down shell of what remained of the transport shuddered as the lifeboat powered off. Jack waited until the shuddering quit, then began to make his systematic way to the bridge.

He stopped a last time as the freighter quivered again, and he heard the sound of the Thrakian warship blasting off in pursuit of the lifeboat and its lost company of men.

A miserable, grubby lot of men awaited him on the bridge. They turned pale and battered faces toward him as he filled the bulkhead opening.

Harkness spat.

"It worked," he said. There was blood in his phlegm. "And at least we're alive."

"Now," Jack said, "Let's find our cryo bay while they can still say the same."

Chapter 5

Rawlins tapped Amber gently on the shoulder. She felt his touch as though she had been asleep underwater and even though she opened her eyes, she viewed him through a murky veil. It had been days since she'd first awakened to find the lieutenant following her like a white shadow. She brought a smile to her face and let it shine for Rawlins, though underneath, her emotions knotted. Amber found him smiling back as she came fully out of her meditations.

The air stank now. It spoke of bodies too close together, and water too scarce for bathing, and the air itself, too used up to be recycled well. It spoke, too, of time running out.

Her stomach echoed the speech.

Rawlins grinned as he lowered himself cross-legged onto the decking beside Amber. He held out a savory smelling bundle, wrapped about by a disposable cloth. "Last of the hot food," he said.

"Thank you." She did not have to fake warmth in her voice as she reached out and took her rations. "Did you eat?"

"Yes," he answered, his gaze flickering off toward the quiet people surrounding them.

She thought, in that second, that Rawlins was a great deal like Jack, able to be alone and private even in a crowd where privacy was nearly impossible. She also thought that Rawlins, like Jack, had probably given her a portion of his dinner. She would not insult him by asking further, and she ate her gift with swift, clean bites.

Rawlins flexed his back as though tense. Amber swallowed the last of the meat pie, then said, "What's wrong?"

His shockingly blue eyes flickered back to her, then he frowned. His brows were almost as milk-blond as his hair, but he'd darkened them with a liner. She could see the dye across the fine hairs. Then she realized part of what was so startling about his eyes: the lashes were nearly transparent, giving him a wide-open look.

Rawlins cleared his throat. "We've had no word from the freighter."

"Have they picked up our homing signal?"

"Not that we can tell."

"What do you think it means?"

"It means that, if Thraks did attack, the freighter may not have survived. Or that they can't get within range to find us. Or . . . we're on our own while they decoy the Thraks away."

"Or," Amber teased, "the world ended yesterday and we just don't know it yet."

He flushed. "And you're not worried?"

"Yes. But Jack has a way of surviving, even when he shouldn't. And we're alive today. So that counts for something. And I've just had dinner. That counts for a lot." Amber grinned.

"Is it true what the guys talk about?"

"That depends." Her grin faded. "What do they say?"

"That you're a street brat. That you grew up in under-Malthen."

"That I did. So my philosophy is easily explained.

Live for today. Tomorrow, take care of tomorrow. Or something like that.''

Rawlins shook his head. "It must have been tough."

She paused, squinting her eyes in recall. Rolf, the man who'd kept her and trained her, had not been a good person. But she'd had her freedom most of the time . . . a wild, flighty creature who would be recalled to her accounting only at sunset. A fey thing, with flashes of intuition that kept her alive, and successful, and protected her from Rolf. Her mind could, and would, kill. She'd almost killed Jack the night he had reached for her in love. The fear that she had, had driven her away in Bythia, straight into the arms of the holy madman Hussiah. The guilt burned her still. How could she face that happening again? There was no way of knowing if she had purged herself of the instinct to kill without intention . . . until the moment came again. Amber brushed her hand across her face as if looking for a stray bit of hair that tickled. The movement brushed away her thoughts. "It was . . . different," she answered. "How about you?"

"I'm a timber man. Or was, until I decided to become an officer. Then when the Knights expanded, I applied to join them."

"That's rare. Pepys doesn't like to recruit out of Dominion ranks."

"I know. But I'm good in armor."

She appraised him. Jack had mentioned Rawlins' ability many times. But the young man's soft declaration now was not boastful, merely confident. "So I've been told."

He colored then, and ducking his chin down, turned his face away.

Amber laughed, and put her hand on his arm. "I'm sorry, Rawlins! Really."

"Don't worry about it. Here I am with orders to

be a tower of strength for you, and you're the one comforting me."

"Orders?"

He looked at her. "You know."

Indeed, she did. Jack thought of everything . . . but had he thought of the fact that she would find Rawlins strangely appealing? That he awoke in her an echo of what her feelings for Jack awoke? This was dangerous, Amber thought, and did not continue to meet his gaze. "Tomorrow," she said, "you can be a tower of strength for me." With a deep breath, she dropped back into her meditations, not only to control her usage of air, but also to calm the turmoil of emotions rising within her.

Rawlins watched her consciousness recede until he could no longer reach her. Around them sat or lay dozens of people in similar conditions, though Amber was a master of the deep trance. St. Colin had instructed them all on meditation in an effort to conserve air and keep stress under control.

He had no place else to go, and he wanted very much to be where he was, so he made himself comfortable and tried to drift away.

"There she is," Harkness said grimly. "We'll be in docking position in about six hours. It's going to be tight, commander."

Jack stood behind him, looking over the pilot's shoulder, at the com screens. "Better late than never," he said.

"Maybe. Maybe not. Depends on how levelheaded our lot has been. Pinned up in those three labs . . . we're going to have a squirrelly bunch."

"A good number of the evacuees are soldiers," Jack told him. "I think I can vouch for their actions. And St. Colin is quite a man. If you haven't seen him in action yet, I recommend you do so. He'll have been talking with them."

"I've seen you in action," Harkness growled. The purpled mottling of his face had deepened, but the swelling had gone down. "That's enough for me. Shall we mark the homing signal and let them know we're coming?"

Jack's gut tightened reflexively. He would like Amber to know he was close to her, but he did not want to give the Thraks any more information than he had to. "No," he said.

Harkness' head swiveled about to look at him, one frizzled eyebrow raised.

"No," Jack repeated levelly, meeting the pilot's gaze.

"Right," Harkness said, and looked back to his command. "Right." He cleared his throat. "We're close to a sand planet."

Jack had been on his way out. He stopped in his tracks as though he had been shot. "Which one? How close?"

"Opus. One of the last the Thraks took. I understand the nest ain't been too successful. It's damn near abandoned. We might be able to find some supplies if we go in."

"No. No, dammit, that's probably where that warship's from. Let's scoop up the lifeboat and get the hell out of here before they track us. Our call for Needler coverage has been out long enough. They should be close now."

"It's a gamble."

"One I'm willing to take."

The pilot chewed on the inside of his cheek before answering slowly, "Then it's one I'll take as well."

Jack looked at Harkness. Animosity was banked inside the bulky body as though it were some kind of slow-burning fire. "I'll see," he said, "that your freighter is re-outfitted."

Harkness took the information with a nod. He

was the first to turn away. Jack waited another moment to see if the pilot had yet another bomb he wished to drop in Jack's lap, but the pilot said nothing more. Jack ducked back through the doorway and left the bridge.

What was left of the transport had been thoroughly cleaned down, but the stench of Thrakian dead seemed to have permeated everywhere. Jack found himself snarling as he walked back through the hulk to the vast gym.

If she had been here, Amber would wonder with Harkness why Jack hadn't destroyed every Thraks he could get his gauntlets on. He didn't know if he could explain to her that he did not want to send other Thraks into a frenzy of vengeance, that his only goal had been to make occupation of the freighter too expensive. Setting loose the second lifeboat had ensured that the Thraks would cut their losses and go after their remaining search party while they could. The Thraks were not berserker fighters. They had a calculated strategy behind much of what they did, even if it was incomprehensible to their enemies.

They were, after all, Jack mused, alien.

It was more surprising to him that there had been a sand planet one could classify as a "failure." Had it been too close to the Dominion territories? Had the Thraks been unable to complete terraforming? If so, why? A defeat to the Thraks was a victory for the Dominion and the Triad Throne, even if accidental. The trick was to find out what had happened so that it could be duplicated. Was what had happened the reason the Thraks stopped expanding so suddenly and sued for peace?

He stopped before his armor and eyed it critically. He'd been unable to strip and service it properly since leaving Bythia. Traces of warfare from two engagements stained it where he'd been unable to cleanse it better. Jack reached out and traced over the crudely painted over insignia on the suit's chest plate. There would be a day, soon, he promised himself, when he'd show that insignia again. When he returned to Malthen this time, he did so with full knowledge of who had been responsible for ordering Dominion troops abandoned on Milos.

Pepys, emperor of the Triad Throne. He hadn't been emperor then, of course, but the savage losses of the Sand Wars had been one of the major factors propelling Pepys into power.

And when Jack faced Pepys again, it would not be as a loyal Knight reporting to his monarch.

And Jack knew that Pepys knew it.

Bogie awoke under Jack's feather-light touch as he brushed the insignia. *Jack.*

He did not respond to his alter ego. Bogie's mental strength washed over him like an inexorable tide, probing, and then ebbing away into silence as the being sensed that he did not wish to converse.

The quiet left in Bogie's wake was shattered by a tone from the intercom monitor.

"Commander, it's not necessary to come up, but I'll feed this to you. We've never seen anything like it."

Again, Jack thought, as he went to the monitor and watched it flicker into life with the computer's projection. And this time, as last, the vision chilled his blood.

His silence was his answer and after a brief moment, Harkness said, "You don't recognize it, either."

"No."

Alij put in, "That sucker's big enough to inhale us and never notice it."

"Moving how fast?"

"It'll overtake us before we dock."

Jack looked at the screen. The Thraks had nothing in space like that as far as he knew, and neither had the Dominion. But the Thraks hadn't been to war openly in twenty years. Who knew what they could have been developing? He wet his lips. "What's their course?"

"I don't think they plan an intercept." The intercom was silent a moment before Alij added, "They don't need to blow us out of the water."

"I know." Jack stood a moment, hating the feeling of being totally helpless. "Leave the intercom open. I want to see the computer simulation of that the second it becomes more than a blip."

"Will do."

Jack sat down and waited.

He waited until the hour when the computer simulation came on and showed him outlines of firing turrets. Then he went over and suited up, unsure of what else he could do. Then he went to the bridge.

Harkness noted his looming presence at the bulkhead, and gave a nod. He said to Alij, "How close?"

"Mark, one half hour."

"How close are we to rendezvous?"

The brown-skinned navigator gave Jack a nervous look. "Do you want me to split hairs?"

"If necessary."

"It should be simultaneous. But . . ."

"Yes?"

"But I don't think they intend to ram either us or the lifeboat." Alij laughed a little too sharply. 'That's just a theory."

Harkness gutturalized deep in his throat and spit into a cup at the side of the control board. The pilot said nothing, deeply intent on the computer simulation of a docking process happening at his control screen.

"Why do you say that?"

"Because, well, because we'll be making some minor adjustments in speed and trajectory to match those of the lifeboat. And I don't see the unknown making adjustments. If they continue on their course, and we continue on the course Harkness has set, they'll just brush over the top of us. We'll miss by maybe two hundred feet."

The hairs prickled at the back of Jack's neck. He watched Harkness simulate a docking.

"Then we'll just have to wait and see."

Harkness' lip curled then. The computer showed a successful interlock, its picture flashing in triumph. He looked over his shoulder at Jack.

Jack nodded. "Nice job, pilot. When it comes time for the real thing, don't forget to account for the wash of the unknown's drive . . . if they miss us."

Harkness blinked. Then he nodded in return. "Will do, commander." He turned back to the screen. "Alij, you'd better be tracking very closely."

Amber awoke to a prickling of every sense in her body, all over, like a heat rash. No veil clouded her eyes as she looked up and then stood. Every hair on her bare arms stood out and she rubbed her forearms gently for warmth. Across from her, Colin awoke as well. He got to his feet agilely for an older man who'd spent much of the last twenty-four hours cross-legged in meditation. He patted down his blue overtunic and searched in a leg pocket of his miners' jumpsuit for a candy. He broke it in two and gave half to her.

"What is it?"

"I don't know," she answered. Around them, less sensitive people began to come awake, still groggy in the bad air. The candy brought moistness back to her dry mouth. Information had been scanty, and she knew it wasn't entirely the fault of those who had taken over the running of the lifeboat. Some of the equipment had apparently been in

disrepair. They were running blind and would stay
that way until rejoined with the freighter or . . . or
until they ran out of supplies.

The decking underneath her feet reverberated as
though they'd hit a bumpy road.

Colin put his hand out and they steadied each
other. Rawlins broke through a mass of sleepers
and waved at her from the other side of the bay. He
trotted over to join them.

"Sergeant Lassaday says it could be a tractor
beam or a docking maneuver."

Amber smiled at the word sent by Jack's bullet-
headed sergeant. Colin's hand on her shoulder flexed.

"Can he tell for sure?"

"No. The screens are out. But he'll swear by it."

Lassaday swore by his nuts, Amber thought. She
smiled widely at the memory. A giddiness swept
her. Then she thought, *It's nothing but bad air.
Euphoria. I should know better.* Aloud, she said,
"Do you think it's Jack?"

"I pray it is," Colin answered. He let go of her as
suddenly the vehicle shuddered under heavy and
clumsy contact. Metal sounded.

And when it should have been quiet, the bay
continued to shudder and echo violently. Denaro,
the militant Walker, came to his feet. He'd been
shorn of his weapons belts for cold sleep, but his
posture now told that he could use hands and feet if
nothing else. He was prepared to fight. Colin snapped
his fingers and Jonathan left his side with a quickness belying his massive build. When he came to a
halt, it was to overshadow the young and rebellious
Denaro.

Like an earthquake with no end, the decking
rippled under her feet. It brought her to her knees,
Colin tumbling down with her, and those still standing screamed and lay down in fear. The bay was

filled with cries of panic which tailed off to a sullen, sobbing quiet.

The side of the bay gave out a ring as though it were an instrument that had been struck.

Then silence.

Amber knew the bulkhead was opening. She could almost hear it. Sensed it with other than the five senses DNA had given her. She stood up, alone, and headed to the bulkhead.

If it was Jack, she wanted to be the first there.

She prepared her mind.

If it was not, she wanted to strike with the only weapon she had.

Chapter 6

Guthul was still cursing the cleverness of his enemy when his adjunct entered his quarters. The adjunct's quivering face plates signaled his excitement.

"What is it?"

"We have a sighting, general. I've been requested to bring you to the bridge."

The general stood. Even for a Thrakian warrior, he was impressive. He arranged his mask into one of dominance and victory, no little feat considering his defeat at the hands of the Dominion Knight. The adjunct quailed as the general passed him, headed for the bridge nest.

Guthul was aware of the attention directed on him as he loped into the bridge and stood erect once more. He eyed the sensor screens. No one had to point out the object of concern. It ruled their sector of space as he did the control nest. His face plates shifted as he put on a subtly inquiring mask.

"What is it?"

"Our grids have been unable to identify. It is a deadnaught of unknown origin."

Guthul homed in on the sighting as he came closer. His chitin rustled. "Between us and the Dominion freighter."

"Yes, general."

"And between us and the Opus crèchelands."

An audible gasp hissed through the control compartment. Guthul looked about him in anger and surprise. "Had you forgotten? I have not. A sign of leadership is to remember our defeats as well as our victories. We conquered Opus . . . but our nests have failed. Still, the crèchelands deserve our vigilant protection. Queen Tricatada expects nothing less from us. Adjunct."

"Yes, sir."

"Continue pursuit." Then, as Guthul swept around and prepared to leave the bridge nest, he added briskly, "And be equally prepared to break off pursuit if necessary. I'll not risk another defeat this trip."

The adjunct brightened. "Yes, sir!"

So much sweat pooled on Harkness' brow that Jack wondered how the pilot could see. Leoni bent over and mopped his employer's brow, but a new puddle beaded up as fast as he wiped the last one away.

Alij looked to Jack. "They're almost on top of us."

"Any sign that the turrets are moving into firing position?"

"None, but . . . smaller weaponry is activated easier and faster. We may not get that notice."

"I know." *Goddamnit*, he knew. Knew better than the navigator. This close the alien ship didn't need its big guns to blow them apart. And this close to the lifeboat, Jack didn't want to engage in protective fire without clear sign of hostile activity from the unknown.

Alij had returned his attention to the screen and said, "Uh-oh."

"What?"

"I'm getting an echo from behind the unknown . . . that or—"

"Or what?" Jack leaned into the bridge, shoulder armor scraping the bulkhead. Bogie protested. *Watch it, boss. I don't like crimps.*

"Or the unknown's so big it's been eclipsing another ship." Alij gave the computer another set of coords, and the viewscreen shifted slightly. "Damn. There it is."

And this one the two of them recognized. The Thraks were right on their heels.

Harkness interrupted, "I've got it."

Alij called out, "They're close enough to spit on us," but Jack barely heard him, already on a run to the interconnective bulkhead as the transport clamped its lifeboat back into position.

The docking crew worked in deepsuits, and motioned him forward as the bulkhead began to open.

Rawlins reached Amber's elbow, but she shook him off as the bulkhead creaked ominously with pressurization from the other side.

"We don't know who's boarding. Get back," he urged in her ear.

Amber swung on him. She didn't know what he saw in her eyes, but it was enough to make him draw back slightly. "Get the others back," she said. "I'm staying here."

Lassaday was propelling the evacuees gently into the crowded bays behind them. Rawlins hesitated, then went to join his sergeant. Amber pivoted back around and waited. A trickle of sweat made its way behind her ear and down her neck.

The bulkhead eased open, revealing a flash of white, and it took no more than that for Amber to be certain. "Jack!" she cried and threw herself forward.

The massive battle armor suit gathered her in as though she were a fragile doll. Even as Jack caught her up, a rumbling and trembling began and the lifeboat shifted suddenly as though not secure in its newly reestablished berth. The bay filled with screams.

"What is it?"

Jack smiled grimly. "We're being buzzed," he said.

"The Thraks?"

"We don't know who," Jack answered. "And they're in no mood to be asked. Let's hope this junker holds together."

Amber held on tight, her hands clasped at the back of Jack's neck, so glad to see him she forgot to be angry, and when she remembered, too frightened to keep it up. Pressure plates groaned and creaked until it seemed the freighter would split apart. Then, she realized, it had peaked and was beginning to ebb.

Gradually the rumbling and shaking quieted, and then all was silent. Through the open bulkhead, voices called, and the din began again as the evacuees realized they had been rescued a second time.

Jack carried Amber through the doorway and into the main body of the freighter. She thought she could hear his heart pounding in his chest, but knew that was impossible. Flexalink armor and equipment was between them. The odor of blood and sweat and ash seemed to be embedded in the suit. She wrinkled her nose.

"You've been fighting."

"The Thraks boarded us shortly after we jettisoned the cryo bay."

Amber looked at the tense line of his jaw, saw the pulse jumping, and knew he did not want to answer the questions she needed to ask. But she did anyway. "Why did you have us brought out of cold sleep? You knew we'd expend supplies."

"If we couldn't get back to hook up, I couldn't

just leave you adrift. Awake, you had a chance. Asleep . . ." his voice faded.

Asleep, she'd have been locked into the nightmare Jack himself had lived. No. He wouldn't have condemned her to that. She pinched the back of his neck. "Well, next time you think of heroics, don't think of doing them without me."

"Unless you're thinking of enlisting, there won't be any way you can join. There's a war on."

"Mmmm." Amber caught herself as he swung her down outside the bridge entry. She could hear Harkness' thickened voice giving orders.

The massive pilot turned and motioned to Jack. "Commander, you'll need to see this."

Amber helped Jack shuck the armor and they left Bogie lying in the corridor, seams open, as the control com screen filled with an incredible sight.

"What the hell is that?"

"The unknown. It's just irradiated Opus."

Amber caught her breath as she watched the corona flare out around a planet, dominating the screen. She did not register its name, only its demise.

"Who did it?"

"We're pretty sure the unknown vessel, but not positive. The Thraks are still in range, but we can't view them now, they're on the far side of the planet."

Jack wiped his hand over his face. There were reddened crimp marks over his bare, sweaty torso where leads had been clipped on. His tanned skin was streaked with dirt and ash, his sandy blond hair darkened to brunette by hours of perspiration within his helmet. Amber was caught by the way his presence dominated everyone on the bridge without effort and without intention, and she caught herself thinking, *He's twice the man anyone here is,* even as he said, "How bad is it?"

"We don't know. We'll keep the readings, but we'll have to find an expert dockside to examine the readings. One thing for sure . . . there's no Thraks alive down there now."

Jack watched the corona flare into a subtle aura. This was different from watching a planet burn—he'd seen that, too. He did not know if he was watching homicide—or suicide.

He could think of only one thing to do. He tapped Harkness' shoulder. "Let's go home."

Chapter 7

Interlude

He came to her when the ship had quieted, to the tiny cubbyhole given to her as private quarters. She had her caftan slipped down off one shoulder, her bare arm out, as she applied a balm the nursing staff had given her. The brilliant blue tattoos remained unaffected, but their heat diminished and Amber was basking in the calm, when she suddenly caught her breath.

She sensed him beyond the metal portal. His warmth washed through, touching her, sending her thoughts into turmoil even as the bulkhead opened and he stepped through, massive in the battle armor, smelling of sweat and war . . . and something more, a musky undertone.

He stopped, wearily, and looked down at her as she caught up the fold of her robe and brought it back up over her shoulder. His tiredness showed in the depths of his rain blue eyes, shadowed by the dimmed lights of downtime. But her senses, heightened by her ordeal on Bythia, caught much more and she came to her feet involuntarily, her hand out to him, even as he said, "I'll leave if you want me to."

"No." Her fingertips brushed his gauntlet. Bogie's senses as well as Jack's flooded her. She shrank back at that—Bogie had changed so much she scarcely recognized the sentience. Wisdom encompassed his ferocity and though she knew he overrode Jack's emotions now, it was with Jack's permission, for they were no longer parasite and host, but companions. So much had happened to Jack on Bythia that she felt that she rather than the alien Bogie was the stranger, the outsider.

Jack pulled back, as if perceiving her hesitation, and Amber stammered, "Don't go."

He dropped his gauntlet back to his side, brushed the glove over his helmet, and then stood there ill at ease. Amber closed her eyes briefly as she felt what he did.

He found the sight of her suddenly hitting him like a swift blow to the stomach, stirring feelings he almost did not recognize. Her tawny hair was disheveled and tumbled about her shoulders along the silken caftan and the glimpse he'd had of her made him tense his jaw for a moment.

She opened her eyes to see the tiny tic along his cheek.

Jack cleared his throat. "I wanted . . . I wanted you to know why I did what I did."

She stood in front of him, glad the caftan concealed the trembling that had begun in the hollow of her stomach. "I know why," she answered softly. "Didn't you know that I would?"

"Let me talk."

"If you'll let me talk about what happened between us." Without trying, she caught his thoughts again, musky flashes of emotion that seared her as, suddenly, he wondered what the tattoos looked like under her robes. He had an intense desire to trace the designs with his fingers, wherever they might go. The wonderment surged through him and Amber's head jerked up, and her eyes met his quickly, widening in amazement.

She took a step back. "No. Please. Last time. . . ."

The sweetness of the last time surged through him, melding time and place until he no longer knew if he was in memory or in reality. He shook his head to clear his thoughts and got out, "That wasn't your fault."

"It never is! But that doesn't mean that I can . . . that you and I. . . ."

"It doesn't mean we can't." He found himself moving forward. Amber put her hand out to stop him.

For an electrifying second, the three of them were one. One pulse raced in desire. One heat rising to the inevitable as they moved into each other's arms.

Amber drew back slightly. "I refuse to make love to more than one man at a time."

Jack stopped, his mouth agape. She tapped his armored chest. "I think this is one experience Bogie doesn't have to share with you." Deftly, she began to strip him of the armor until he stood alone. Jack kicked his gear to one side and reached for Amber.

He held her so close to him now that he could feel her heart pounding wildly in her chest, her nipples quickening through the fabric of her caftan. "I'll have to leave you behind again, I won't have any choice. And I can't promise you I'll come back to you."

Her breath grazed his chin as she answered, "I know."

"I think we've waited long enough."

"God," she whispered and looked up at him, her neck arching gracefully and a pulse beating in the curve of her throat. "What if I—"

He did not let her finish her protest. His mouth covered her last words, and she met his embrace with one of her own, and his body felt the sense of her from her long legs to the fragrant strands of her hair. When she moved back, it was to let her caftan drop to the deck. She stepped out of it, bared to his touch.

He hesitated a moment, drinking in the beauty of her young body, breasts high and round, her thighs smooth beneath the blue patterns of the alien artist, the hair of her pubes just as golden and fragrant as that about her face. Wordlessly, she reached for the fastenings on his pants and he let her undress him, feeling his hardness surge forward as she stripped his breeches away.

Then they moved close together, he tracing the feathery, erotic designs upon her skin, and she following the bunching of muscles and tracks of scars from other wars and other times until she gathered in his maleness and he bent to trace his lips rather than his hands about her breasts . . . and from there, he could remember little thought as their heat swept them away.

He awoke, her silken body curled next to him. The room was still darkened and her soft breathing soothed him. He could not sleep without fitful awakening, haunted still by the nightmare of being trapped in dreams without end. As great as his need for Amber was, having her did not cure him. He lifted his head slightly to look at her sleeping next to him and knew that even her love could not sate his need for vengeance.

There wasn't a part of each other they had not caressed or claimed, and he lay with his eyes half-open, consummated, yet somehow still lacking and wondering why. Amber moved her head along his bicep, her cheek brushing his arm, then turned and curved in another direction. Gently, he eased his arm from under her.

Amber had given him new life. Always, from the moment he had met her. He was reluctant to leave her now, but, compelled, he continued to ease his body away from her until he could stand.

As he stood, enveloped by the musky smell of her balm and their lovemaking, he realized what it was that drove him away. Amber had made love to a man with only half a past, and not much of a future. Bogie had the key to the other half, and Jack could not rest until it was restored to him. With that past in his grasp, he could offer Amber a future of her own.

And find a way to extract his revenge upon Pepys and the Thrakian League.

With the stealth Amber herself had taught him, he dressed and left her alone.

Chapter 8

It was an ill-kempt, sour-looking group that was cut away from the evacuees upon docking on Malthen. Pepys watched his security force neatly separate the ones he'd called for from the rest of the group after the old transport landed and then cracked open like an old, rotten eggshell.

As motley as they looked, unbathed, tired, the man he sought stood head and shoulders above the crowd. Even without his armor.

Pepys made a noise in his throat. He was unaware it had been heard until a hand fell on his shoulder.

"That is him?"

"Yes."

The captain was in dress blues, his own perhaps or someone else's, poorly fitting, his muscles pulling against the seams. He'd put on bulk since leaving for Bythia. *Just a boy, still growing,* Pepys thought. *What would it be like to be growing into your prime once more?* As the World Police troops quickly rounded up the man and the lithe girl by his side, and the group of Walkers led by Colin into a second car, he saw Storm pause and look over the docks.

It was as though he were a hunter or a hound and he'd winded something. "Look at that," Pepys cried fiercely. "He sees the staging. He knows."

"Knows what?"

"Knows we're readying for war."

The man behind him said blandly, "A soldier's soldier."

The camera work faded out as the vehicles pulled away toward the palace.

Pepys paced his inner rooms. He wore a shirt of flowing sleeves to hide his spindly, birdlike arms, but his hands hung out like those of a gangly adolescent boy, and he flopped them unconsciously when he walked. His trousers and boots were plain, but of the finest material. Wealth gleamed deep within their manufacture. He pulled up short to stare at his new minister. Baadluster did not return the piercing look, he was in a world of his own. The minister was homely, tall and pasty pale, with lips too thick and ears too large, poking out from limp brown hair, but the man had eyes of coal black that, once focused, could burn you to the core.

Pepys erupted back into motion before Baadluster could focus on him. He had needed a new minister, now that the Thrakian League had declared war. Baadluster assumed those new duties overtly, and, covertly, those of Winton, Pepys' head of the secret service, who had died on Bythia in Jack Storm's hands.

Literally, if the reports he had gotten were true. Jack had taken Winton's head in his gauntlets and squeezed until it had exploded like a ripe melon.

Pepys was unsure how to credit those reports. The Knight was an enigma to him, to be sure, but he had never sensed a violent or brutal streak in the man. Still, Winton, being Winton, had perhaps elicited that response. Winton would have made a saint come undone.

The Emperor of the Triad Throne stopped at that

thought, and ran his liver-spotted hand through his hair. The frizzy red strands rose with a static electricity all their own as he did so. Pepys reminded himself of a legendary Medusa, every hair on his head determined to snake about as though alive. He kept his own hair because it pleased him to do so . . . gave him a disarming and boyish look . . . kept his foes from staring him in his cat green eyes and realizing the schemes that lived deep within them.

He worried for a moment about what Winton might have told either Jack Storm or Colin of the Blue Wheel before he had died. He had not sent Winton off to Bythia to attend to either the Knight or the saint; the man had been about his own machinations, but that did not make him less knowledgeable about Pepys' intentions. And, then, of course, there was always the question of how much Jack already knew before Winton exposed himself and suffered the consequences.

He told himself this was no time to worry about losing power.

Pepys impatiently looked over the local bank of scanner monitors. The emperor took a deep breath that spasmed somewhere inside.

"I've cleared my agenda for him. I don't have time to waste."

Baadluster appeared to wake, though his eyes had always been open. "Perhaps traffic. . . ."

"Traffic!"

"The man has returned from a planet caught up in civil war and out of the hands of the Thraks to report to you. He *will* be here."

Pepys looked up, into Baadluster's eyes. The minister met his gaze levelly for a moment before looking away. Because he looked away, Pepys did not have to hide his smile of triumph. But he said, "Of course, you're right, Baadluster." He lowered himself to a chair built to suit his wiry, slight frame. "We're agreed on this course of action."

"Yes, emperor."

"Do you think it wisest?"

Baadluster considered him. The coal dark eyes stayed flat. Cool. "Not wisest, perhaps," he said, "but best. And that's all we can do, is it not? Make the best choice available at the time."

Pepys' attention was riveted on the minister. "And what, do you think, is the wisest?"

"Kill them both. Though, in retrospect, that might make a martyr out of Colin, which you would want to avoid at all costs, even if the evidence pointed toward the Thrakian League as the murderers. A spiritual network such as the Walkers have can endanger your own."

Pepys said nothing aloud but his eyes reflected his thoughts. *Yes, it would. And I don't want that.* He had never wanted that. Damn the Walkers. They'd seemed harmless, but during the decades of Pepys' reign, they'd been everywhere, looking for archaeological proof that Jesus Christ had gone on to walk other worlds. The religious affirmation had yet to come, but the sites being investigated had other, more tangible importance. The digs had established outposts which had gone on to establish frontiers, all steeped in Walker philosophy. Pepys could point at a half dozen major treaty infractions with the Thrakian League over the last decade that involved Walker sites. And when you had a saint who could actually work miracles, as Colin had. . . .

"There'll be hell to pay, Baadluster, if we're wrong."

Baadluster did not answer, but his black eyes fired up even as security rang through to tell Pepys that Captain Storm had arrived.

The Knight arrived alone, as requested, separated in the outer halls from his companion. Colin would also arrive separately, later. The vibrancy of the uniform faded his eyes to an honest blue. His sandy blond hair was beginning to recede slightly above his brow. He was young, half the age of the man he was destined to replace, but Commander Kavin had had implicit trust in Storm's abilities.

Pepys cleared a drying throat at Storm's appearance. Winton had had no such trust. *The man is one of our lost Knights,* he'd told Pepys. *I'm sure of it! He knows what we did in the Sand Wars.*

Then where had he been for the last twenty-five years, showing no sign of the passage of time?

Where?

In the hands of the Thraks, perhaps?

Or one of the several factions working very hard to put Pepys and the Triad Throne out of business permanently? Sweat broke out in the emperor's armpits as he thought of the Green Shirts.

He had not bothered to tell Baadluster that he and Winton had already tried to have this man killed several times. Storm was too damn lucky to die.

Pepys got smoothly to his feet. Jack still wore his insignia of captain, his promotion to commander not official yet.

"Emperor!"

As Jack saluted, Pepys leaned forward and snapped off the insignia and held the gold-threaded decorations in the palm of his hand. He felt gratified at the mild surprise awakened in the Knight's eyes.

"Commander," Pepys answered. "You'll have your new rank emblems before the day is out. Bureaucracy is always slow to keep up with field promotions."

"Thank you, sire." Storm inclined his head.

As he looked up, Pepys indicated Baadluster. "Commander Storm, I'd like you to meet my new

War Minister, Vandover Baadluster." He guided
the soldier to a pair of waiting chairs.

The two men sized each other up. Pepys admired
Baadluster for the noncommittal expression retained
by the minister. He might know nothing of the
soldier beyond the ordinary barrack gossip. Storm
showed only a mild curiosity.

Jack turned back to his emperor. "How ready are
we?"

"Congress drags its heels, but we'll be ready. The
Thraks have not yet officially declared war, but
they've been busy dismantling their diplomatic posts.
We'll hear soon. Or perhaps just slightly after."
Pepys smiled maliciously. With the Thraks, one could
not depend on being told until after the first strike.
"We, of course, are doing the same."

"In the meantime, Thrakian cruisers are still in
the trade lanes, where the Treaty allows them to
remain." There was disdain in the new commander's voice.

Pepys looked at him with a long measuring glance,
then said deliberately, "I made that Treaty. I'll see
it enforced as long as it still has life. If there is a
way to turn back after all this . . . if it can be done,
I will see it done."

A normal man would have flinched. Storm returned the Emperor's look levelly and answered,
"The Thraks have no such compunctions. Never
have had, never will."

"Nor, sir, had you. Without your actions, we
might not be in the position we're in now!"

Baadluster stepped between them with a movement so smooth it seemed almost accidental. The
minister forced Pepys to sit back in his chair.

"My actions," Jack said, "have always been with
the Triad Throne and the Dominion in mind."

"I know that," Pepys answered impatiently. "Else
I would not give you the Dominion Knights."

Storm stopped in his tracks as though momentarily taken aback. Pepys' gaze met Baadluster's with a gleam of triumph. The emperor knew the soldier now knew he was going to be offered the command of the Dominion Knights, and that he had not expected it originally. Pepys had him where he wanted him.

The soldier shifted his tall muscular form in a chair built for Pepys' comfort. Jack placed his hands on his thighs and leaned slightly forward. "And what do you want me to do with them?"

"The Dominion Knights will be fully reinstated. We've stepped up recruitment and training. I don't anticipate any problems from the Dominion Congress accepting either our troops or my leadership of them." Pepys gave a tight-lipped smile. "They may call us mercenary, but the Congress knows what we can do. We both know this war won't be fought in the sectors of space. We can try to put weapons' platforms into orbit outside each and every target we wish to attack or defend, but that is a logistical impossibility. No. Like the Sand Wars, this will be fought planet to planet, without destroying the land we both covet, and we'll have no choice but to follow the Thraks' lead. We need the infantry to fight this war, commander, and the Knights are the best we have to offer."

Jack watched Pepys, realizing the electricity with which the fine red hair rose and fell as though on a tide, was a signal of the man's level of intensity. He was intense now. Very intense. But not over Jack and Jack was grateful for that, aware he tended to give himself away too easily even with Amber's street savvy training. Jack inclined his head in slight affirmation of his emperor's statement. "I accept."

Pepys sat back in his chair. "You understand, of course, that your command of the Knights will be secondary to my and Baadluster's orders, and also probationary until you give me proof of your ability to win in the field. I don't, however, anticipate problems in that area."

"The Thraks were all but unstoppable before, sire," Jack answered levelly. "They may prove so again, but I can guarantee our best effort."

"Good! All I can ask. Our relationship with the Dominion is an odd one, but we are all human, and that binds us together. We are woven like a net, a fishing seine, and the Triad worlds are the floats that keep the net buoyant . . . but the Dominion is the strand that makes the weaving. If the strand comes undone, eventually we, too, will be left adrift." Pepys blinked furiously and Jack was astonished to see dampness well in his emerald eyes.

The emperor shook off his mood as Baadluster cleared his throat. Jack looked to the tall, pasty-complected man who towered over them and who had no chair to sit in. The new Minister of War returned Jack's gaze, and Jack saw the heat smoldering in the depths of flat black eyes.

He knew then that Vandover Baadluster could be as terrible as Winton had been.

"Commander," Baadluster said. "Please tell me, in your own words, what happened after Bythia."

For a moment, Jack felt a stab of panic, razor sharp. Technically, he was now an officer stripped of rank. Pepys could do that to him, if he wished. Jack had no illusions as to the strategies the emperor might employ, but he let his breath out slowly, giving way to the rationale that this was not one of them. Just the same, Baadluster noticed the flicker of his gaze toward Pepys. And misinterpreted it.

"Come, come! Don't look to him for permission to answer. I'm your commanding officer now."

Pepys, however, wore a pleased expression. "Don't

badger him, Van. He's my man, as he should be. That's what it means to be a Knight."

Jack felt bile at the back of his throat. Pepys had no idea of what it meant to be a Knight. The amputation scar of his little finger went livid as his fingers pinioned his right thigh. If he had been able to bring alive out of the Bythian disaster the man who'd told him that it had been the Triad Throne itself which had ordered the fireburning attack on Claron, Pepys would not be sitting across from him. No, Pepys had no idea of what it meant to be a Knight. Jack hesitated too long in answering and an unfathomable expression flickered across the emperor's face.

Pepys lifted his chin slightly as Baadluster intoned, "He says it without words, but he says it none the less. He wonders if you know what it means to be an emperor."

The faint sheen of sweat on Jack's brow turned icy.

A silence fell on the room.

Pepys smiled tightly. "And now, Minister Baadluster, you may leave us."

The limp-haired man had been hovering over Jack. He straightened and looked at his emperor. For a moment, Jack thought he was going to argue. Then the thick lips thinned, and Baadluster turned and left the private hall.

Pepys keyed his remote and the taping banks shut down one by one. Jack watched the displays go dark, knowing the gesture was being made to impress him, and knowing that nothing kept Pepys from recording secretly. But he was supposed to think that Pepys would not stoop to that, although Jack knew he would.

The emperor waited for several long minutes,

bright green eyes peering at Jack over the steeple of
Pepys' hands. Jack forced himself to wait coolly.

"Why did you murder Winton?"

Jack looked into Pepys' shaded eyes. "I did not
murder him. I killed him in self-defense."

"A man in battle armor against a man without?"

"Winton was not helpless."

The emperor dropped his hands into his lap. "No,
I suppose he was not. He was not the sort of man
who would ever be. He did not trust you, Winton
didn't."

They stared into one another's faces. Jack thought
of Amber and how much she would relish this game
of words and facades. He did not. He shifted his
weight in the chair from one lean hip to the other.
"Why?"

Pepys' hair crackled upward. "I'm sure I haven't
an idea. He was in charge of the World Police. It is
possible he thought you were a security threat."

"I haven't been on Malthen long, your highness—
but I've never heard that the WP was shy when it
came to arrests or trials."

"No." Pepys gave a twitch of his lips and looked
away briefly. "Your interest in the firestorming of
Claron always bothered him. You championed it
when you first came to me. The . . . incident of
Claron was a regrettable one. For reasons of security, what happened there can never be revealed,
and yet you don't strike me as one who would
accept that as an answer. Give me reason to believe
that Winton was wrong about you."

Although Jack's face did not twitch, his gut screwed
tight. Damn Pepys for making him trade off Claron's
lease for new life against the greater good. Damn
him. It was the Thraks or Pepys, and Pepys could
thank god that he was the lesser of two evils at this
point. He made a choice. "No."

Pepys' face went whiter still, verging on gray, but

his eyes lit up and he leaned forward in the chair. "What do you mean?"

"I mean, your highness, if my service as a Knight is not evidence enough for you, I can't please you."

"Can't or won't?"

"My point is made."

"But not mine. Do you like your commission?" the emperor asked abruptly.

"I appreciate it," Jack answered.

The emperor thrust himself out of his chair and began pacing. "What am I to do with you, Jack Storm?"

"Send me wherever you want the Dominion Knights to be stationed. Then let me do my job."

Pepys turned at the edge in Jack's voice. "You imply, without interference."

"If necessary. You tried to keep Kavin on a short leash. To paraphrase, he hung himself on it. He died fighting, not the enemy, but Winton."

"I know that."

"Then you should not have allowed it to happen."

Pepys brought himself up. His pointed chin trembled for a second, then dimpled as he fought to calm himself. "As if anyone could control Winton. He plotted against everyone. Even me."

"A dangerous man."

"Less dangerous to have under one's nose than a galaxy away." Pepys cut the air with the side of his hand. "I won't be judged by you."

Jack did not respond.

Finally, Pepys dropped back into his chair. "What happened after Bythia? What do you know about the Opus incident?"

"Only that the monitoring equipment aboard the freight transport was primitive, at best. The Thraks had done their best to board us. I couldn't allow that to happen. I think they intended on taking hostages. When they attempted to overtake us, an

unknown interceded and shortly after, our readings
indicate that the planet was irradiated."

"The Thrakian League claims it was done by
you."

Jack could not keep the surprise from surfacing.
"What?"

"They've filed an official protest."

"We've never operated like that. And Harkness'
scow is incapable of such an action. Did they mention the unknown?"

"No. I have only your report that such a vehicle
existed and, under the circumstances, it sounds as
though you are trying to smokescreen the situation.
General Guthul claims that the transport had jettisoned a lifeboat and appeared to be on an erratic
course, out of control, coming out of hyperdrive.
When he attempted to come to your aid, he was
fired upon, missed—and the weaponry used annihi-
lated Opus." Pepys drummed his wiry fingers on
the chair arm. "He has support in the Dominion
Congress. He has just enough of the truth to give
credence to his claims."

"A Knight would never jeopardize planetary environment to win a battle."

"Yes." Pepys gave him a long, slow look. "Yes,
there is that. And, small though it was, you seized a
victory for us. I won't forget that and I won't let the
Congress forget it either."

"There may be other advantages to the encounter."

"Such as?"

Jack barely hesitated, then continued. "The Thraks
stalking me seemed to have difficulty sensing my
armor. If there is an advantage to be had from the
encounter, other than beating them at their game, I
believe it is the discovery that there is a property
peculiar to norcite which baffles their sight."

"Really?" Pepys' impatience faded abruptly into

curiosity. "Are you asking for permission to research and test this further?"

"I think the project has merits."

"All right then. Proceed. But obtaining Thrakian subjects for field tests are your responsibility. Brace yourself for a long week. Baadluster has arranged for a visiting senator to oversee the drills."

"From Congress?"

"Yes." Pepys looked perversely pleased. "May I remind you that politics has been the death of more good soldiers than war?"

"I'll try to be discreet, sir."

"I'm counting on it." The emperor turned his back on him, and Jack knew he had been dismissed.

Jack left. He knew for certain they had been recorded, for Pepys had feared to ask him the obvious questions. Who was he? Where had he come from? And was he going to try to topple Pepys from his ill-gotten throne?

Chapter 9

Over the years, Emperor Pepys had received St. Colin of the Blue Wheel in many different ways. He'd been hustled in the moment he'd asked for audience, and he'd been ignored for months. He'd been both paraded in and hidden under cover. He'd been received with respect and scorn and, once or twice, desperation.

He'd even been met once by the secret police, their shackles ready.

So he was prepared for almost anything when Pepys summoned him the third day after his return from Bythia.

Raised to conspicuousness from humble beginnings, Colin wore miners' jumpsuits under his brilliant blue overrobes. He kept the jumpsuit pockets filled with many things: credit disks to satisfy filching hands on the street, religious tracts, a hand beam and even a handgun. Today the palace gate screening discovered the gun, a WP man removed it, examined it critically and gave it back.

"What if I shoot him?" Colin asked mildly.

"Then we'll know you did it," the guard answered sourly. "He's waiting for you in the private audience room.

As Colin threaded his way through the magnificent, if cold, rose obsidite corridors, he reflected that he knew the private audience room well. The location of their meeting gave him not a clue as to Pepys' frame of mind. It could not, however, have been good. Colin had been the Ambassador Pro-tem on Bythia. He should have been summoned the first day back, regardless of his age and need to rest.

At that thought, Colin pounded to a stop and harrumphed at himself. Age, indeed. Just a step past middle-aged.

Of course, death throws a long shadow and he'd nearly met it months ago.

As he rounded the bend, he could see that the door to the audience room was thrown open, and golden daylight from outside windows cast a gleam across the flooring, making it the color of a glorious sunrise. He gathered his thoughts and his life in his hands, and entered.

The twilight of the catacombs embraced him as General Guthul listened to the buzz of protest left behind at the end of his address before the councils. They sounded as though they had just left the nest, he thought to himself, even as he arranged his mask into one of triumph and confidence. And they might well be outraged. He had just laid before the League a plan of such outrageous action that they might as easily behead him for treason as rustle their chitin in amusement.

And, if he were very, very fortunate, one or two of them might have the military background to call him genius. It was those one or two upon whom he now staked his whole career.

They clicked him back into the assembly much sooner than he expected, shaking him out of his hum of meditation upon the whole, and he hastily checked to make sure his facial planes were arranged properly before returning.

One or two nearest him took offense at his mask
and rattled their bodies angrily, antennae up and
trembling. He took no note. They were conserva-
tives, always the first to rattle and the last to take
action. They seemed to consider taking alarm part
of their contribution to the council. The rest of his
peers he found alert and resting on their forearms
across their slanted benches, awaiting his next words.

"Continue, general. We have considered your
speech and decided that it is not the prattling of a
deranged being. We have weighed it and found it
worthy, if unorthodox."

Guthul pulled himself up, aware that he was a
fine specimen of military breeding, and he looked
about the semicircle of the assemblage. "There is
no more to say," he husked. "I am done. Either
back me or court martial me. I demand my due and
I demand it now. The time for hesitation is past."

Another trilling ran through the council. "You
suggest putting us well within reach of the enemy if
we strike as you demand."

"Yes. It is the only way to draw out Commander
Storm. The risk is great, the advantage considerable
if we can put the commander down now. I must
remind you, however, that if we attack on the Dominion fringes, where we are safe to hit and run, we
also put ourselves within reach of the Ash-Farel.
That the great and ancient enemy is upon us once
more."

Parthos, the newly recalled ambassador to the
Triad, opened his face mask and then closed it
tightly, a shocking display of emotion and anger. It
generated the effect he intended as attention immediately swung from General Guthul to the diplo-
mat. As Guthul was a fine specimen of warrior
breeding, Parthos was an equally fine one of diplomatic genetic structure. He snapped his lower man-
dible into place and the strength of its clack echoed

throughout the chambers. "I suggest we vote for Guthul's plan. I stand in favor of it, knowing that if Guthul is to fail, he will pay the price, and applauding that he is Thrakian enough to risk all."

As Guthul heard the speech, he was very careful not to let the joy and personal triumph he felt move his mask of leadership. But it was difficult. Very, very difficult.

Now he could contemplate squashing the Dominion Knight like the plasmic worm he was.

The samovar of tea had cooled, cookie crumbs had been swept away, and Pepys' fine hair had crackled down to a moderate aura before the emperor's emerald eyes fastened on him with their usual predatory stare. Colin put his cup down.

"Animal, vegetable, mineral, or friend or foe?"

The emperor rocked back, visibly startled. "What?"

"The game we're playing today, my friend."

Pepys caught the joke and laughed before putting aside his cup. "Neither," he said. "You're here because it was necessary to talk to you before removing you as ambassador."

"I removed myself, already."

"So you did. But as my subject, it's necessary for me to formalize it." Pepys stayed lolled back in his chair, watching as Colin rose and strode to the window. The window held a rare view of a singular aspect of Malthen . . . untamed land ranging over a sere group of foothills. Colin thought of Bythia.

He turned round.

"You did me a great disservice, Pepys."

The emperor nodded. "And myself as well."

"You urged me there, with several hundred of my most militant followers to protect our findings. That gave you leave to send a like number of your Knights, to keep an eye on me. But did you anticipate that my men would be slaughtered and your numbers halved before we got out?"

Pepys put out a freckled hand and played with the gold rim of his teacup. "No," he said shortly. "Your men, yes; mine, no. I knew the Thraks were playing a deadly game there. I did not know the Bythians were on the brink of holy war."

"On the brink no more. They blazed through my ranks like wildfire." Colin sighed. He shoved his hands into his thigh pockets as he leaned against the windowsill. "I know you. I should have seen it coming."

"The militants were doing you no good, Colin. We weeded them out before. I merely saved you the job of doing it again."

"Militant or not, they were men with souls! Sometimes I think you think very little of that."

Pepys did not answer, through the movement of his finger upon the cup's rim sent out a tiny belling. Finally the emperor looked up and he smiled, a gesture that did not warm his eyes. "Very few men would talk to me as you do."

Colin ignored the warning. "Very few men have the resources to frighten you," he responded. He stood up, removing his hands from his pockets, and in one change of posture went from a benevolent, fraternal man to a man of dignity and fathomless potential.

The pupils of Pepys' eyes widened at the change. The emperor straightened in his chair. He lifted his hand from the teacup. "I want Denaro."

"What is he to you? He's only one of a handful you failed to have wiped out."

"Give him to me," said Pepys.

"No."

"Then I'll take him for treason."

"You couldn't prove the charge."

"No, but I could tie up your time and attention doing so, and have him anyway."

Colin felt the lines at the corners of his eyes deepen. "What game is this you're playing?"

"The game of empire. Denaro's as dangerous to you as he is to me. Give him over and we'll both have done with him."

Colin thought deeply. The sunlight at the window had shifted a fraction before he finally answered, "I'll let you know." He headed for the audience room door even though Pepys had not dismissed him. He heard Pepys' voice, at his heels, as the door closed.

"Do that."

Denaro stood at attention before Colin, his muscular body bulging the seams of his jumpsuit, belying all attempt of the humble cloth to make him seem a simple Walker disciple.

Colin sighed and looked down at the hardcopy Denaro had brought him. The implications were obvious and the man's request not unreasonable.

Not unless the prelate were to consider Denaro's militaristic tendencies and the splinter factions threatening to tear the Walker religion apart. Perhaps Pepys had been right in trying to arrange for the collapse of the Walkers. God knew that Colin feared a holy war among the Dominion worlds and other outposts of mankind far more than he feared anything else in his lifetime. If he sent Denaro on his way to set up a dig, the hotblood would be free to build his army as well as set up a frontier outpost to support the Walker investigations. And then, there was Pepys' request.

The emperor and the reverend had been friends once. Colin had seen his friend grow apart and disappear into a mesh of alliances and entanglements, a web where every word and action tied into another, pulling here and there until he had become an emperor.

And what had Colin stayed behind to become? A minister, thrust into sainthood by a miraculous action he could not explain and had, only once since then, been able to duplicate. If he had not become a saint, would the Walkers have held together? A question he could not answer and yet asked himself time and again. Should he, as Denaro and others insisted, pull together the strands of their influence and make a genuine empire of their doctrines or should he continue to hold those strands loosely and let fate bear them where it would? He knew Pepys spied upon him as a rival.

However, it was Denaro's chafing that occupied him at the moment.

Colin rubbed at his weary eyes. He did not have the energy of his youth, and the incident at Bythia had drained him far beyond expectations. It was worth it to have healed the heroic Rawlins, but Colin wondered if he would ever regain his own vigor. Perhaps it was not meant to be. Perhaps this was the price God extracted from him for resurrection. If so, then the next would be his last . . . if ever there was a next.

The hardcopy report fell into his lap. Colin shook his head. "No, Denaro, I do not think this outpost a fit assignment."

The youth said nothing at first, but a nerve jumped along the thick sinews of his neck. As the silence drew out, Denaro broke it. "Doubtless," he said, "your eminence has some other position in mind for me." He showed his surprise as Colin smiled kindly at his words.

"As a matter of record, I do," the older man said. Lines of character deepened in his cheeks and about his eyes. "Come with me."

Chapter 10

Communion. Storm watched the troops moving below and moved as one with them, and Bogie overrode his thoughts until the blending edge between his personality and the alien's disappeared for a moment. He brought himself back with difficulty.

We're ready, Boss.

"To fight? Nearly."

The being responded with surprise. Jack shifted inside the Flexalinks, saying, "First we must have an enemy."

Thraks!

"Maybe."

Another thrill of surprise from the deep warrior voice echoing inside his mind. Jack smiled widely in spite of himself, a grim smile. "We're waiting for them to declare themselves."

There was a split second of humbled silence, then Bogie rumbled, *Thraks declare themselves the moment they crawl out of their crèche.*

"Yes."

You fence with words.

"Sometimes it's all that keeps us from being as savage as the enemy."

Sometimes being as savage as the enemy is all that will allow you to defeat them.

Jack made no answer to that, and Bogie's mind-speech lapsed as if the being knew he wished to be alone with his thoughts.

He'd had precious little time to be alone with himself the past few days. Around them, the equipment shops and immense hangars being erected for staging filled the training grounds with such a din of noise it was only possible to find quiet with a helmet on and the mikes off.

There was a muffled vibration behind him. He turned and saw Colin entering the bridge, his grayed and balding head bowed against a wind only the Walker prelate seemed to feel. Jack took off his helmet and closed the observation booth windshield, baffling the sounds so they could talk. The reverend carried a report under his arm, plastic edges ruffling as he walked. He straightened, saw Jack watching him, and came to a halt, wearing a calm if worried expression.

"What brings you here," Jack said, "past security points that ought to have stopped you."

"I have friends in many places," Colin chided him. He looked down off the bridge. Jack, following his gaze, saw Rawlins at the gates looking up to make sure that Colin had reached his goal before re-securing the grounds.

The two men looked at one another. "There's a story between you and Rawlins," Jack said.

"Perhaps. He saved my life. That sort of action often forms a bond." Colin set his lips together and made it apparent he was not going to say anything further.

Jack looked back to the grounds. Below, armor flashed, glinting in the Malthen sunlight. Colin seemed content to let him watch the drilling for a few minutes, then there was a rattle of papers. Jack turned back.

"What can I do for you, Colin? I've got an appointment in a few minutes."

"Then I'll get to the point, Jack. Take Denaro in as a Knight."

His newly fashioned composure as a commander broke. "You want me to what?"

"Accept Denaro into training."

"As a Knight? Or as a Walker?"

"Both. Denaro is willing to swear allegiance to Pepys. But I feel that . . . that in the undertakings ahead of us, we are wise to have formally trained personnel. Bythia would not have been the disaster it was if the men we'd had posted there had been trained militarily as well as spiritually."

"Pepys would never allow it."

Colin looked past Storm's broad shoulders to the training grounds. "He has already given me permission."

Jack thought he knew a lie when he heard one, but he had never heard Colin lie before. "Impossible."

"No. Not really." Colin smiled. "I quote, 'It's better to have your enemy under your nose than a galaxy away.' He said you would find the quotation familiar."

Jack made a noise at the back of his throat. His armored presence dominated the control booth, but Colin did not seem intimidated. Jack had a sour taste burning in his throat. "If the emperor has given his permission, then you don't need to talk to me."

"No need perhaps, but I wanted to."

"To explain why you're handing me a live wire?"

"That. And," Colin handed him a copy of the printout he held, "this."

Jack took it in his gauntlets, handling the plastic copies as deftly as with his bare hands. He skimmed it. "Looks like a survey report."

"It is."

"Anyone else seen this yet?"

"No. Walker surveys are quite confidential."

Jack tapped a wavy line. "You're going to establish another dig site."

"If finances and personnel allow." The Walker prelate paused a moment. "And if I have the coverage I need."

"You're expecting trouble again?"

"You showed me the signs yourself. Look here, at this spectrograph. These hills here . . ."

"Rich in norcite."

Colin nodded. "Probably. And that means. . . ."

"For whatever reasons, Thraks will probably be as interested in the site as you are. At least they were on Lasertown and Bythia."

"And it also means I'm not likely to find the archaeological evidence I'm looking for. We may find . . . once again . . . something else."

Jack looked at Colin. "But you're willing to take the risks."

"I must. Those other sites may not be what we're looking for, but I can no longer blindly ignore the evidence. There is a pattern here, there must be. And if there is another sentient, space-faring race, I can't turn blind eyes to it. Can you?"

"No," Jack said. "Nor can I give you Dominion protection."

"Not overtly. But I think I can guarantee you that Denaro will go AWOL as soon as he feels he is proficient in a suit."

Jack scrubbed his armor gloved hands through his dark blond hair. "I don't need that," he said.

Colin sighed and answered, "Neither of us do. But I can't think of another way. With the Thraks about to declare war, we may be way out there all by ourselves."

Jack shook his head. "I won't let you go all by yourself. All right. Denaro is in. Lassaday's in charge of Unit 3, it's just begun training. We'll install him in there. But if he turns up missing, I don't want to remember we had this conversation."

"Nor I," returned the saint, with an unheavenly glint in his mild brown eyes. He left when Lassaday climbed to the bridge.

The sergeant looked after the reverend as he left. "And wha' did he want?"

"He blessed the recruits."

"A practical man, that Walker." Lassaday rubbed his callused palm over his tan, bald, and profusely sweating head. "I'd give my left nut to have a thousand more like them."

Jack did not let humor twitch the corner of his mouth as he looked at the training grounds. The sergeant was too right. They needed a thousand more like this. "Don't let the senator hear you say that."

"A senator?" Lassaday's lip curled. "Jesus, commander, that's all you need. If I were you, I'd weld him to Baadluster and let the Minister of War take the heat."

"I would, but it seems Baadluster's done just that to me. They're getting restless down there. Better get back."

"In a minute. I heard some scuttle."

Jack took a moment to look closely at the veteran. He'd been through Lassaday's none too gentle but capable hands for Basic. On the grounds, Lassaday wore a silver mylar jumpsuit to catch the eye, but his sun-darkened face wore a no nonsense look now. "What is it, sarge?"

"I got the word there's a lot of subspace chatter going on. My son is into it, posts to th' bulletin board all the time. It looks like the Thraks are massing."

"Really?" Jack smiled tightly at that. Would fortune smile on him twice by tipping the Thraks' hand? "It would be nice to anticipate an attack before they break out."

Lassaday beamed. "Thought you'd like that, commander. Be there waitin' for 'em, a little reception committee, like."

Jack nodded, and Lassaday left the podium, passing by a brilliantly coated gentleman who was approaching the bridge. The man could be none other than the senator, short and compact, with arms and shoulders that looked as powerful as a bulldozer, fair-haired and with the florid complexion of a short-tempered man. Well-muscled thighs drove the man across the bridge to Jack's side where, though much shorter than a man in armor, he was not out-massed.

"Commander Storm."

Jack offered a gauntlet. "Senator Washburn. Your aides?" He looked around, anticipating a brace of aides/bodyguards.

"Sent them away. Told them you'd either be responsible for me or you weren't worth the price of scrap for your armor."

Jack found himself with a genuine smile for the short, feisty gentleman. "So that's the way of it," he said. "Good. I have no more time for you than you have for me."

Washburn's thick blond eyebrows wagged up and down. "Commander, I have all the time in the world for you, but I appreciate the frankness. What have you got for me?"

"Team drills. This is Unit 1, the team I went through training with, and we're all fairly seasoned now, but most of us had to be reequipped coming out of Bythia, and new suits take time to get used to."

"Any trouble getting the optimum out of your gear?"

"No, sir. I think you'll be pleased." Jack waved his left gauntlet and the troops waiting below went into motion.

At the end of an hour's time, Senator Washburn turned to Jack. "I'm impressed. But what makes you think this type of land war is what we need?"

"Senator, we all know maneuverability in space is greatly hampered. Basically, we have one pass and that's it. We'll be slugging it out on land because that's what matters to both us and the Thraks. We don't breed in vacuum. On the whole, we don't nurture our young out there, nor grow our crops or mine for manufacturing. We're still land-based and that's where we'll be fighting because it's our land they covet. If we fight them from space, we'll be polluting the very terrain we're trying to save."

Washburn's right eyebrow bristled up. "It's the old Sand Wars mentality."

"Perhaps. Who says it was wrong?"

He grumbled deep in his throat, and said, "My colleagues won't be easy to convince. We were soundly beaten in the Sand Wars."

Jack could say nothing back to that. A familiar ache of having been betrayed and left without hope arced through him, but he did not let it show in his expression. He remembered Lassaday's information.

"Perhaps," he said, "I can arrange a demonstration."

"That would be greatly appreciated, commander. And don't be shy with the budget. Get yourself some new armor—that set looks a little worn to me."

Jack's lips twitched a little. "It has its purposes."

"Don't stint yourself, commander." The senator gripped the railing, leaning forward until his nose pressed against the windshield. He took a deep breath. "God, I love a wartime economy."

Baadluster's pasty complexion pinked. "You want to what?"

"Follow the lead that the subspace call-board is

giving us. I want to be entrenched on that planet when the Thraks hit. I want to be waiting for them."

"We've got no confirmation that Stralia is targeted. We're still waiting for an official declaration."

"And that attitude gives them first strike capabilities."

"Perhaps." Baadluster's teeth nipped at his too thick lips. "Stralia is under our noses. Surely the Thraks would have better sense than to attack us there, scouting activity notwithstanding."

"I have a hunch otherwise."

The minister stood there, his slender hands twitching at his sides for a moment, before he pivoted to look at Pepys. He did not fling his hands into the air, but he might as well have.

Pepys put a hand up to his chin, somewhat disguising the amused set to his expression. "Just what," he mumbled out of his half-hidden mouth, "do you propose to do?"

"If we go, we go now. Even though we're closer, we'll have no way to beat them out of subspace if we don't. I'll take Rawlins as my second and leave Lassaday here to keep taking the edges off Units 2 and 3. I'll leave Travellini as my back-up officer."

"The Knights could be ruined almost before they've been reinstated."

"Never. And Washburn intimated that the Dominion Congress doesn't want to hire ineffectual, outdated troops. He all but told me they wanted to see us in action."

Baadluster hissed in disgust. Pepys waved him quiet. "How soon can you be ready?"

"By the time you have a transport ready for launch. The suits are already in the shop being stripped down and repowered—that's customary after any training exercise. We can be on a shuttle before nightfall."

"Then," and Pepys' red hair crackled with the

force of his words, "You had better say your good-
byes. You just be sure to give me Stralia and give
them their victory."

Jack saluted. "I'll do my best, your highness."
He turned to go, remembered something and turned
back. "I swore in a new recruit this afternoon. He'll
stay behind with Lassaday."

"A single recruit?" Pepys' eyebrow went up like
a fuzzy red caterpillar. "Who is it?"

"A former Walker by the name of Denaro, your
highness. Colin brought him to me. Said you knew
all about it. He shows a lot of potential."

Baadluster's frustration seemed to boil over about
then and Jack thought it wise to retreat.

Jonathan lumbered into the middle of Colin's
afternoon meditations, a harbinger of reality. Colin
looked up at him, saw the knifelike frown creasing
his aide's ursine face, and dispensed with scolding
him for interrupting.

"What is it, Jonathan?"

"Commander Storm is here. He demands to see
you."

"Ah." Colin nodded. "Give me a few minutes,
then send him in." He stood up and stretched, then
reseated himself. He had thought to himself more
than once that the commander's name was not so
much a name as a prophecy and he thought it again
now, knowing that Jack would be bristling with
indignation—and rightly so.

The room shuddered slightly when Jack entered,
though he was dressed as a mere soldier and not in
battle armor. Colin set his teeth. The resonance of
the meditation room would bear the shock waves of
the commander's obvious anger for days.

"Jack. I've been expecting you."

"You're damn right you have. How long did you
think you had before I found out about Denaro?"

"Not much longer than this. All I needed, actually, was long enough to get him sworn in," Colin said mildly.

Jack halted in the middle of the room, in front of the burled wood table and the chair where Colin sat. His light blue eyes had darkened and the wind had torn through his straight hair, tumbling it about. The man had few lines on his face . . . his shoulders broad, his frame erect, but Colin could never shake his feeling about Jack—the eyes were older than his mid-twenties body. He had a maturity about him that belied his youth. There was a mystery buried somewhere in that man that Colin was not privy to, and Colin wondered if he would live long enough to see it unfold.

"I don't like being used, especially by someone I consider a friend."

"And if I had told you, would you have accepted Denaro?"

The commander hesitated. He frowned, the expression pressing lines into a face that did not yet have them permanently etched in. "I don't know. But you didn't give me a chance to make that decision, did you?"

Colin stood up. "No," he said, regretfully. "I'm afraid I didn't. And you're right, Jack. I should have. I should have known you well enough."

"What happened?"

"Pepys wanted Denaro."

"Why?"

The Walker prelate strode a few steps away, to look at a mood painting on the wall. Its swirl of blue colors formed and dissolved in a constant, if gradual, shifting. "I'm not sure why except that Denaro is a militant, and Pepys is afraid. He wanted him where he didn't have to worry about him anymore.

"Maybe Pepys is right." Jack's voice was calm

now. "Denaro has and could cause the two of you a lot of trouble."

"Could. Just as you could cause him a lot of trouble. I'm sorry, but it's not in me to condemn anyone for what they could do. But I couldn't disobey, either. After all, Pepys is my emperor. So I gave him Denaro in the best way I could." Colin tired of the blue painting and turned. His blue robes fluttered, giving Jack an eerie sensation that the older man was just an extension of the painting's possibilities.

"Denaro is safe from persecution as long as he's a member of the Knights."

"Yes. I think so."

"What about when he leaves us?"

"We'll have to face that when it happens. In the meantime, Pepys has a war to run. He should be sufficiently—distracted—I hope, to forget about Denaro."

"Never," Jack told him. "The man never forgets an enemy."

Colin paused, then said, "I'm sorry, Jack. I did not mean to add this to your burdens. You're right. If you wish, I'll recall Denaro. We'll let Pepys take whatever course he intends."

"No." Jack made his way to the room's entrance. He stopped at the door. "He's one of mine now, and he's going to be good. But next time, saint," and Jack smiled crookedly. "Talk to me first. We might both be on the same side"

Colin returned the smile warmly as Jack gave a half-salute and left. The older man's smile faded. Unlike Jack, Pepys did not know a good man when he had one. It might be the death of his friend.

Chapter 11

Amber stared around the immense compound, an uneasy feeling at the nape of her neck, which she couldn't dispel. Since returning, the pace of their lives had been frantic. The entire barracks was on alert, packing for shipping out even as they trained. She chafed her bare arms as she waited, tracing the feathery blue patterns drawn there. As long as the alien dye permeated her skin, alien senses invaded her soul.

She sensed the visitor before he reached the front portal, had it open, and was waiting as the street savvy urchin darted out of the courtyard shadows, beyond the view screens of the panning security cameras and within arm's length of her.

He skidded to a halt and tossed a palm-sized package at her. "Here's your jammers," he said. His upper lip curled in a sneer.

Amber suppressed her smile, knowing that she'd surprised him, but he wasn't about to reflect it. She flipped him a three credit disk. "Thank Smithers for me," she said.

"Don't bother with it, lady. He's sending you the bill."

"I'm sure he is," she returned, but the boy had pivoted and dived back into the shadows, his grubby hand closed tightly about the money.

She'd embarrassed him because he thought she'd seen him coming. What would he say if he'd known he'd set off every sense she owned: smell, touch, hearing and thought, as well as sight? Amber palmed the door shut and stood a moment, her eyes half-closed. These were extensions of the sensory perceptions Hussiah had given her. Would they wear off with the tattooing? Or would she be driven insane first?

Amber forced her eyelids up and ripped open the package the street brat had delivered. Two jammers blinked in her palm. One discreetly placed to the fore of the suite and one to the rear . . . even though the apartment had been swept, she knew that the jammers would keep long-distance ears from hearing them. With a wry smile, she paced the double suite and installed the chips, knowing that Jack would never have thought of it.

Paranoia can be good, she told herself, and returned to the front door, her silken caftan flowing about her as she paced tensely back and forth until she again sensed a visitor.

His heat flowed out ahead of him like a swiftly moving fire. Amber hesitated as she went to the door, knowing it wasn't Jack unless he was furious—and Jack did not have that temperament unless he was in armor and linked with Bogie. Then who—? She keyed on the viewscreen.

A rawboned man halted in front of the door, brushing his limp brown hair to one side with an impatient hand. His thick lips pursed as he reached out. Amber instinctively disliked the look of the man, but she recognized the cut of his clothing. One of Pepys' courtiers, probably. What would such a bureaucrat want here?

She opened the door cautiously. The caftan sleeve slid along her slim arm as she did so, revealing the blue tattooing. His black eyes drifted toward the sight, took in the phenomenon with a ferocity of interest that almost seared her as he looked back.

"I'm looking for the young lady who accompanies Commander Storm."

"That would be me." She blocked the door with her form even though the man hardly looked as though he would force his way past. Looked, but not sensed. No. She felt his heat wash over her. Heard the race of his pulse. Could pick out a stray thought even though he kept his mind locked down well. He would do whatever he had to to get what he wanted. She braced herself. "Jack is not here at the moment. He's working with the troops."

"I know. If you would allow me . . . I'm Vandover Baadluster, the new minister." She said nothing, but the man's dark eyes glittered as though he knew what she'd been thinking.

He waved a long-fingered hand. "May I come in?"

He set her teeth on edge, but Amber inclined her head. "It's your street," she said, her words an echo from her past.

"Street? Ah. Yes." Baadluster eased himself in. "From that standpoint, I suppose it is, but the emperor would never want you to feel as though these apartments were other than yours."

Amber said nothing. Whoever he was, this man had not come here to make her feel at ease on the palatial grounds. Nor had he come to be silent.

Baadluster rocked back on his heels. "Have you settled in?"

"As well as can be expected." She moved back uneasily, knowing that the man had not come to her to exchange pleasantries. "I . . . am busy, Minister Baadluster. If I can help you?"

"Perhaps. I have been investigating the records of my predecessor, Commander Winton. I was distressed to see that you were implicated in several assassinations."

Amber felt her skin grow cold and pale. "I was not found guilty. Evidence suggests that the assassin who died on Bythia when he murdered the Ambassador was the same man who struck here."

"Unfortunately for you that evidence is never to be available to us again."

"I can't be tried!"

"No. And there is probably no chance you ever will be. But," and Baadluster held the word in his teeth a moment. "But future transgressions will not be so easily dismissed."

"I'm not an assassin."

He looked around the apartment for a moment. "Winton suggested otherwise."

"Winton was crazy."

"Perhaps. It would have been easier to tell if Storm had brought him back alive, wouldn't it?" He looked back to her. Then, so quickly she couldn't evade him, he grabbed her wrist. His fingers felt like live coals on her skin.

"You come from under-Malthen," he said. "You've no implanted ID. You come and go past the security systems as if they don't exist."

She wrenched her arm away. "Old habits die hard."

"Indeed. Are you and Storm a team, or are you using him?"

Amber palmed the door open. "Get out."

"I've not finished our talk."

"I have."

Baadluster flushed, a purple mottling of his pasty flesh tones. "You play, but I do not."

She straightened and threw her head back, feeling her chin settle into pointed stubbornness as she did so. "It would really be naive of me to think that we're on the same side, wouldn't it?"

"Yes," the Minister of War answered. "It would. And it would be even more naive to think that Jack Storm will not suffer for his association with you. Or you from his."

"What do you want?"

Baadluster curved his plumpish lips into a semblance of a smile. Amber concealed a shudder as the nape of her neck tingled. "A word now and then," he said, "might convince me of your loyalties."

She stood for a long moment, running through the possibilities of what Baadluster wanted, then fixing on it in shock. "Why?"

Vandover smiled. "Because you will want to."

Amber gathered her thoughts. Jack would not be surprised that they were suspicious of him—they had to be, after these last few years. But without proof, and with Jack in the position he was in, with war looming on the horizon . . . he'd probably never been safer. She cleared her throat. "I won't do it."

"Of course not, my dear. I didn't think you would."

Her stubborn chin dropped slightly.

Vandover Baadluster smiled widely. "But it was worth a try, and neither will you tell him I contacted you. Pepys is a liberal emperor, but nothing in regulations says that a soldier's whore has to be allowed to stay with him."

"I'm not his whore!"

"No?" His brow arched. "Perhaps they have another word for it in under-Malthen."

Amber moved away from the portal as Baadluster neared it. "And I'll give you this, for free." Her angry gaze met his amused one. "Just like me, you aren't safe anywhere, either."

For the briefest of moments, she thought he was going to hit her, and fought every muscle in her body not to pull back until she sensed the muscular heat of his arm bunching. But Baadluster did not move. The darkness of his eyes seemed to flare but whatever it was he might have done, Rawlins interrupted.

So filled had her senses been with the man before her, she'd never heard his approach, but the young Knight filled the doorway suddenly, his milk blond hair tousled from the wind, and his fathomless blue eyes drinking her in.

"Amber. The commander has word for you." Rawlins blinked slowly as he looked from her to the minister. "I'm sorry," he said, "if I interrupted you."

"No matter, lieutenant."

Amber cleared her throat to say, "Rawlins, this is Minister Vandover Baadluster, the emperor's newest adviser."

Rawlins saluted.

"Lieutenant. I'm finished here. For now."

She held her ragged breath as the man inclined his head slightly and left Jack's apartments. Even with the portal closed and locked behind him, she could still feel the feral heat of his body and his thoughts.

If she could have, she would have disinfected the room.

Amber pressed her hands to her lips for a moment and found herself trembling. Angrily she dropped her hands to her sides and clenched her fists. They would never have dared approach Jack like this. Never.

And because he wears armor, Amber thought. *You won't jerk him around because he wears the armor!*

Rawlins looked thoughtfully out the portal as he opened it to leave himself. "Trouble?"

"No."

"You're sure?"

"Yes. What does Jack want?"

"He'd like you to come out to the training grounds."

She frowned. "Why?"

"He wants to talk with you."

A chill ridged up her spine. "Why didn't he use the com?"

Rawlins would not meet her eyes as he said, "Some things are better said face to face."

Amber shivered as the coldness from the room seemed to gather inside her. Rawlins sensed her withdrawal and moved back from the door. He made as if to touch her comfortingly on the arm, but did not complete the gesture.

"It's our job," he said.

"No." She returned his gaze, thinking of Jack and how far they'd come to reach this point. "No, I think it's his destiny."

Chapter 12

Intercepted

Baadluster shadowed the emperor as Pepys looked over the subspace call report.

"Have you made a record of this?" he asked of the minister.

"Nothing official. You won't be able to keep it down long. There's bound to have been other messages that were gotten out."

Pepys sighed. As he looked up, he rubbed his fatigued eyes. "It will be blamed on the Thraks."

"I think so. But there's no doubt in my mind from the description given here that it's someone else. Perhaps even a twin ship of the unknown Storm encountered."

Pepys blinked his eyes back into focus. "Another planet gone. Hundreds, no, thousands of colonists . . . so far out on the rim that we barely had contact. Why?"

"Shall I inform your officers?"

The emperor sat there, caught by the stark realization that there might be somebody out there bigger and badder than the Thraks. Were they waiting around to pick up the pieces? Or did they even care if there were any pieces left?

"Your highness."

"What? No. I don't want anything official said about this. Let's wait and see if any other messages got out. Perhaps not. This . . . massacre . . . seems to have been pretty efficient."

"Your highness, I'd suggest the star fleets be notified, if not the Knights."

"No."

Baadluster drew himself up. "Very well. Good night." He withdrew, his gangly shadow mingling with, then dissolving among the other long shadows in the emperor's private chambers. Pepys scarcely noticed his leaving.

Chapter 13

Jack looked up from his reports as a flicker of movement outside his private berth caught his eye. He keyed the tapes to pause and a faint hum of static filled his ears as the audio dimmed as well. The shadow of movement coalesced into Rawlins, waiting nervously beyond the privacy panel, and Jack made a movement to let him in.

"What is it, lieutenant?" Disapproval faintly edged his words. With the ship nearing their destination, they had barely enough time to prepare themselves for the coming drop. Rawlins should not be wandering around.

The young man came to a stop. His milky white hair spiked back from his high forehead, and his blue eyes seemed to beg Jack for reassurance. Jack did not need to hear any words to read the unease in Rawlins' eyes. Forty-eight hours would not be enough to prepare this man for war. Maybe a lifetime wouldn't.

Jack hated to go into battle with hesitation like that riding his men. But he knew Rawlins wasn't a coward—he had never seen that in him before. So it was something else that gave the young man doubts. Evidently Rawlins thought Jack had an answer, or he wouldn't be here.

But Rawlins stood poised, his fear unvoiced, as though speaking of it would give it shape.

"Come in, lieutenant. There just might be enough space for you to sit down if you do."

That thawed his second's vocal cords. "Yes, sir." Rawlins stepped in past the privacy panel's track and squeezed his lean hip onto a chair flap. "Did I disturb you?"

"Just going over the terrain. We'll stay in orbit on the far side, keeping the planet between us until the Thraks commit to a landing pattern. Then we'll position the drop. I don't know where it'll be, but I have a good guess based on past performance." He had a damned good guess and he didn't need the tapes to inform him. His communion with Bogie was feeding him a storehouse of information. Now he had more than his instinctual gut level hatred of the Thraks to fight them with. More than his nightmares of locked-in cold sleep. More than Baadluster's vague stratagems. And he could only pray it would be enough.

Rawlins stretched his legs out restlessly. He looked up at Jack from under dark brows. "It all depends on us, doesn't it?"

"No."

The brows went up in surprise. "But I thought—"

"You thought we had something to do with gravity and magnetic attraction, with rain and wind and fire and DNA? Come on, lieutenant. The only thing depending on us is whatever sector of land I give you to hold onto. That's it.

"I've never seen a sand planet, sir, and I don't want to. Claron was bad enough for me. But I thought that the Dominion . . . that Congress' support of the war . . . the whole circuit . . . was in our hands."

Jack took his tapes off pause and shut the whole system down. He took his headset off. "I don't think any Knight alive is armored well enough to carry that kind of load, do you?"

"Well, no, sir. Not really."

"Then you can relax, soldier, because you're not being expected to." Jack leaned forward slightly. "What you are being expected to do is study your briefs so that when I give you your assignment, you can carry it out."

Rawlins' color came back, and so did the glint in his eyes. He nodded. "Yes, sir. I can handle that."

"Good. Now get out of here or you'll wish Lassaday had come along instead."

Rawlins grinned in tribute to their tough and feisty NCO. "Yessir!"

Jack watched him go and sat for a long moment as the privacy panel closed after him, leaving the berth in silence. As he finally moved to replace his headset, he thought of what rested on his shoulders, and what didn't.

Amber had had little for him in the way of good-byes other than the immense sadness welling in brown eyes flecked with gold. She had stood in the curve of his arm for a long time after his words had died away, and they watched the training grounds empty of troops eager for combat, until there was nothing left but dust whirls and the spartan barricades. Because of Bogie, he felt her presence through his second skin, every nuance of movement and heat.

He felt the sighing moving through her just before she said, "I don't mind you going so much . . . it's just that I always get left behind. And I never thought I'd be jealous of a pile of scrap . . . but Bogie's the lucky one. I may share your bed, but he shares your soul."

And with a faint whisper of a kiss, she'd left him on the command bridge to make ready to go to war.

She'd been right, of course. And that was one more wrong he carried with him until he found the Thraks who could purge him.

Chapter 14

"No, no, you stupid son of a bitch," Lassaday bellowed, his voice breaking into static over the com. "Keep that up and you're going to blow your ass off! Now step in line and remember, the suit's carrying you, you're not carrying the suit. Quit flexin' your muscles like some overgrown ape."

Denaro fought the wild gyrations of his armor to a standstill as the sergeant's rough voice washed over him. Beneath it, he imagined he could hear the jeers of the other recruits. His heart thumped loudly with anger and he took a deep breath, retreating into the meditations of the Blue Wheel to compose himself.

St. Colin had promised him a hard but rewarding road to travel. How hard, the old man could scarcely have guessed. But, and Denaro steeled his jaw, the empire would not get the best of him. He had been given his mission and he could not fail in it. He was in exile until he mastered the armor or it mastered him. Sweat dripped off his brow and down his bare torso, where leads pinched uncomfortably to his skin. He took a deep breath and, almost as if Lassaday sensed he had composed himself and was ready to try again, the sergeant rasped, "Get the lead out, boy."

*　　*　　*

The session over at last, Denaro stumbled into the tunnel corridors leading to the locker rooms and the shop. Jostled and bumped around by recruits more in tune with their equipment, he sagged against a wall and let them run by him. He ached in more muscles than he thought God had ever created as he reached up and unscrewed his helmet.

Malthen air poured in, tinged with a smell of hot concrete and dirt, but it was sweet compared to the sour aroma of his own body.

"Rough day?"

Denaro was startled, in spite of himself, and smothered a groan as a calf muscle threatened to cramp. He half crouched down to rub it, realized he couldn't get to it through his armor and settled for stomping his foot on the ground several times until the muscle unknotted. He glared at the woman who shared the corridor shadows with him, until he recognized the commander's woman.

His mother had taught him that the ungodly feared a fight and to "stare the de'il in the eyes until He backs down." The commander's whore was no exception and so he stared at her until she came out of the shadows and he could see her better.

He had stayed away from her on the evacuation transport. There, Jonathan had been by St. Colin's side and it had been Denaro's job, in the background, to keep the evacuees away from the prelate. He had been in disgrace, the majority of his company overrun by Bythian snakeskins until less than one man in twenty had survived. It was none of his business that the reverend seemed to enjoy the woman's company. It was, perhaps, a minor reflection of his humanity and flesh that he did. But Denaro did not like to profess such a weakness himself and though he stayed rock-steady as she glided within arm's reach of him, he could feel his nostrils flare.

The thundering passage of the other recruits faded away and the two were left alone in the corridor without even an echo to disturb them.

The woman jerked her head slightly, indicating over her shoulder. "They have an advantage over you."

"Three weeks of training," he said warily. He knew the Devil was going to offer him something and he wondered what it might be.

Amber smiled. He saw then she was no older than himself. "Jack said you had potential."

The Devil himself! But Denaro felt a tinge of pleasure at the praise, nonetheless. "Did he?"

The girl-woman said nothing further, but began to circle him slightly until Denaro had to crane his neck a little to keep her in view. She unnerved him.

"I've been with Jack a couple of years," she said. "You might say I've got the theory while you're getting the practice."

"Theory?"

"On how the suit works. How it should work, how to mesh its power with your ability."

Denaro froze as she went behind him and then returned. The dim light of the tunnel caught the feathery tattooing on her bare arms . . . she wore her jumpsuit with the sleeves cut off as though daring people to look upon her disfigurement. He shivered even as he made his mind up that he'd let the imp tantalize him enough. He straightened and tightened his grip on his helmet.

She laughed, a breathy, mocking sound. "Denaro! I think you're afraid of me."

He shot her a look that lesser disciples of the Blue Wheel would have quailed at, and she laughed at him a second time. Then, astonishingly, she stretched out her hand, palm up as if offering peace.

"I could help you through the rough spots of the next few weeks," she said.

"You? Why?"

"Colin has been very good to me. Let's say I owe him."

Denaro relaxed slightly. "St. Colin is a man of many virtues."

"You can say that again."

He scarcely noticed as she entwined her arm about his Flexalink sleeve and began drawing him down the corridor with her. As the perfume of her tawny hair dazzled his senses and blurred his vision slightly, he was deaf to her last words:

"And I've always wondered what it would be like to wear armor myself."

The staging hold vibrated as the ship began to descend into an orbit. Around the shop, soldiers in various stages of hook-up looked up briefly. Their glances flickered toward their commander. Jack was aware of it and ignored it as he continued donning his armor. Steadied by his presence, the men went back to their tasks. Most of them had never made a wartime drop before and it did not help that the few who had were keyed up. Jack tried to ignore the shaking of his own hands as he wired himself to stay in the suit, plumbing and all, for the next few days.

The surging through his nerves was not fear though, it was adrenaline. Pure, unadulterated. His pulse sang throughout his body as he outfitted for battle. His ears rang with the buzz of his readiness, and with Bogie's tide of ferocity which grew by the second.

"Commander Storm."

"Yes, Whitehead." Jack looked up. The fleet pilot's face filled the screen, his helmet masking all but his wide nose and dark eyes. The pilot looked unhappy.

"We're approaching the far side as requested, commander, but we've picked up a blip."

Jack's skin tingled. "What is it?"

"I'm not sure, sir."

"Give me your best guess or relay the picture."

Whitehead gave him a measuring stare over the com. "I'd say there's somebody waiting for us."

In a corner, one of Jack's men muttered, *"Shit."*

Jack stood up and finished shrugging into the suit. "Give me the overview."

The pilot fed it in.

The shadowy blip grew in size until there was little doubt.

"It's a trap," Rawlins said.

Jack felt himself growing cold. The Thraks were waiting for them. But he smiled. "Good."

Chapter 15

"Good?" echoed Rawlins.

Jack ignored him. "Whitehead, are they in orbit or maintaining a fixed position?"

"Doesn't look like they've got much drift."

"Okay, then pull a right angle turn here. Put us in orbit, but keep them on the edge of vision. I want to know the second they move."

Rawlins was still in shock, his half open suit making him look like some kind of exotic flower. His piercing blue eyes were fixed on Jack. "Sir."

Jack said to Whitehead, "Give me a picture of those sectors we were looking at earlier." With a brief glance over his shoulder, he said, "Thraks dug in are a lot easier to find than Thraks being dropped in. We may not catch them coming out of hyperdrive, but this'll do just as well."

He scanned the data coming in over the screen. "Freeze it there." The computer obeyed. "There's sand. Not much. But a Thraks never digs in for a fight without some sand. They store their food in it, like a larder. This is where they're dug in tightest."

Rawlins thawed out, shrugged into his sleeves, and sealed his armor to the neck. "Then that's where we hit."

Jack shook his head. "No. That's suicide to hit

'em there. We'll land here and here," he windowed the screen. "And spiral inward. It won't be easy. That's rough terrain and they'll hit us with everything they've got once they see we've pinpointed them."

"How do you know that's them? Maybe that's a desert or something." Garner, dark bushy hair in disarray and with disbelief on his feral face, moved across the bay. He and Jack had been at odds during Basic, but Jack had won his loyalty once before, and Jack did not fear having the soldier at his side now. Garner's face showed no malice, but he looked to Jack for an answer.

"It shows on the spectroscope. Believe me, it's Thrakian sand. *I know*." And he did.

"Yes, sir," Garner acknowledged. "Then what's below it?"

"Depending on how long they've been here . . . nests, an armory, and possibly even catacombs. It doesn't take them long to dig in." Jack picked up his helmet. He looked around the ship's hold. Fifty-nine men paused to meet his eyes. "Whitehead, put me on broadcast."

"Yes, commander. Tied in."

He was now being watched on the two other ships by another 120 men. Jack said, "We're ready for drop. The Thraks are here, waiting for us. But they don't know that we don't care. We're ready for them. And we're going to take them out. This is how we're going to do it. Listen carefully. Drop time in twelve minutes." And he began to detail the drop zones, sector assignments and ever-tightening spiral they were going to throw around the heart of the Thrakian infestation.

When he was finished, there wasn't a man who doubted they could do it.

He smiled tightly, a grim smile for which he had,

unknowingly, begun to grow famous. "All right now. First team drop units, Red Wing, Blue Wing, Green Wing, let's go."

He made a motion and Whitehead cut the com screen transmission. The pilot's face filled the screen once more.

"Break a leg, commander."

"Don't worry," Jack said. "I want you to watch that mother ship. Turret movement or orbit change. If it flinches. . . ."

"I'll go in and burn its tail feathers for you." Whitehead bared his teeth in anticipation.

"Do that," Jack said. "But don't forget you've got to haul our asses out of here when we're done."

"Commander." Whitehead sounded mildly aggrieved. "That junk is no match for a needler."

"The general of that junk may surprise you." Jack said nothing else as he locked his helmet on. The ship shuddered as Whitehead took it down to where Jack wanted it. Team One went into the drop tubes. It would take six passes for Whitehead to get them all down. Jack wanted to be on the first one, but he was scheduled for the last, just in case the Thraks had changed techniques.

The Thraks hit them as soon as they chuted in. Jack was pleased. It gave him a chance to blood his men right away, rather than have them walking about the landscape all spooked until they met action. Wondering about the enemy was more dangerous than facing them. His com was crackling with messages as he plummeted in, cut the chute and let his power vault absorb the shook of hitting.

"Quiet down out there and get to work," he ordered, cutting across the chatter. The com lines went quiet. Then Rawlins, with Unit 3, called out, "Oh my god! Here they come!"

And it was busy after that.

*   *   *

He doubted if any of his men had really seen a warrior Thraks. The Thraks that came in on the trading ships were really drones, mottled gray or sable, impressive enough until compared to their bigger brothers. But a warrior Thraks was bigger, more massive, his natural body armor far denser, his ability to run slope-backed on all fours making him much more agile than the drones. They were most insectlike when still. In movement, they became vicious carnivores and Jack didn't want his men underestimating them.

"Red Wing. We're being flanked."

"Then turn. Keep your grids on, and put your locators on memory. We'll fall back into pattern later," Jack said.

"Man down! Man down!" a voice shrilled, and cut off abruptly.

Jack waited. "Rawlins, Garner, Peres. Anybody know who that was?"

A young voice quavered back, "This is Simons, Commander. That was Joe Henkley. He had trouble after the drop . . . something inside the armor broke loose . . . he'd been trying to get it hooked back up."

"All right, Simons. Thanks for the data. Keep your chin up and your eyes peeled." Jack let the rosy glow of the holo bathe him as he searched for movement. He wasn't disappointed. In two seconds, he was very busy, as the choppy, green-brown terrain of grass, brush, and hillocks, suddenly exploded with Thraks.

They didn't go down the way they used to. Bogie sang in his blood as Jack fired and ran, fired and vaulted, return fire ricocheting off the armor. He saw one stumble down in the wave of chitin rearing up against him, even as he turned and ran, drawing them after him into the arms of his soldiers holding the sector behind him. Bogie roared his disapproval of the maneuver until Jack turned and stood, flanked by Rawlins to his left and another Knight to the right.

He pointed his gauntlets and laid down a spray of fire. Another Thraks tumbled, but a dozen more jumped it, throwing themselves over and coming up mean.

"Holy shit," Rawlins muttered. "What stops 'em?"

"This does," said Jack, and blew the leader's head off. It took a precise throat-shot just below the mask to do it. But it could be done. He took the legs off three more and said, "Let's go."

Bogie roared his approval as Jack ran toward the Thraks, vaulted their line and came down behind them, sending havoc into their ranks.

From the chatter on the com, he could tell that his men were settling down from their first startled reactions. He cut into the transmission, saying, "Don't waste your fire. Now that you know what they're like, make every shot count."

Garner huffed back, "Jesus, commander, these bugs are *tough*."

"Yes," Jack returned. "But you're tougher. Remember, Garner. We're here to kick ass. We want 'em to think twice about going to war with us."

He began firing single shots until the Thrakian line either went down or fled.

Then, still smiling his grim smile, he set his locator to find his original destination and resumed course. Ahead and behind him, flanking him, just within hailing distance, his men did likewise.

Third day. His mouth felt dry and the sweat trickled persistently, maddeningly, through his chest hairs and down to his sweatsoaked trousers. At his back, the chamois that was Bogie's regenerative form lay coolly against his shoulders, absorbing heat and moisture there, and protecting him from the chafing the field pack always created on an armored back.

He almost hadn't ordered field packs. He was glad he had. Thraks had been bred tougher. They fought better than they had in the first Sand Wars. They'd taken their beatings and learned their lessons.

But then, so had Jack.

Twelve percent casualties weren't bad. And they were now targeted toward the interior of their spiral pattern. From the attacks in response to their raid, he knew he was right about the location of the nests and main armory. Wipe that out, and the mother ship just over the horizon would pull out in a hurry. Whitehead and the two other needlers and been doing a little dance with the Thrakian behemoth, nothing serious, but most of the bombing to soften up the Knights had been kept to a minimum. So far, so good.

Although, if he had it to do over, he'd have Lassaday here as well. And Travellini. Holding 180 hands to get his troops through this was tougher than he'd thought. His throat had gone dry and raspy sometime last night and Bogie had mournfully informed him that morning that their water supply was depleted. It seemed the old suit had developed a minor leak. The recycler was keying in on the leak as humidity and drying it out almost faster than it leaked, leaving Jack without water and with a paper dry throat.

It made it difficult to give orders. He'd spread himself too thin, knowing himself to be the only true veteran among the suits. There were mercenaries, of course, who'd been through a variety of actions, but nothing in a sustained, contained situation like they faced now.

All in all, they'd done well. He was proud of them. Any minute now, the Red Wing should hit the leading edge of the sand as the spiral tightened. When they did, with Peres leading them, Green Wing and Blue Wing would have to get their asses in gear for Thraks would literally erupt out of the ground, determined to protect their headquarters. Not too long now.

Jack licked his lips and wished he could mop the sweat off his forehead.

Almost as if reading his thoughts, Peres said, "What's it going to be like, again?"

Jack checked his tracking grid. Peres should be southwest of him. That put him facing into the wind. "Grit," Jack answered. "In the wind first, like dust. Then you'll get close enough to see patches of it on the ground. Eventually, you'll hit the dunes and from there, Robbie, you're going to be too busy to be a tourist."

A short laugh. Jack added, "And I don't want anybody slowing down for souvenirs. I only need one body and I'll handle picking that up. Everybody else concentrate on clearing the field. We blow the armory and get out."

"Yessir." He heard a wave of echoes.

"Anybody showing a red field?"

"No, sir."

"Good." Inwardly, he was greatly pleased that no one had exhausted their power supplies though he had suspected there would be dead suits. Although technically they could stay in the field much longer, in reality it depended on how much firepower they'd expended. And how much firepower they'd expended depended largely on how inexperienced and scared they'd been. They'd done very well to get this far.

Peres said, "There's grit on the wind, sir."

"Good." Jack checked his gauges over. "Give a yell when you hit the first patches. All Wings, all sectors. Listen up. When Peres signals us, tighten the ranks. We're going in. Any of you with expended field packs, *drop 'em*. I want you lean and mean. Got that?"

An echoing wave of assent.

Ten minutes later, Peres' hoarse voice came over the com. Jack never heard what he said, but he launched forward into a run, closing up the ranks and bringing his spiral pattern into a stranglehold.

He heard the whoops and cries as Thraks exploded out of the scrub brush and dunes of sand, intent on protecting their last holding grounds.

The Knights crossed the leading edge of sand that encroached on the Stralian soil. The line of Thraks wavered for a moment and gave way. Jack could not see far enough over the dunes, but in a few hours, he should be able to meet with Peres as their deadly circle closed.

He kept firing and striding, breaking the ranks of the Thraks before him, his boots doing almost as much damage as his gauntlet fire. His left gauntlet muzzle jammed, leaving Jack with scorched fingertips inside the glove as it overheated. With a mild curse, Jack pulled out his laser rifle from his field pack and cradled it, the first time he'd had to use the pack. He'd been saving it for the coup de grace, but no matter. Nothing was going to stop him today. He saw Rawlins following him in, and then picked up ground sight of the rest of Blue Wing. Laser fire dazzled his sight as another wave of Thraks reared from the ground and charged.

Their bodies crunched when he strode over them. Flecks of green and yellow ichor flew up to splatter the white armor. White. A deadly shade of armor unless one were buried to the hips in white and beige and pink sand.

Then, he became part of the landscape, unlike the sable and more somber colors of armor the others wore. Jack's armor had always been designed for war with the Thraks. He was going to win this one. He had no doubts.

Not even when the ground opened up right under him and he plunged into darkness.

Chapter 16

"Shee-it, commander!"

Jack's ears echoed even as he dropped and hit the power vault to land. He landed, and went to his knees, Flexalinks complaining. It had been like falling off a cliff. Even worse had been the plunge into Bogie's thoughts—the berserker clawed at him from the inside. He swam in raw panic. His breath rasped through his clenched throat as he fought to take possession of his mind, of rational thought. Bogie weakened and Jack immediately squelched the light sensors, not wanting to advertise his position, and came to rights.

I'm blind, boss.

"Loosen up, Bogie. I'm not."

Then he broadcast, "I'm okay. Nobody panic. I'm in an underground cavern or catacomb. Maybe Thrakian, maybe natural, hooking into their network. I'll take one or two volunteers with me, the rest of Blue Wing go on to their rendezvous." His voice sounded normal, even cheery to himself, no thanks to Bogie's fear that still attempted to claw its way out of him and take over everything he knew.

"Ah . . . commander?"

"Yes, Rawlins."

"What are you likely to run into down there?"

Jack smiled tensely. "I'd say, lieutenant, I'm likely

134

to run into a lot of Thraks. On the other hand, if they're coming out after you, I may just run into a lot of luck." Bogie's panic bled away as Jack began to examine his surroundings. He stood cautiously, thinking to himself that the new suits had automatic sounding equipment, with periodic readouts. His armor had it, too, but he had to instigate the function. He'd been just too damn busy to bother.

Getting old, boss.

"Not me," Jack answered him. "Just you."

Maybe. The sentience's inner voice was weak. The suit's gauges were swinging into low. Was Bogie feeding off the suit's power and causing both of them to run short? *It's cold.*

"And dark." Bogie would no more admit his emotional lapse than apologize for stepping on a Thraks. Jack cut the conversation short, as he relocated his original path and saw the cavern widen out in front of him accommodatingly. All right then. He'd take the low road as long as it led where he wanted to go. The berserker's mental shiver acknowledged his decision.

At his back, two heavy thuds announced recent arrivals. Jack panned the rear view—one was Rawlins. The other a new recruit by the name of Aaron. Aaron was a curly headed, snub-nosed kid with innocent blue eyes that shaded the devilment hiding just under the surface. But Jack hadn't seen anybody technically better with a suit, even if he wasn't as athletic as some. Aaron made a lazy salute before casting about the cavern. He then dimmed his lights to follow Jack's lead.

Rawlins was an ebony shadow among the darkness. His visor glinted briefly, then a low beam issued out.

Knowing he couldn't ask for better men at his back, Jack went into the unknown.

*   *   *

It was like being swallowed whole, Amber thought, as she stepped into the fawn-colored armor. It smelled, too, and she wrinkled her nose slightly, thinking of sweat factories and other memories from her not too distant past as a street hustler.

Denaro's face had pinked. "There's no plumbing for—ah—someone like you."

Amber peered out at him over the neck rim as she finished sealing the seams. She had to crane her neck to do so. She was tall, but Denaro was vastly taller even for a soldier and the suit was greatly oversized for her. She thought that, suited, Denaro would be bigger than Jack. "That's okay, Den. I'm not going to be in here all day . . . right?"

"Ahh. Right." The Walker shifted his weight from side to side.

Amber waved a slim hand at him. "Don't worry, Lassaday won't catch us. Besides, you've been authorized to log extra practice time."

He cleared his throat. "Just don't . . . ah . . . dent it or anything."

"You'll have it back in no time. Come on, walk through the tunnel with me." Frowning slightly, Amber concentrated on slipping her feet into the boots and her hands into the sleeves and gauntlets, where a mesh of circuitry immediately gripped her fingers and, for the first time, she understood a little about the gauntlet weaponry. *Just like pointing a finger,* she thought. Strange that her first time using a suit would be in ordinary armor, not Jack's where both Jack's presence and Bogie's could embrace her. She'd been in armor before—under extremely cramped and difficult circumstances. This was entirely different. A feeling of power swept her.

"Are we powered up?" she said, aiming her right index finger at the locker room wall. Before Denaro could answer, the laser rayed and a pan-sized area blackened.

Amber jerked her hand out of her sleeve in reaction and stood, wide-eyed, looking at the sooty wall.

"Yes," Denaro said, his voice anticlimatic. "On low power, but be careful." He held out the helmet. "You'd better put this on. If you're spotted like that, they'll know it's not me in the armor . . . but they won't be able to tell through the visor screening who it is."

"Don't worry," Amber said grimly. "We won't be spotted." She reached for the helmet.

Jack had never known Bogie to feel cowardice, but as he strode through the earthen caverns, he could feel the presence quaking about him. The chamois along his shoulders and the back of his neck fairly shivered, sending harmonic feelings along the tiny hairs back there. "What is it?"

Cold, boss. Cold and dark.

Jack looked over his power gauges. There was a nearly imperceptible drain. He wasn't expending that much energy in the suit. "Bogie, what are you doing?"

I . . . don't know.

"Watch my power outage, okay?"

There was no answer, but another tremor upon his shoulders.

Behind him, Aaron and Rawlins matched his steady walk. Jack surveyed the cavern as well as he could with the amount of illumination he wanted to use. Dirt wall, unshored . . . as if a gigantic mole had dug it. Under their feet was a layer of clay sediment, broken by small rocks and pebbles, all dry. Perhaps an underground flood wash, of some sort. No rocks or minerals to speak of. He could feel a deep-rooted vibration overhead.

"What is it?" Rawlins broadcast.

"I know what it is," Aaron's still high, very young voice answered.

"Aaron?"

"Yessir. That's the rest of Blue Wing. There's a rhythm, like someone jogging."

Dust and pebbles shivered down from the roof. "If you're right," Jack murmured, "watch your heads. We're liable to have visitors."

The cavern narrowed to two abreast width, then made a Y. Jack paused at the fork, checking his map. The screen flashed him a direction, and he went to his right, slightly off course by a degree, but then again—no one had promised him a direct road.

The vibration overhead paused. All three of them came to a stop.

Jack tilted his head even though it did no good . . . the mikes were directional . . . his stance was unconscious. "Fighting," he told the two. "Come on, we're missing all the fun." Bogie's chill had transmitted to him and as he surged forward, his teeth began to chatter. His sweat covered torso had gone icy. He charged into the tunnel, certain that they were almost within striking distance of the Thrakian nest.

Amber skidded to a stop at the tunnel mouth. Her heart pounded and her pulse sang. The Bythian tattooing—which had faded to a tenth of its original intensity so it looked like a network of fine veins marbling her fair skin—burned with her delirium as power of one kind spoke to power of another. "Oh, my god," she murmured to herself, for she'd left Denaro in the dust. "Jack must feel like a god." She leaned against the left seam of the suit, heedless of the circuitry and wiring poking into her.

Denaro came panting up. His dark hair stood all

on end. "Milady!" he cried, as if she were deaf inside the armor. "Are you all right?"

"I'm fine. Don't get your bowels in an uproar."

His ashen face now grimaced at her retort. He wiped his forehead with the back of his hand. "I've seen a recruit blow himself away in a suit. Perhaps you could use a little more theory, too."

She ignored his sarcasm. "Don't forget, Denny, my boy—I'm the brains and you're the brawn. Now what direction do I head this scrap heap in?"

"The obstacle course is that way."

Feeling invincible, she surged out of the tunnels and on to the fields.

Feeling invincible, Jack spotted the light curving from the end of the tunnel, alien though its illumination was, and knew he'd been right. "Use everything you've got, boys," he said to Rawlins and Aaron. "Including your boots. Stomp what you can't laser. Don't let 'em tear your field packs off, you'll need your rifle." He took his out of the cradle of his right arm and lifted it. "Let's stir up a hornet's nest."

He broke into a run for the fifty yards remaining, his momentum and the power of the suit carrying him at an incredible rate. Thus it was that the three of them broke into the underbelly of the Thrakian occupation force, kicking through wafer thin cellular walls, ignoring the cocooned nets hanging from the ceiling as they fired. Aaron let out a squawk of indignation as one bundle swung into his helmet and Jack heard an "Oh, shit! That was part of Fielding!"

Rawlins ducked as a Thraks picked up what was left of a fellow warrior and threw the blasted torso at him, ichor spraying wildly. "How the hell can you tell?"

"I'd know that hairy, tattooed arm anywhere! What is this?"

Storm waded through bodies, kicking and shattering anything that twitched as a chittering wave of Thraks backed away from him. "Let me give you a hint, Aaron," he got out as he laid down a spray of fire that seared chitin and left a smell like burning hair on the air. "They don't take souvenirs, either! This is their pantry."

He thought he could hear Aaron gagging and added, "Keep going, boy! Watch 'em. Here they come at two o'clock!"

The Thraks boiling away from them were unarmed and frightened. The Thraks flooding downward from the other end of the tunnel were armed to the masks and madder than hornets. They did almost as much damage to the unarmed Thraks as the three Knights did.

Jack swung his field pack around, grabbed two grenades, tore the pins and chucked them as far ahead as he could. The concussion battered the suit and the mikes, waving his ears ringing. Two blurs to one side of his helmet told him either Aaron or Rawlins was following his lead.

He got his heading. Bits of chitin filled the air even as the first of the line to get through reached him. He set his rifle in his armpit and laid down an even spray of fire. "Rawlins, Aaron. I want you to kick your way out and get up there!"

"What?"

"Use your power vault and grenades, dammit! Get dirtside and do it *now*."

"Yessir!" they chorused as Jack set his teeth and boots. Provided there was nothing alive at his back, he ought to be able to hold this tunnel mouth indefinitely.

Or at least as long as he still had firepower.

The ceiling came down behind him and for just a

moment he was cloaked in a fine cloud of smoke and dust. The Thraks piling into the tunnel drew back in wonderment.

For just a second.

Then, with a terrible clacking of mandibles and spurting of their rifle muzzles, they plowed forward again.

Jack smiled. It had obviously been a long, long time since any of them had faced a Dominion Knight.

Chapter 17

"You ought to be proud of our boy," Pepys said, swinging about in his chair. "He's handed us a decisive victory."

Baadluster's upper lip tightened as though his teeth gave him some deep and stabbing pain. He paced away for a second or two, then turned and faced his emperor. "That he has," he said grudgingly. "And now Stralia's fate will be decided quickly in the Appellate Courts. The sooner it is freed to be colonized, the better it will be able to defend itself. Or had you overlooked that piece of property?"

Pepys shrugged indolently as he threw the report over one shoulder where it slumped to the ground and lay, plastic sheets akimbo. "I gain more in the long run for the Dominion to have confidence in me as a war leader and provider of troops. My claim to Stralia was poor at best and fourth or fifth in consideration. A wise man, my dear Vandover, knows when to cut his losses and take what he can get. And look what our commander's given us! Just look! Damn near one-handedly."

"Then," and Baadluster drew near. An unhealthy pallor cloaked his skin. "Perhaps you'll consider what I have to suggest. You face a full Congressional hearing with regard to the budget and appropriations."

"I do," Pepys agreed. "All it takes is enough of them to decide I have them by the monetary shorthairs and we'll be providing no troops."

"Send in your hero. If we work with him, we should be able to overwhelm the Congress with emotion, sway the dissenters, and get the budget through before anyone notices that we're going to own them completely."

Pepys' indolence faded rapidly as he straightened in the chair. He looked keenly at Baadluster. "You're talking about giving him a public forum."

"He's a soldier, not a politician. Feed him what you want him to say."

Pepys tickled the corner of one eyebrow with a fingertip. "Storm," he replied slowly, "is his own man. But it could work."

"Surely he's not naive enough to believe all we require of him is to fight Thraks."

"I think perhaps he is."

Baadluster smiled. "Then we can't allow him to stay that way. There are concerns he must deal with . . . building the troops and generating the propaganda necessary to authorize their use. I have leverage I can use if your highness finds it difficult to persuade him."

"Leverage, Vandover?"

The Minister of War towered over the emperor. Pepys waited for enlightenment, but none came. He smiled tightly. "I see you've been busy filling Winton's shoes."

Baadluster gave a slight nod.

Pepys sighed. "Well, then. I suggest you get hold of our hero. We have only a few weeks to make preparations." He waved his hand, dismissing Baadluster. The minister lingered a few seconds longer than was in good form, as if to show Pepys that he did not have the control he wanted. Pepys watched the lanky man's disappearing form until the closing

portal hid it from sight. Then he took a deep breath.
He had stayed true to his adage that it was better to
have an enemy under your nose than out of sight,
but he wondered if he had done a wise thing. Rumors reached him now and then. Rumors that
Baadluster had belonged to a splinter faction of the
Green Shirts though Pepys had not been able to
unearth recent activity. Had the Green Shirts been
too radical for Baadluster . . . or not radical enough?
Pepys closed his eyes, thinking that when he had
been younger, he could not rest until he had the
throne. Now that he had the throne, he could not
rest keeping it.

Lassaday stalked about the locker room. "Dammit, Trav," he muttered to Captain Travellini. "Do
we tell 'em or not?"

"We have no proof that anyone's been breaking
in. The security systems show nothing."

"I know that! I'd give my left nut to know who—"
he broke off as a buzzer rang in, overriding his
words. "What is it?"

"Moussared here, sir. The racks check out."

"Right." He looked to Travellini. The captain
stood at attention, slender, darkly handsome, a single wing of premature silver along one temple. "Nothing there. But I know what I know, even if I can't
prove it."

"Then you'll have to tell the commander and let
him take over, sarge."

Lassaday's thick chest rose and fell in frustration.
"Th' freebooters'll wait for no one! By the time I
get enough proof, they'll be gone, and our suits
with 'em!"

Travellini spread his hands out. "Our only other
choice is to shut down training altogether until we
find out where the missing suit is, and who's been
breaking in. I don't think we can afford to do that."

"Damn right. Well, th' commander's back tomorrow. I hear the emperor's got a call in for him. I guess we'll be next in line, eh, Trav?"

As the good-looking captain nodded assent, Lassaday slammed a locker door in frustration and left, eyeing the security camera with an evil glare for its failure.

Jack hardly had two words for Amber when he returned. He went to see Pepys first and then Lassaday cornered him, and when he came back to Amber, telling her that he would have to leave with Pepys in a few weeks, all she had with him was the night . . . and the night she shared with Jack's nightmares.

He rarely slept through. She knew that from years of association with him and the one or two times she'd nursed him through injury and illness. But she thought perhaps it had lessened, or even faded altogether, that night-startling bolt from sleep into wakefulness, his eyes wide and his breath shuddering in his chest. He did not fear death, she knew that. He feared the inability to be allowed to live . . . his dreams deep scars from the seventeen years he'd been locked helplessly in cold sleep. She tried to soothe him back to rest, but their lovemaking had already spent his energy and though he lay down beside her, she wasn't asleep when he got up and left.

She knew where he'd gone. Her slender fingers kneaded at the blankets as his warmth faded from beside her. He'd gone to the suit, to Bogie, to commune in a way he'd never reached out to her.

Amber threw herself out of bed as if to follow, then stopped herself at the bedroom door. She couldn't follow. She knew that. She turned her restlessness into pacing, then stopped. Bitterly, she repeated what her hated Rolf had often told her: "You can't lose what you never had."

She returned to the now cold bed. She might not have him now . . . she might never have him . . . but she would not let him face his destiny alone much longer. At the back of her closet, behind a false door, hung a suit of armor that she was very close to mastering.

Lassaday grimaced. It sent rivulets of sweat running down his bald pate. "I don't like yer leaving so soon, sir. Not with the trouble and all."

"It can't be helped. I don't like it either." Jack looked out over the parade grounds. The troops looked good, but he knew after Stralia that they had a hundredth of the manpower they needed, and with the attrition rate of training . . . he might never have the Knights at full muster. He disliked the duty he'd agreed to perform for Pepys, but it had one advantage. The Knights would gain the publicity they needed to gather new recruits. And the Stralia incident bothered him more than he wished. He could not shake the idea that the Thrakian League had been waiting expressly for him. Did they think that the Knights were nothing more than an extension of himself, now that Kavin was gone? If so, he must do everything in his power to make sure they were not right. Lassaday, Garner, Travellini, Rawlins and the others must be able to step in. He was the last true Dominion Knight . . . and it was in his power to correct that, to make certain that it did not remain true.

But it would take time, time he found hard to gather. The upcoming trip would delay him even more.

Yet he had also found evidence on Stralia that he could not ignore. The Thraks had not just been waiting there for him . . . from the depth and size of the catacombs, he was certain the Thraks had been based, on and off, on Stralia for some years

while the Dominion Congress argued the coloniza-
tion and ownership rights. He did not like the impli-
cation of the infiltration which had taken place right
under the noses of the Triad Throne and the
Congress.

A buzzer sounded and Lassaday grimaced again.
"Th' bugs are ready, sir."

Jack looked down at the portion of the parade
grounds that had been sectioned into a blind maze.
Shields thinly glazed with norcite were set in place
among the other walls.

Lassaday sighed. "We've got a bloody fortune
down there, sir."

"I know." But it would be worth it if he could
prove what he hoped to prove about the Thraks. If
they had a blind spot he could capitalize on, the war
would come to a quick and speedy halt.

They'd brought three Thraks back and, so far,
kept them alive. Now he heard the portal doors
opening, loosing the warriors onto the parade
grounds. Lassaday leaned over the bridge railing
with him, knuckle-scarred hands tightly gripping the
bar.

"What if this doesn't work, sir?"

"Then we try again," Jack said. He watched as
the Thraks stumbled out into the white-hot light of
Malthen's ever-burning sun. For a moment, he
thought he saw confusion on the masked faces.
Then the Thraks fell on each other with a fury that
saw two tear each other apart. The third turned and
made a gesture to Jack and that was indisputable,
despite the language difference, and tore its own
throat out and toppled, splattering ichor onto the
parade ground sands before anyone could stop the
suicides.

Lassaday growled deep in his throat. "Nasty beast-
ies," he said. "Well, that's the last of 'em."

Jack stepped back, gorge rising in his throat in spite of himself. He wondered if he would have exhibited similar courage under Thrakian captivity. He swallowed hard. "There'll be another time, sarge. Store those norcite shields where they can't be vandalized. We'll find a way to use them."

As he stepped down from the bridge, he tried not to let the failure bother him. He could not be wrong about what he'd observed aboard Harkness' freighter. He could not!

Chapter 18

"We're on final approach now, your highness."

Pepys wiped off the fine sheen of nervous perspiration from his forehead. He looked askance at his cabinmates, Storm and Baadluster. Storm looked calm and composed, almost meditative. Baadluster's attention was fixed on the viewscreen showing the descent.

Pepys wrenched his thoughts from his nervousness and focused on the screen. The cloudy luster about the planet faded for a moment, as if a wedge had been cut into it.

"The shields are down," Jack said.

Pepys looked to the windowscreen. His air sickness fled in the moment he realized that the center of the Dominion was wide open, vulnerable to their descent. He smiled wryly then, thinking of all the times in his dreams when he'd willed such a thing to happen for his attacking troops, and had never been able to force it. The shields could be brought down, that was true, but at great risk and expenditure.

It was not surprising the Thraks struck only at outlying, ill-defended planets.

The shimmer returned. They were through. Pepys cleared his throat, rapidly picking up composure as they returned to his element. His battlefield, by necessity, was the Congressional hall awaiting them.

Dreams of conquest here were disguised behind his politics. He took one last look at his Dominion Knight and hoped to god he and Baadluster had not underestimated the man.

Baadluster seemed to sense Pepys' thoughts. He turned from the viewscreen as the capital came into sight, its visibility partially veiled by scattered clouds and a light drizzling of rain over portions of the immense city. "Rest today, Storm," the minister said. "Tomorrow we go back to work."

Jack looked at the city, thinking that the Dominion capital was everything Malthen was not. Clean. Beautiful. Unfettered. Green streaked the walkways and park areas as if the forest had returned, unconquerable, to the pavements. The domed rooftops of the many buildings glittered in cobalt blue or in the green patina of weathered bronze. Pink and white tile. And windows, everywhere windows, as if the restriction of mere walls were too much to bear. He liked what he saw. He looked forward to the following day.

Pepys said, "Good timing. The Thraks have formally declared war. Now let's see if we can get the Dominion to join with us in answering them."

A shiver of anticipation ran down the back of Jack's neck.

The chamber was huge. In hushed tones, Baadluster said, "It's said to have been patterned after the old Terran Congress."

Home World. A beginning so far away that, in the end, only it might be safe from the Thraks. Jack felt himself squaring his shoulders back as he stepped into the wing, awaiting his introduction.

The senators and representatives were anything but quiet. Many sat, listening to the speech being presented to them, but equally as many conferred in groups, sitting or standing. There were young

men and women at com lines, taking notes or trans-
mitting messages, calm islands in the benevolent
chaos. Overhead were the trade logos and city state
banners as well as world flags of the Dominion, the
Outward Bounds, and the Triad Throne.

Jack sucked in his breath, calming himself, and
rethought his decision not to wear his armor. He
missed the edge of Bogie's righteous anger but not
the subtle power struggle that underlay their communication. Diplomacy was going to be difficult
enough. He caught sight of Senator Washburn, a
prism of activity, settling a wing of senators in their
seats, hovering over each one and speaking confi-
dentially before moving on to the next.

He also saw Pepys, sitting in the visitors' gallery.
The red-haired emperor had worn his regal robes,
and was outfitted as Jack rarely saw him, in red
stones and gold threads that made him look like a
barbarian throwback. In the midst of all his splendor, he looked a bigger man than he was. Five WP
men rayed around him in formation. Jack recognized three he'd had dealings with under Winton's
regime; he felt his lip curl in instinctive dislike.

At Jack's side, Baadluster intoned, "I'll be leaving you now. I must join Pepys. You're sure you're
set? Have the speech with you?"

Jack nodded. He palmed the disk lightly, thinking that he still did not feel comfortable with the
contents hammered out by Pepys and Baadluster.
Senator Washburn stood up straight and looked at
them. Their time must be close. Baadluster hissed
something under his breath and faded away from
Jack's side.

Jack's tension left with the minister. He looked
across the hall, wishing that he could somehow find
and isolate Amber's face in the ocean of faces, but
knowing he could not because she had been left
behind. As he saw the security and broadcast cam-

eras panning the hall, he knew she'd not have felt at ease here. Anyone appearing here would be forever stored in too many master systems. As he looked up into the domed roof and eyed those cameras, a thought occurred to him and began to slowly expand.

One of Washburn's aides came up behind him. "Almost ready?"

He looked at her. Expectancy shone from dark eyes set off by warm brown skin. He nodded.

She took his hand. "Just feed the disk into the podium as you step up. The speech comes up on that transparent screen down there . . . the words are color-coded to be invisible on the broadcast. Looks spontaneous, but isn't. You can move your eyes slightly, the screen moves with you to a certain degree. Unless, of course, you have your speech memorized."

He nodded again.

She smiled widely. "Say something," she said. "The senator will have my head if you've lost your voice from stage fright. Destinies are decided in here."

"Damn all Thraks," Jack rumbled in amusement.

The aide laughed. "Good enough for me."

The audience hall began to applaud and the noise moved in waves, baffling off the accoustics of the chambers. At first, Jack thought they might have been heard, then he saw that Senator Washburn had gained the podium and was preparing to introduce him.

The thought that had begun grew until it seized him, and he scarcely heard Washburn's speech leading up to his introduction.

The aide pushed at his right elbow lightly. "That's it, you're on."

Jack stepped out of the wings and moved toward the podium. A hush rippled across the floor following applause for Washburn's words. *What has*

Washburn promised them in me? he thought briefly, as he stepped onto the dais. He felt a catch deep in his throat, a momentary flutter of nervousness that he shrugged off. The AV equipment responded to his weight in front of the podium and flashed READY, awaiting his disk to be fed in.

The audience had quieted, awaiting him, and as he hesitated, they began to clap again, as if urging him to relax and deliver his words. He looked across the floor, where Pepys' planned splendor caught his eye once more, and then a grim determination settled over him along with a deadly calm.

He held up his right hand, four-fingered like a badge of courage, and knew the cameras were broadcasting close-ups of him, and the speech disk winking in his palm. To hushed murmurs, Jack flexed his hand and the disk folded into an unusable mass. He tossed it to the foot of the dais.

Instantly, the air became electric. The audience knew whatever they were about to hear was not a prepared speech. Uncontrolled. Alive. Anticipation snapped toward him, and he knew he had better not disappoint them. Baadluster half rose to his feet in the visitors' gallery. Pepys dragged at his sleeve and brought him back to his seat.

"Congressmen and representatives, ladies and gentlemen, and honored guests."

His voice brought quiet to the chambers. Even without the sound system, he would be heard clearly. No one, short of an assassin with Amber's powers, could stop him now.

Joy filled his voice as he began to speak.

"I have been introduced to you as a commander in the Dominion Knights, the battalion newly reformed by Emperor Pepys. I'm his sworn man, a soldier who wears battle armor. Many of you will listen to my testimony with bias, believing what you have already been told is the truth.

"You've been lied to."

Voices raised in pandemonium. To one side, Jack could see Washburn pounding a gavel for silence. Pepys sat up straighter in his booth, his auburn hair a crackling halo about his grim face.

"I swore to Pepys, but before him, I was sworn to another. A man whose name since his death has come to mean defeat and shame. I'm an honorable man, but I can hear you asking how can a man be loyal to two masters? If you're not, you're all damn fools."

"But I know where I stand because I never swore to the man, but to what he offered."

"First let me tell you who I really am."

"I was born on Dorman's Stand."

Another burst of noise and disbelief. The senators still standing about in the back galleries began to move closer, finding seats. He could see an aide racing across the upper balcony, in pursuit of what, he wondered briefly, as the audience calmed yet again to hear him.

"You heard me right. There's been no human born on Dorman's Stand in the last twenty-five years. It fell during the Sand Wars. It's a sand planet, lifeless for our people. But I was born there, and I remember the way it used to be, and I grew up there following in my father's footsteps until it came time for me to believe in another man." A fleeting, wry smile, passed over his lips. "I was a raw recruit then."

"I enlisted as a Knight under Emperor Regis."

This time, there was no wave of noise. Instead a deadly silence fell over the people before him. He caught sight of their faces and knew he had them.

"I'm probably the last living true Knight still in commission."

Baadluster and one of the WP men abruptly left the visitors' gallery, but Jack felt a keen edge of joy, for it was too late now.

"I enlisted to fight the Thraks, thinking we could stop them. I was sixteen and and you must understand what it was like to be me then."

He took them back, among the finely threaded memories Bogie had given him, because he had no choice. Otherwise they would never believe him. He was unsure if they believed him now. He only knew that no one stood any longer, and that even the aides at the com lines had turned to him, listening, their lips and fingers stilled.

"And so, I swore to Emperor Regis.

"And so it is that I'm here today. For if we had not been betrayed on Milos, if the Knights had not been left without backup, we could have held Milos. We could have stopped the Thraks then and there.

"But Regis wasn't secure in his power, evidently, and there were factions working to unseat the old warrior. We Knights became the pawns in a petty struggle and Milos was the mortal blow."

An incoherent shout interrupted Jack. He paused and looked toward the wing from which the sound had issued, but no one followed it up. He took the opportunity to press his fingertips along his brow, mopping up a few drops of sweat he hadn't known had rested there. He took up the unseen challenge.

"How do I know? *Because I was there.* I was one of the thousands scheduled to be left behind. The fleet was ordered out and the Thraks swept in. I was one of only a few hundred to make it to the three transports that somehow managed to come in. All three of them were hit heavily by Thrakian fire while trying to lift off."

His gaze swept them now. He challenged them. "I can see you remembering. Facts, you might tell me, easily scanned on any library computer. Perhaps. But I lived them.

"Two cold ships never made it past the League offenses. A third did . . . so heavily crippled it went adrift, its cargo locked in cold sleep. Eventually, its damaged systems could no longer function. Backup systems faltered. Those asleep died.

"Seventeen years later, the ship was found and one man remained alive—alive, but not untouched."

Jack held up his scarred hand. "I suffered frostbite. Cold sleep fever. And they tell me I could have been saner. I lost an entire lifetime while the Thraks took the planets they wanted, and Emperor Regis became a defeated old man who fell prey to an assassin.

"I spent four years in the Knights. Seventeen asleep. And the last five years learning the truth.

"The truth, ladies and gentlemen, is that the Thraks have no regard for your right to life. The truth is that we once had the means with which to stop them. To teach them respect for dealing with us. And we have those means again. I swore, not to Regis and not to Pepys, not to an emperor.

"I swore for peace through war.

"I stand by my oath.

"And I ask you to give me back the means with which to achieve it."

With those words, Jack stepped back.

There was an absolutely stunned silence. He dared to look at Pepys, knowing that both the expressions on his face and the emperor's would be covered by close-ups. The emperor sat motionless in his booth.

Haltingly, the applause began. It grew in spurts, hampered by the sound of the audience getting to their feet. They stood in waves until not a man was left sitting.

Not even Pepys.

Chapter 19

"A goddamn pacifist."

Jack sat down wearily, throat dry after hours of interviews following the Congressional speech. "Why else would you make war?" he said quietly and tried to ignore his emperor pacing before him.

Pepys came to a stop. His face went through several expressions before settling on a frown. His mouth likewise opened for retort, then closed. He looked to Baadluster.

"All is not lost," the minister said. "They're still debating out there."

Pepys shook his head, his frown obscured by a cloud of fine red hair, and stalked away again, his ceremonial robes practically afloat. He cast a look of loathing at Baadluster as he passed him.

He stopped at the far end of the room as though he had needed to put a distance between himself and Storm.

"I am your emperor," he said, his voice modulated with effort. "Why did you not tell me?"

Jack looked up. His eyes of rainwater blue met Pepys' cat green ones. "I thought you already knew."

Pepys made a gesture with his hand, the side of it cutting air as though it were a sword. "How can I trust you?"

"Or I you."

"Don't fence words with me! You weren't found by one of my ships or I would have been told."

"I'm a Dominion Knight," Jack said. "That should be enough. I am what I am, and I do what I've been trained to do. No more. *And no less.*"

"That's all I get? That's all? I could have you removed as commander."

Jack inclined his head. "If that's what you want. But I don't recommend it." He stood up. Under the lines of his dress blues, his frame carried the powerful muscles it took to wear and use a suit of battle armor. "Now you know me for what I am. Remember that I have always known you for what you are."

Pepys' body had been seething with indignation under his ceremonial robes, but the tone of Jack's voice froze him in his place. Baadluster cleared his throat as inconspicuously as he could, yet the emperor shot him a hard look and the minister shifted away from him slightly.

"Are you threatening me?"

"No," Jack said, as he moved closer. "But I think it's time we understand one another. Winton feared me, but for the wrong reasons. The Thraks didn't have me. If I was in the hands of the Green Shirts, then they couldn't accomplish what they wanted to. It had already been done, my emperor, by seventeen years of cold sleep, locked into a debriefing loop. I have lived and relived an eternity of betrayal. I know who I hate." Jack paused. His hands flexed. "Give me the freedom to go after the Thrakian League."

Pepys had been holding his breath. He relaxed now, nearly imperceptibly. "And then?"

"Reclaim Claron. Winton had it firestormed to rout me out. He duped you into okaying his actions because of the survey showing Thrakian infestation."

Baadluster said, "What kind of accusation is this—" but Jack gestured, cutting him off.

"Winton used freebooters. They can't be controlled."

Pepys sighed. He pulled out a chair and sat down, suddenly. "I bear the onus," he said. "All right. Terraforming for Claron. However long it takes, whatever the expense."

"In exchange for what?"

"Your silence? No." Pepys took a deep breath. "I am, in spite of all you might suspect of me, still the emperor of the Triad Throne. You can't prove what Winton ordered, I know that, but that does not mean I condoned it. Then or now. Let's just say I'm doing what I am doing to gain your loyalty."

A tiny muscle ticked along the line of Jack's jaw. He straightened. "I am a Knight. You either already have my loyalty or not. I can't be bought."

"No," Pepys answered him, smiling tightly. "Perhaps not." Anything further he might have said was interrupted by Senator Washburn bursting into the room. He was followed by a slender young man in the uniform of an aide.

"This is my son, Brant," Washburn blurted. He inserted his square, massive frame between Pepys and Baadluster. "Jack! Jack, my boy, I couldn't have done better myself!" He turned to Pepys. "Brilliant! Absolutely brilliant! His tongue would snap if he tried to lie! And a pacifist at that."

Pepys said irritably, "What is the news, Washburn?"

"What else could it be? Pepys, you astound me. No wonder you sit on the Triad Throne. If you'd given us a warmonger, we'd be out there arguing still . . . probably until the end of the session. But when you gave us a peaceful man who knew the time had come to fight—well, you lasered the opposition in their tracks."

Baadluster interrupted. "We have the appropriations?"

"Yes! Yes! We have a probationary war, gentlemen."

Jack watched them from across the room. He had won the battle for Claron, but he felt curiously hollow inside. It was not victory enough. Amber would probably have agreed with Washburn's assessment of his tongue and lying. He had learned long ago not to lie if he could help it.

So he simply had not told all of the truth. Pepys seemed reassured, but he would not be if he knew Jack's thoughts. First the Thraks. Then the emperor.

Chapter 20

"Drop in twenty minutes."

Jack rubbed the back of his neck and tried to ignore the computer voice. He keyed back, "Just get us in there."

The fleet pilot came on with arrogance in his voice. "You think this is easy?"

"I think," Jack formed his words deliberately, "that the bulk of the enemy is dirtside and if you want to fight a war, you've got to get us where the action is."

The warship waggled, and every man in staging found it hard to keep his footing. A buffeting followed and Jack knew that last burst had been close.

The pilot made a noise of contempt and closed off the com line.

The man suiting up nearest Jack paused. He frowned. "They never give us any respect."

Jack shot back, "Just do your job. We get in there, clear the sector so the shield crews can be dropped and get pylons built and the shields back in place. That's what we're here for. Do your job and the respect will follow."

The soldier's face paled a little under Jack's harsh tones, but he nodded. "Yes, sir."

Jack lapsed into uneasy silence. He looked across staging and realized he knew very little of the men fighting with him this run. Who would watch his back? Garner, across the bay, his spike of blue-black hair standing up defiantly, had his back to his commander and was instructing a green recruit on the niceties of a first drop. Jack could not hear what was said. He touched the cherry picker that held his own suit.

Boss. Are we ready?

"Nearly."

It's been a rough campaign.

"I know." This was Jack's third drop in five days, but they were going to regain Oceana and get the shields back up, dealing the Thrakian League another severe loss.

They can be beaten. A step at a time, but they can be beaten!

Jack opened up the seams, picked up a probe and began to test circuitry, automatically, out of habit, even though Bogie had been fully powered and tested twenty-four hours ago. He frowned. There were minute power shortages. Bogie had been pirating again. Jack rubbed his temples. The finding strengthened his resolve to get new armor fitted when they returned to Malthen. His old suit was no longer reliable . . . and there was another being fighting him for control of it. He couldn't tell Bogie yet nor could he predict what the sentience would do if he found out Jack would no longer share the suit or companionship with him.

Would it be the death of Bogie? Jack knew that the possibility existed, for the sentience was struggling now to regenerate as he had never had to struggle before. Perhaps the being was more closely related to a parasitic Milot berserker than he realized. Perhaps it needed more than Jack's warmth and sweat.

Perhaps it needed to begin feeding.

Jack jerked the probe out of his suit irritably.

Across the way, Fostermeir, his NCO for this drop, began the countdown. "Gentlemen, suit up! And let's not forget the dead man circuit, boys. We don't want any Thraks pulling armor off the casualties to take home and have fun with."

Premonition prickled at Storm. *Well,* Jack thought. . . .

". . . there's no time like the present." Denaro straightened, his helmet under his arm.

Amber shook her head. "I can't go with you."

"You damned well can't stay here. We may have five thousand recruits roaming around now, but I can tell you that they *know* there's been rogue activity. It's just a matter of time until you're caught."

Amber's mouth curved just a little. Denaro glared at her. He threw his shoulders back.

"All right, all right," he said. "I've been a pain in the ass. I have my duty to St. Colin and the Blue Wheel. And I'll admit I thought you were a she-devil at first, come to tempt me with all your wiles. But I'm a soldier and you're a soldier, and the emperor's army is no place to be caught. If you're going to fight, fight a war that counts. With someone honorable."

"Jack's honorable."

His jaw moved, then the man said, "From what I've seen of him. But Pepys is not, and a Knight has to be the emperor's man. Come with me."

Amber hesitated. Then she said softly, "No. I won't leave him. But you needn't worry . . . no one will find out from me where you've gone."

Denaro stood poised one second longer as if arguing with himself, but his lips clamped tightly on the words he might have said, and he ducked out of the locker room, leaving Amber alone with the words she might have said.

She stood alone with the echo of receding footsteps and wondered if, when Jack came home, he would come home to her.

Or would he really be coming home to his obsession with the armor and his fight against the Thraks?

Since the day of his speech to the Dominion Congress, her loneliness had been incalculable. It was as though a ten-meter metal plate had dropped between them. She had finally moved out of his bed, into the second bedroom in the apartment, and he had not even noticed.

Or worse, if he had, he had not objected.

"Ah, damn," she whispered, and the strangled sound of her own voice startled her. What was she lacking? What was it that she couldn't give Jack? If she could only find out.

She hung her helmet on its hook, thinking that it looked more than ever like a disembodied head, and began to strip her armor from her body.

"Red Wing down! My god, they're all gone."

"Pull yourself together, Garner."

"Jack! They're gone!"

"I've registered the hit, mister. Now pull your team together and get out of there." Jack moved his chin and took a sip of water that did little to ease the ache of loss he felt. The Thraks were getting used to fighting them again. They were taking a terrible toll.

He moved forward, tall buildings blocking his soundings and his readings on the target grids. Broken concrete and twisted beams prevented him from getting a fix on either his men or his enemy. Tile and fallen brick obscured doorways. Window shards lay scattered on the ground, sliver sharp and jewel bright.

This had been a city once, before Thrakian bombardment reduced it to rubble. Jack moved through

it and tried to keep the devastation from moving
him to despair.

Bone shards were almost as prevalent as glass
shards. Evacuation had come too late for some.
Ruins of transports and hovercars lay on their sides,
gutted with fire, lanced with skeletal remains. He
was all right as long as he did not remember they
had been human. The countryside was scarred even
worse: the Thraks had spent days knocking out the
power systems and the shields. Days before the
Knights could get here. Days and nights of aggres-
sion against a planet unprepared for the act of war.
He did not look down as he strode through an
alleyway, his mikes echoing the sound of his own
steps back at him.

His gauntlets tingled at his wrists, reminding him
they were powered up. Jack halted just before the
intersection with the main tube. He had a hunch the
Thraks that had taken out Red Wing were now
realigned out there, waiting to ambush Blue Wing.

He looked at his mapping grid. "Fostermeier,
Blue Wing, count off, with street positions."

"Yes, sir, approaching corner of Tenth and
Galway."

"Garner, angling up eighth toward Galway."

"Peaches here, in the alleyway intersecting Men-
doza."

"It's Aaron, sir, and I'm scaling a foundation . . .
I think I'm near First Street."

And on down the line, as they all approached
Galway.

He called it a hunch. Amber would call it intuition and curse him if he paid no attention to it.

"Don't enter the tube. I think we'll run a little
interference first. Back off."

"What is it, commander?"

"I think they're in the subway junction under the
Galway Main tube. Thraks like to go underground."

Jack felt the rightness of it the moment he said it.
Yes, of course, the subway system! Like home to
the Thraks. The moment Blue Wing entered the
main street, they would boil up out of the subway
entrances just like they boiled up out of sand.

The question was, what was he going to do about
it?

Static buzzed in his ear. A faint transmission fed
in. "Commander Storm, this is Gold Wing."

"Who's that? Where's Captain Bosk?"

"He's down, sir."

"Dead?"

"Well . . . he wasn't, sir, but the dead man circuit got him when they pulled him out of his armor."

They wanted armor. And they wanted it badly.
That confirmed Jack's fears. No longer would the
Thrakian attitude of natural superiority be on Jack's
side. The Thraks were going to find out all they
could about the enemy they were facing.

"Commander?"

The young voice pulled his attention back. "Who
is this, mister?"

"Lieutenant Vega, sir. We're on the outside of
the city, near the open country. I remembered the
lectures you gave, sir. There's sand around here
somewhere, there's grit in the wind."

Already. Jack made up his mind. "Hold on, Vega.
We'll be backing you up just as soon as we can pull
out of here." He toggled onto his main frequency.
"Fostermeier, I want a river of flame down there."

"What?"

"Fossil fuel, whatever you can find. Or, a volun-
teer with all the grenades he can handle."

"That's a death sentence, commander."

Jack felt the sweat trickling down his back. "Not
necessarily, sergeant. I'll do it myself, if I have to."

Aaron came in over the com. "Ah . . . commander? I'm presently standing on the first floor of

what appears to be a brewery. The storage tanks are still intact."

Alcohol? Not a very hot burn, and difficult to start, but their lasers ought to be up to it and it was better than nothing. "Garner, get over there and help him. Peaches, you, too. I want to funnel it down in flames. The rest of you men, home in on me. We're going to be decoys. And Fostermeier, if anything happens, I want you to take the rest of Blue Wing out to Vega's position. Where there's sand, there's the main infestation. It'll have to be taken out. All right, let's go. We're on a timetable for the construction crew drop. I want those shields back up before they can bring their mother ships down!"

They formed a wedge. They marched, the shocks from their armored boots vibrating through the asphalt and pavement. Jack smiled grimly. He knew that the Thraks knew they were on their way.

He only hoped they couldn't count that well.

Garner came on. "We're set here. Shit, Jack. This stuff is 120 proof . . . but we can pour it right on top of 'em. We've stopped the storm drains, the street will be full in a second."

"Then it'll burn well. We're almost in position. On my mark . . . now." Jack right-angled, making his way toward the brewery.

A fighter streaked overhead, leaving a sonic boom in its wake. Jack craned his neck back, helmet cameras catching its blurry image. At the edge of the city, explosions erupted, and he could see a dark cloud of smoke and glowing ash rise crimson against the destruction.

"We've got no time left, they're bringing in the big guns."

"It's on the way," Fostermeir said.

Jack strode out onto Galway. Two degrees to his left, he could see the cavernous mouth of the subway stairs. He was in a concrete canyon, with no-where to run if his tactic failed.

Amber liquid washed past him, curling about his boots, and swirling on down the street, blue alcohol flames nearly invisible. It spilled down into the sub-way, where it burned hotter and he could see the gout of flames turn orange and roar back up from the mouth of the underworld. Thraks filled the stair-way. Jack braced himself and began to shoot, cutting them down as they attempted to hurdle the wall of blue and orange flame.

Something slapped at the armor. He staggered back.

Boss, they're using projectiles. I suggest we not make a target of ourselves!

Beside Jack, Fostermeier blossomed. He dropped, visor down, into the dwindling river of fire.

With an angry whine, something slapped at Jack's armor again. He felt the pinch of crimped Flexalinks along his upper arm. "Sergeant!"

He's gone, Boss.

Jack hit the power vault, clearing the NCO's still form easily. The alcohol flames, quickly spent, gut-tered out. He scanned his screen, saw another two of his men down in the street. A field pack lay burst open between them.

With two strides, he reached them. Jack plucked out three grenades. He turned and headed for the subway entrance.

I don't think I'm going to like this said Bogie.

"I think you're right," Jack answered. "Garner! Head for the outskirts, now, and that's an order! Home in on Vega and go for the nest." He keyed the start sequence on the grenade and, even as he walked into the field of fire, he wondered when Bogie had gotten a sense of self-preservation.

Something slapped him high in the left shoulder, hard enough to pivot him around on his boot heel and leave him staggered. He righted himself and keyed the second grenade, then lobbed them both.

Smells flooded the suit as if he'd cracked his helmet, yet he hadn't. Sounds followed—an earfilling chittering of Thrakian alarm. A wall of Thraks reared in front of him as Jack punched in the last code. He rolled the grenade across their front, hit the power vault, and was in the air and behind them when the shock wave hit.

He could smell the explosion. The scorched chitin. The hot ash. As he hit and landed, a racking pain skewered his left shoulder.

"Damn," he said. "I'm hit."

No kidding, boss. You're leaking.

Projectiles. The norcite coating on his armor had taken him farther than Fostermeier and his other two men, but he wasn't completely invincible. Jack got to his knees and then stood up. The constrictions of the armor prevented him from surveying the exterior damage.

From the inside, it felt gooey. He started to look down and thought better of it.

"Get a patch on it, Bogie, and let's get out of here."

The chamois which always lay along his back and neck, edged over to his shoulder. Jack felt a gentle warmth begin to drive away the icy pain. He turned and panned the street. It was empty.

He broke into a jog, the battle suit eating up the distance. The throb in his shoulder kept time with the jolt of his boots.

He wasn't going to go unless he could take the nest with him.

Bogie settled gingerly over the torn flesh. He was cold, always cold now, and the power reserves of Jack's armor no longer fed him the energy he needed to maintain a status quo, let alone to regenerate.

Blood welled up around him, soaking naturally into the porous nature of the chamois. Bogie refocused from the battle they fought to his own inward nature.

He tasted life. He knew the flavor. It sang in him, gave him heart.

He knew that Jack was dying, even as he sensed that he had begun to live again, for the first time in long, cold months.

It was the blood. The crimson fountaining up from the damaged flesh. It had to be.

He stemmed the life flow. He dared not taste it again.

He dared not.

Jack's pulse thundered in his senses. He could heal Jack somewhat, set the edge of puckered flesh next to the edge of puckered flesh and begin the healing. Clot the bleeding, scab the wound.

And he could carry Jack to safety within the shell of the battle armor, if there was safety to be found anywhere on this planet.

Or he could touch life himself and grow again.

His soul trembled.

The chamois quivered. Tiny cilia erupted. Hairlike. Feather light. Questing for the life font it desired. No, craving was not strong enough! In every particle of his newly reforming body, Bogie had to have what he had tasted.

Bogie pulled back from the wound, not trusting himself. Jack neither knew nor cared as he cried out hoarsely, "I have the sand targeted. All Teams, all Wings, home in on me, we're going in!" even as he staggered forward.

Jack's destiny was moot, Bogie decided. He let the cilia creep forward in quest of whatever life might be left.

Chapter 21

Amber woke screaming, her voice clawing its way out of her throat, her bed covers thrashed and wet with sweat—or was it tears?—about her. She shivered into silence, her throat as lacerated with her terror as if she'd tried to swallow a power blade. Her chest heaved for air, and then she *knew*.

"Oh, god. It's Jack!"

She threw aside the covers and, in pitch darkness, stumbled out of the bed. There was no time, no time to waste at all. She opened the com lines to Colin and prayed for a speedy answer.

It was the middle of the night, but the Walker prelate answered on the second ring. She recognized his meditation chamber surrounding him. His eyes were tired, he was still fully dressed, and she realized he'd been working late.

"Amber. What is it?"

"It's Jack. I know it is. Oh, god," she got out, before a paroxysm of fear stilled her.

"Where is he?"

"I don't know! Fighting somewhere. But I think he's dying . . . or dead."

St. Colin closed his eyes briefly, as if in remorse, then looked back at her through the screen. "He's a soldier, dear heart. He knew the risks."

"He can't! It's not his time yet. Not without me. He can't!"

"What do you expect me to do?"

And in that moment, hope seized her nearly as keenly as the fear had. He had not said, *there's nothing I can do.* He'd asked, *what do you expect me to do,* as if he could do something. With one hand, she swept her disheveled hair back from her face.

"What can you do?"

He winced. "A prayer, perhaps?"

"I'm not religious.

For a long moment, he closed his eyes again, before looking deeply into hers. His deep sable eyes were pensive. "I'm helpless, Amber. If I were with him, perhaps . . . but he's far beyond my limited capabilities."

"I can help."

"You'd have to be with me. Do we have much time?"

She snatched at the remnants of her dream. "I don't know—but it's better than nothing. You stay—I'll get there."

Colin keyed off as she broke the connection and his screen went dark. He sat back in his chair. He'd been up most of the night in his meditation chamber, not worrying, barely thinking, merely atuned to the elements of the room. Renewing himself. Perhaps even readying himself. When the natural time for sleep came, he had used a light trance instead, waking when Amber called. *Did I know?* he asked himself. There were those Walkers who would insist he had . . . the ones who called him saint. But there were others who would disagree, the same Walkers who would have felt that Denaro had defected. He knew there might be trouble at any moment, precipitated by the militant's actions. It was only logical to stay alert.

And there were a precious few who would say,

what happened, happened. Why question it? Simply accept it as you find it.

Colin rubbed his temples, thinking that he preferred to side with the last group. He knew he had erred in speaking with Amber. A deliberate or an unconscious error? Was it recognition of some unvoiced feeling that if he could save any friend he had, he would save Jack? Perhaps. What was done, was done. He slipped back into his trance and it seemed like a matter of moments before a sleepy, rumpled Jonathan was escorting Amber into the chamber.

Her very presence resonated in the chamber. She wore her Bythian caftan and had tied her tawny hair back in a knot, but tendrils of it had escaped to frame the tense lines of her face. She barely waited until Jonathan left, then she crossed the room and grabbed his hands. Her fingers were chill.

"He's still there," she said, and her voice was husky. "But I'm losing him."

He made her sit beside him, and then he said, "You think I've promised more than I have."

Amber looked closely at him. "I think you have promised all that you can do."

He knew she had caught him. He was silent for a long moment. "Very well," he said. "Do you know why I am called a saint?"

"I looked you up once," she answered, with a mischievous grin that was far more like the old Amber he knew than this worried young woman who sat next to him. "You were rumored to have raised the dead."

"No rumor," he said, feeling uncomfortable. "But he'd just died in my arms. Doctors do it all the time."

"But you were at a Walker outpost."

"Yes. Relatively primitive conditions, and don't ask me how I did it because I don't know. I just know that, suddenly, I was filled with this outrage that he should have died, and I was determined that he shouldn't suffer the indignity of his broken body . . . he'd been in a cave-in, trying to reach a group of school children who'd gone in to see some artifacts just as a minor quake hit. They were frightened but safe, the area they were in had been shored up well. He was killed in an after-shock. I was very young then. I was angry that someone so good should have died so horribly." Colin looked away from her then, filled with the memory. "I remember holding him very tightly as I prepared the body for his widow to see. The esophagus had been packed with dirt. I cleaned him out, straightened broken limbs, and washed him. Then the outrage hit and I held him tightly one last time, thinking—and I've never told anyone this—thinking how pissed off I was at God that it had happened."

"And then he began to breathe in my embrace."

Colin took a deep breath himself and turned back to Amber. He had not quite told her all of it, but some things were between himself and his God.

"And so that's why they call you a saint."

"I presume so. It cannot be for holding my temper in check. Amber, I cannot guarantee it would ever happen again. It would be a mockery to do so. God heals, not I. I can't guarantee God's manifestations."

She pushed the silken sleeves of her caftan up in determination. The light blue tracing of her tattoos seemed alight. "Maybe not. Now tell me what happened to Rawlins."

His jaw fell. "What do you mean?"

"What do I mean? What do you think I mean? The two of you walk into an ambush at the Thrakian embassy and the two of you walk out alive? The only thing wrong with you was broken ribs. I knew something had to have happened to Rawlins. He was in a daze for a month, and now he follows you around as though you had a psychic leash on him. We all have our histories on Bythia. I simply couldn't figure out what yours was."

Colin shook his head. "He took a chest shot meant for me. I healed him. He . . . was not dead."

"But dying."

"Perhaps." He felt very old, suddenly. "Amber, I'm not the man you took adventuring to Lasertown. I'm not even the man who went to Bythia. It . . . it takes a toll, perhaps one I can't begin to pay any more."

"That's why I'm here. Please. You've got to help me try. Together."

Colin looked at her. Night pressed in about the room, even though there were no windows. He could feel its presence, very close. Her heat warmed his right side, but nothing could keep the iciness of a soul at ebb tide from his left. "All right," he said quietly. "Take my hands and see if you can find your way to him."

Amber took the older man's hands in hers. She could feel the age in his skin. Wrinkled. Not elastic like hers, springing back after each touch. And the pads of his hands were calloused and broad, like a man who had worked with them each and every day of his life. She wondered at that even as she felt the tiny drum of his pulse under her fingers. Anchored by his steadiness, his age, and his wisdom, she flung herself into the void in search of Jack.

She expected cold. She received nothingness, a stretching of herself until she felt vast and incredibly transparent, a sprinkling of mortal dust that the first solar wind could scatter irretrievably. She had to make the effort to pull herself together before she mingled forever with the infinite possibilities of the universes she encountered. She was a kite, soaring, and Colin was the flier, far behind her, yet connected by a tenuous string of simply *being*.

Her perception of herself and Colin was so altered from what she'd expected, that she had no idea of how to look for Jack. Would he be dust also? Or a rock, like Colin?

No, she thought. She remembered him from her first impressions, locked in his white armor, hot with vengeance. *He was a sun*. She knew that and went in search of a planetary flame that burned as brightly as any solar disk.

Condensing herself, she trailed across worlds in a track that had no signposts, no maps, no indication of where she had been or where she was going. She found a flame or two, tasted them—not Jack . . . not even human. She flew onward.

There was a tug at her string. She looked back and saw Colin's anchoring of her self grow a little weaker. Time had no meaning. *How long*? she thought. And then, *how far*? He reeled her in until she hovered, not in her body but close enough to see out her eyes and once more feel the touch of flesh upon flesh. Her ears were filled with song, a thousand notes and vibrations, some discordant, most melodious.

"Here," Colin was saying, and his voice was so thin, so far away, she could barely catch the sense of it. "Amber, can you hear me?"

Her lips opened. "Yeeesss," she whispered.

"Jonathan's located the current campaign. Star maps will do you no good, but I have something. This was made for me by a Walker congregation from Oceana. Use it to home in on."

He pressed something into the palm of her hand. Her impression of touching it was double-layered: the faint, gritty impression of rock and cloth upon her palm, and a closer, much more intent impression upon her ethereal body. She grasped it and flung herself away again, this time with a lodestone for her direction.

To that, she added pain, for, previously, she had forgotten to look for war, and although every planet she touched echoed with strife, she looked for immolation.

She reached a world and slowed, uncertain, felt a gigantic brush of another body past hers, and saw, was seared by, the impression of an immense warship coming to, turrets swinging around, and the planet below trembling under the blast it received.

She quailed from the uprush of death and pain and fear, alien though it was, for the planet being destroyed was not inhabited by humans. She heard their cries in her mind and tumbled away, letting the backlash of the weaponry sweep her away.

Quiet hovered behind her. The warship thundered out of orbit and left, the planet wrapped in an aura of radiation. Amber held her lower lip between her teeth as she took one last look back, over her shoulder.

Sand, she thought. A sand planet but sand no more. Its atmosphere rippled in a prism of color.

She had no time to wonder. The lodestone in her hand jerked to the right, and she soared, and found another solar system.

The white flame she sought guttered low. Fear coalesced in Amber's ethereal body as she drew near, and found a physical world, torn by battery placements and shelling and laser fire—all scars that would heal quickly, unlike the world she'd seen irradiated. Below her stretched a cityscape, half in ruins, flames licking at it, gray pavement streaked with crimson. Beyond it, she saw countryside, its green trampled, ground broken, trees snapped and flung aside. Men in armor ranged it, moving quickly. She saw the sand waiting on the horizon, sand and the abhorrent touch of Thraks.

Drawing in upon herself, she swooped down, no longer having to search for Jack. She was air and he was fire, and he sucked her in as though she existed only to fuel him.

Her last gasp was to reach for Colin.

Colin felt the sharp jerk on his soul. It nauseated and frightened him because it felt as if something was trying to suck him out like a raw egg from its shell. Amber's chill hands convulsed within his, and then he was gone, his mind ripped out of his body, and he found himself confronting . . .

It was not death. He knew death. It was Jack and something different, something primitive and feral, something desperate to do anything to maintain its life . . . yet something with an ultimate form that shimmered on the edge of Colin's senses like a golden curtain of intelligence and benevolence. He was reminded of an embryo's selfishness in its mother's womb, launched toward a life it could not possibly comprehend yet.

Amber enveloped him. *Can you help? Dear god, hurry, I'm losing it . . .*

Colin sensed Jack's wound, but the second presence fended him off, would not let him near, and, worse, this thing knew and understood the plane they inhabited, the spiritual self. It could and would destroy Colin on this plane. He approached again, and was rebuffed so solidly it made him gasp and pant in his physical form and his senses whirled, torn between what he experienced in his two selves. He was fading from Amber's grasp. All he could do was offer the second presence a glimpse of the life awaiting it, before their contact exploded and he and Amber were flung across the galaxies.

Chapter 22

Jack staggered and went to one knee, jarring himself inside the armor. A lead broke loose from where it was clipped to his torso, and he swore. But the sharp pain did some good. It broke the lethargy riding him. His shoulder sent a jag of agony throughout his body, broke sweat out on his forehead, and raised bile to the back of his throat. He righted himself. He listened for Bogie to goad him onward, but the sentience was uncharacteristically silent.

Around him, return fire kept him pinned down. He checked his target grids, uneasily aware that he'd been about to walk right into a crossfire and wondering what his mind could have been on. That's when he knew just how badly he'd been tagged. He was losing it. . . .

"Jay-sus, commander, you've been hit!" Garner hit the dirt field next to him, ducking his helmet behind a barrier of mud and rock thrown up by the earlier pounding the installation had taken.

"How close are we to getting in?"

Garner's helmet swung to face him. Through the sun-screened visor, Jack had difficulty seeing if there was humanity within. But Garner's voice held a trace of his fierce, biting humor.

"You and me and Aaron, and three or four well-placed grenades should do it. They'll be facing a fatal distraction . . . if you can do it."

"Don't worry about me." Carefully, Jack reached around to unsling his field pack. He left it and the laser rifle within it lying at his feet as he stood, keeping the outcropping between him and the main nest.

"Commander—"

"No more weight than necessary," Jack said. "Take what you need and leave the rest. If this works, there won't be enough left of the Thraks to matter. If it doesn't . . . the team coming up behind us can use it. Where's Aaron?"

"He hit the dust over there." Garner pointed. Armor could be seen lying amongst charred and broken ground, grass clumps still attempting to wave feebly despite damage and trampling, like a forlorn banner.

Aaron's young voice came in faintly over the com. "—Com trouble, but I'm ready when you are—"

"Ready." Jack keyed his grenades. "On your feet. I want to see if you guys are good enough in armor to keep up with me." He surged out of hiding and charged the Thrakian battlement.

Bogie felt the renewed heat of Jack's blood. He lay against Jack's skin, listening to the thunder of his pulse as the man launched himself against the enemy.

And within the armor, Bogie fought another war. He felt the touch of something he could not identify, something . . . celestial. It offered him so much more than mere life. It gave him a view of the being he might grow to be out of the baseness he was now.

But not a being sprung out of blood.

No.

And as Jack threw himself at the nest, laser fire

rippling off his armor, Bogie drew back his cilia, denying himself. He did not have the strength to heal Jack the way he once could have. Instead, he worked at stemming the flow by blocking here and here . . . doing what he could to make sure the man who nurtured him might live.

But there was no way either of them could block the barrage from the remaining Thraks.

Jack flung his grenades, hit the power vault and somersaulted in midair, away from the resulting explosions. The burst flung him, as he'd intended, out of the line of return fire. He heard Garner yell and Aaron bite off a curse that sounded much too vehement for his youth. Then the mikes went dead, overloaded by the following blasts. He landed, and a shock wave tumbled him over. Garner landed well. A laser blast blossomed in the middle of his chest plate. Crimson and ebony blocked out his rank insignia and Garner crumpled slowly.

Sound bled back in. Jack stood. He heard the ricochet whine even as the projectile slapped him again and he felt the pain tear through his right thigh. *Damn*, he thought, as he went to one knee, and twisted around. *I'm never going to get out of here in one piece!*

Then, all was was silent . . . except for a piercing screech that became louder and louder. He looked up and panned the darkening sky. A Needler whipped in overhead, lower and lower. He saw the canopies hitting the air below it.

The shield crew.

Jack withdrew his right hand very slowly from his gauntlet and sleeve and wiped his face. His skin was clammy.

Static crackled. "Thank you, Commander Storm. All clear now, shield crews dropping. Stand by for pickup. Acknowledge."

Jack cleared his throat, his thoughts still fuzzy.
"This is Commander Storm. Please repeat."

A laugh. "What's the matter, Jack? That last
salvo scramble your brains? There's nothing moving
down there but Dominion armor. Get your shit
together and make the rendezvous point. I understand there's a few of you guys need the doctor."

Jack blinked. He realized then that the dancing
lightning of laser fire had ceased around him. He
pulled Garner to his feet. The man came up, air bur-
bling in his chest. Jack assessed the damage. He
reached into the armor and made Garner place his
own hand over the wound to staunch it. It wasn't
sucking air, so the man just might make it. Jack felt
a surge of fierce joy as Aaron helped him brace
Garner from the other side. Once more they'd beaten
the Thraks at their game. He heard the Needlers
screaming overhead. "Let's go home."

Chapter 23

Interloper

The warship swept in before the tertiary alarms even had a chance to go off and the factories had no time to download for red alert. Young Brant stood at the con tower, unable to believe his comp readouts.

"It can't be in under the shields."

"Affirmative. Unidentified aggressor, bearing six-zero-niner—"

"Shit," he muttered and hit the manual alarms.

Later, the records would show he was a full thirteen minutes ahead of the tertiary system.

Brant then opened the general com lines. The armory factories could blow half the planet up if they went, and there was no doubt in his mind that the incoming wasn't friendly. As he opened the lines, he said to the computer, "I want a Thrakian ID."

"Negative," the comp replied smoothly. "The unknown is not Thrakian according to data bank."

"It has to be!" Brant stood on one leg and then the other. "Answer the com, dammit! Answer me!"

A low thunder began to rumble. His fair blond hair stood on end. The tower vibrated.

"ETA fourteen minutes," the comp said. "Air to land missile approach."

"What?" Brant's voice went up half an octave. "Oh, shit, oh, shit! *Answer the com!*"

A light came on, but the screen stayed dark. "Good afternoon, this is Washburn Industries. If you wish to talk to personnel, key 1. If you wish payables, key 2. If you wish—"

Brant screamed into the receiver, "We're under fire! Emergency!"

Then he ran for the underground silos. Behind him in the tower, the comp said smoothly, "ETA seven minutes."

And another comp replied, "If you wish to talk to customer service, key 5. Thank you for calling Washburn Industries."

Brant erred. The unidentified assailant did not take out half the planet. But the predominant continent in the northern hemisphere suffered severe casualties. Washburn Industries, along with two grenade factories and Beretta Laser Rifles, were pulverized.

Even the underground silos.

Only the "black box" remained intact to tell the story after the first impact.

Chapter 24

"You can let me walk across the quad. I'm not going to break in two, goddammit."

Amber said scornfully, "An overnight at the hospital and you think you're healed. If you don't behave yourself, you'll be *sleeping* in the quad. Colin, talk some sense into him!"

The Walker stood, Jack's arm draped about his shoulder, looking as though he was bolstering the man's weight while Amber wrestled to set up a four-wheeled cart. The early morning breeze ruffled Colin's light fringe of hair and he took a deep breath. Malthen might actually have rain today, he thought as he inhaled. He no more supported Jack than Amber did at the moment and the two men exchanged a glance.

Face pink, Amber straightened. "There. You sit. Or you go the hard way, facedown on a gurney."

Jack made as if to shrug, then winced and thought better of it. He sat down in the small cart and adjusted the handlebars to a comfortable reach. He started the cart. Colin and Amber did not find it difficult to match its pace as he drove across the palace grounds.

"You know," Jack said, "the medics didn't say this was necessary."

"The medics," Amber retorted. "The same medics who also released Garner this morning? Just before he collapsed?"

"That's different. Garner spent the trip back in a cryo tank. They thought he'd healed more."

Amber stretched her long legs and strode out in front of the cart, bringing Jack to an abrupt halt. She looked down at him. "I hear one more complaint out of you, and I'm going to tell Pepys and Baadluster you're out early, and you can spend the day with *them*."

"Now that," Colin observed, "is a potent threat."

Jack smiled wryly. He held his hand up. "I surrender."

"Good. Now point that thing in the right direction and get going."

Colin caught up with Amber. In a voice pitched so that Jack could not hear it over the hum of the cart's motor, he offered, "You shouldn't be so hard on him."

Her nose was pinched white, belying her attempt to smile. "I know," she answered. "But when a miracle can't even save him . . . when you know there's nothing you can do, that you're absolutely helpless . . ." She stopped at the edge of grass that was brown and brittle, as desperate in its need as she was in hers. "I've just got to knock some sense in that thick farmer's skull of his. I know what it's like inside that suit . . . you think you're unstoppable. Well, he's not. And the sooner he realizes it, the more chance I've got that he's going to keep coming back to me."

Colin took her words in with a deep sigh. He reached out and took her hand, pulling her along with him as he hurried to catch up. "That's why, my dear, so many of us believe in God." At the outside walk to the officers' apartments, he took his hand from hers and gave her a chaste kiss on her cheek. "I'm going no farther. This is a sensitive area at best, and I want no more friction with Pepys than necessary."

Amber threw a look over her shoulder to make sure Jack was waiting for her before he stood up. She looked back. "Have you heard from Denaro?"

The old man smiled. "Now that would be telling, wouldn't it? I'll talk to you two in a day or so." He gave a graceful half-bow, then turned and left them.

Amber helped Jack stand. If he noticed her new strength and firmness of muscle, he said nothing. What he did say was, "Where's Bogie?"

"In the shop. There was a lot of damage, Jack. I went in yesterday after I left you. But he's okay. Just, I don't know. Different."

Jack paused, leaning his weight on her shoulder, his warm breath grazing her face as he talked. "I think he's dying. I can't give him what he needs to grow anymore."

"Jack!"

"I don't know what to do. We could turn him over to one of the university labs, I guess."

"We couldn't! He'd die anyway without us. And what lab could you trust?"

Jack's silence confirmed her fears. She shouldered his weight a little better. "Come on. Let's not stand out here and talk about it." With her free hand, she checked the security seals. All were intact.

He made himself smile. "You just want to get me in bed."

"Keep thinking positively," she shot back, and palmed the door open. He found it necessary to lean on her more than he'd thought as his newly healed thigh and shoulder weakened on him. Inside the apartment, he took a few short breaths to quell the pain and dizziness as Amber left him long enough to lock the door. She left all the shades down and the lights off and he blinked, waiting for his eyes to adjust to the dark.

"Can you make it to a chair?" She thumbed at an unresponsive light switch. "Damn light sensor's broken."

A third voice caught them in the dimness. "Don't bother, Amber. I can see just fine."

When Amber had pulled the shades, Jack could see the golden mesh ocular piece glinting at them. The rest of the face had changed . . . harsh angular lines biting into heavy jowls. The tousled black curls were going a dirty gray. The intruder rested a handgun on his thigh lightly, its red charge button shining at them. But Jake knew the man well. Long ago deserter and underworld scoundrel, Ballard.

He clenched his fist even as he fought to stay upright, solid, menacing. "How did you get in here?"

Ballard glanced at Amber. "She knows we have our ways. She bought jammers a few months ago. Simple enough for me to slip in a microchip that made your home easy for me to unlock. Thought I might need it." He held up a thick hand. "Before you tear me apart, Storm, let me say that I had nothing to do with what happened last year."

Jack had little reason to believe him. "The terrorists carried an unusual calling card. Your prosthetic eye." Sour memories of threats and beatings filled his throat.

Ballard made a noise, half scorn and half as if painful remembrance. "That bastard Winton set them up. Me, too. He tore my eye out, then sent me on my way." He smiled without any warmth. "I didn't think I'd be able to get another one put in. But Winton also paid me well. I found a good surgeon this time. I hid out until I heard you'd killed him on Bythia." Ballard shifted in the chair.

"What made you crawl out from under the rocks this time?"

"The war." Ballard waggled the gun. "I was taking libation in a bar, looked up, and there you were in Congress. You did us proud, Jack. I was the first to call you what you are, the last remaining true Knight. I want you to remember that. I want you to know that I knew who you were, and even with my eye gone, I didn't tell Winton. He had his suspicions, but he never had the truth from *me*."

Jack shook his head. "You deserted and took your armor with you. Don't be proud of yourself now."

Ballard hawked deep in his throat, turned his head slightly and spat on the rug to his right. "Listen, hero. If it weren't for scum like me and Amber, you wouldn't have survived two weeks in Malthen."

Jack moved then. He launched himself across the room so quickly that Ballard could not react, wrapped his fist in the front of the intruder's short jacket and shook him as if he were not even human. The gun fell to the floor and Amber snatched it up.

Ballard's teeth rattled. He blurted out, before Jack could say a word, "I'm wrong there. Amber's not scum, never has been. Dammit, man, let me go. I came here to help you."

Jack staggered back on his heels as he gave Ballard one last shake and dropped him.

The chair cracked as it took the man's weight and Ballard sat, panting. He brushed a limp curl off his gold screen eye.

"Say what it is and get out."

"All right. Amber—" the man's good eye flickered visibly toward her.

"She can take care of herself."

Ballard shrugged. "It's not good, Jack, getting her involved. All right." Gingerly, he reached inside his short jacket. "I brought you something." He flipped the recording disk in the air and Jack caught it.

"What's this?"

"*This*, my Knight, is something you should know about. Rumor has it that the new Minister of War makes Winton look like a saint. There are more things in heaven than you or I can dream about," and Ballard smiled crookedly. "Thank me for it later. If you need a witness, let me know." Ignoring Amber, he got to his feet and lumbered toward the door.

Amber trained the gun muzzle on him. Her finger began to tighten on the trigger sensor. But Jack waved. "Let him go."

She gave Ballard a poisonous look as he reached the portal. "Don't ever confuse me with yourself again."

Ballard paused, a massive wreck of a man. He reached out and chucked her under the chin. "No. I won't make that mistake again. I owe you a sincere apology, little one." His gaze flicked over Jack once, quickly, then back to her. "Let's just say that a small and jealous man can make bitter remarks." Amber wavered uncertainly and he took the opportunity to leave.

Jack held the recording in his palm. "Let's see what the hell this is."

The recording faded into silence. Amber looked up from her kneeling position on the floor. "What's going on?"

Jack stayed in the broken armchair. It had gone lopsided after he'd dropped Ballard's mass into it. He drummed the padded arm beneath his hand. Three fingers and a thumb, drumming, a discordant noise. "It means that whoever it was got in under the primary and secondary alarm systems and past the shields. The computer had to have been right: they couldn't have been Thrakian. It took a week's worth of pounding to break the shields

on Oceana before they got to go dirtside. No one
I know has the technology to circumvent shielding
as if it wasn't there." The face of the war was
changing before his very eyes.

"Then why weren't you told?" Amber countered.

"I don't know. It could be they don't trust me
since Denaro defected. I could kill Colin for getting
me involved in that." He stopped drumming his
fingers and, instead, rubbed his thigh as if the deep
gnawing pain he still felt from the wound could be
eased that way. "It sounds to me like the same
outfit that got Opus."

Her golden-brown eyes widened. "Them?"

"I think so. Don't get me wrong—it could be
freebooters, there's none of them above a little loot-
ing during wartime, when the majority of the fleet
is distracted elsewhere—but there's no one, no one,
with that kind of technology yet." He stood, still a
little wobbly, and made an effort to hold himself
tall. "I think that we're facing brand new players,
and we can't begin to know the rules or stakes until
we know who or what they are. Ballard says he can
get me witnesses. Contact him. I want to meet with
them. I don't think there's a way in hell we can
trust Pepys or Baadluster to tell us the truth if they
even know it."

Chapter 25

Pepys looked at the report. "Another one," he said, wearily, and rubbed his eyes. They had lost their emerald brilliance from fatigue. His freckled face was puffy.

Baadluster stood at the window, looking out to where a light rain attempted to clean Malthen's air, water its greenery, and purge its technology. He held his hands clasped loosely behind his back and, perhaps intentionally, perhaps not, his voice sounded a little smug as he answered the emperor. "No one else has seen this yet, not even the Dominion Security Council. If you wish me to arrange it so . . . no one will."

Pepys looked over a copy of the transmission one more time. Then he said, "What about Washburn?"

"We may have to take him out to keep him quiet. That was his son making the recording." Reluctantly, Baadluster turned away from the sight of the rain.

One carrot-colored eyebrow arched. "Surely someone would notice the absence of four major defense industries."

"Accidents happen. We could release news of a Thrakian strafing."

"On a shielded world?"

"A traitor let down the forcefields," Baadluster said blandly. "Washburn or his son. It would not matter, to the dead." He turned back and missed Pepys' shudder.

The emperor took a deep breath. Then he said, "Whatever is quickest and easiest to arrange. Do it neatly. I want no connections to be made."

"Don't worry," said Baadluster smoothly. "If anything comes back, it will lead to the Green Shirts. Now, as to the other matter we spoke of, I believe it's time to come off the defensive. I think we should look to beating the Thraks on their own territory."

"When?"

"I think we can have the new recruits up to it in two weeks."

Pepys stood up and stretched his wiry body. "What about the new recruiting centers?"

"Up and operational. Commander Storm appears to have a certain amount of charisma. They're still lining up for enlistment. We'll have all three centers fully equipped for basic training by the end of the week. Five thousand more graduates in six months."

That brought a smile to the emperor's face. He stepped to the window, deliberately blocking Baadluster's line of sight. It was, after all, his view. "I never thought I'd see the day the Dominion willingly donated ground to me, to my troops. I wonder if they'll like the flower that grows from that seeding!" He laughed. "All right then. We can afford to take the offensive. What about our new commander? Will he be well enough?"

Baadluster stood behind the emperor. The man was small enough that the minister could easily see over his head. He had, in fact, a better panorama than Pepys did, and he knew it. His too thick lips thinned cruelly. "If not, he would never admit the weakness. One way or another, he'll accomplish what we want him to. And if we're lucky, the Thraks will rid us of him."

Chapter 26

Jack fingered the Flexalinks. He curled a fist and pounded the shoulder plate, unhappy with the feel of it. It might have just been his imagination, but he felt the give in it. The weakness. The edges of certain links here and there retained their crimping in spite of having been pounded out.

Good as new, boss.

He did not answer Bogie. The armor was not as good as new. Could no longer be repaired as good as new. And, he knew from previous outings, its obsolescence impaired his leadership. Leadership, hell, it impaired his very *survival*.

"Ever think of moving, Bogie?"

Huh?

"Never mind." He dropped his hand. What could he do? "Still cold?"

The sentience was slow in answering, then, *Yes.*

He slapped the armor sleeve. "We'll think of something." He turned to leave. The shop was quiet. It was mid-shift, in the middle of the night, and he'd left Amber alone in the bed once again to come here. Soon, even in mid-shift, the shop would be filled as staging began for the operation to invade the Thrakian League. He approved of Baadluster's decision and that filled Jack with the faint-

est of misgivings, but he could not deny himself the
sweetness of a strike at the Thraks. He turned away,
and was caught by the edge of Bogie's thought.

What is life?

Jack said ironically, "You ask me? Maybe I should
haul St. Colin in here and let you grill him."

*I am serious, Jack. When you were injured, I . . .
tasted you. I tasted your life, and it was warm.*

The sentience had to mean blood, not life. Jack
thought of the Milot berserkers and how they were
born into existence. He shuddered. Was Bogie then,
if not an actual berserker, a parasite as he had once
feared? Did he fight the possibility of being first
possessed, then consumed, every time he wore the
armor? He fought the revulsion the idea brought to
him. "You're alive, Bogie. You're thinking and
aware."

*Only through you. Take you away from me, and
I am nothing.*

That was what Jack feared most. Did the alien
sense the inevitable choice Jack was being forced to
make?

Jack took up some tools and sat down, helmet in
hand, while he worked. The feeling of having something to do while he talked settled him. Finally, he
said, "That will change when you've grown."

*I can't grow any more. What will feed me?
Blood feeds you. What will feed me?*

"Blood isn't the only thing that feeds me. I breathe
air. I like the feeling of sun on my skin. A bottle of
good beer and a medium-rare steak now and then. I
need to feel good."

You need Amber's love.

"That's one of the things."

Bogie was silent for a long time. Jack finished
checking the circuitry he was working on. He did a
minute bit of soldering and cursed when he burned

his fingertip. He ought to let the technicians handle this, he thought to himself. It's too bad Bogie wasn't a seed. He could just transplant him. Or a seedling that could be grafted somewhere. He looked up. "Other things grow differently. A seed takes sunlight and water. Photosynthesis. It grows that way."

Explain.

Jack tiredly brushed his hair from his forehead. "I can't explain. Listen. Feel." He reached out and held the armor's gauntlet and remembered his family's agra station on Dorman's Stand. The rows of growing things. The ATH moving down, harvesting, its bulk and its roar. Roots being pulled from the soil. The smell of dirt and heat.

There was a lingering moment when Bogie tried to hold onto him even though Jack was finished and was attempting to pull away.

With a shuddering sigh, he broke contact, and saw the white-hot rays of first sun under the shop door. Half the night had gone in what had seemed a few moments. He stood. His injuries had stiffened and he moved to stretch them, carefully, mindful of the weeks of healing still to come. The gauntlet moved after him, curving for a grasp on his arm. Jack paused and let Bogie touch him, aware of the effort it took the sentience to animate the battle suit.

Let me feel the sun again.

Jack felt the wash of heat against the shop's garage door. "Feel it yourself." He braced his good shoulder against the equipment rack and shoved it across the begrimed concrete flooring, until they were up against the door. He palmed it open and heard the servos begin to whine.

As the door rolled up, Jack blinked. The sun, almost too harsh for human eyes, flooded his senses. He tugged the rack after him and wheeled it outside.

I never realized, Bogie said. Wonderment tinged his rough tones.

Jack felt the new day wash over him. Recent rains had cleansed the air somewhat. No brown tinge hung over the cityscape, cloying the horizon, and the pink tinge of sunrise had already burned away. It was not as beautiful as Dorman's Stand, or even as beautiful as Oceana had been, destroyed though it was.

But it was, indisputably, alive.

What a fool I was, breathed the alien sentience.

Beside him, Jack felt the sleeves move as, haltingly, Bogie held his hands up to the sunlight.

This is life.

It was not the celestial brilliance that had brushed him when he thought of bleeding Jack. But it was of the same stuff, and it flooded him, fed him, warmed him.

"Sunlight?" Jack said. "But you've been out in the sun—" he stopped short. What was different? Why did Bogie feel energized now?

They stood in the wash of the sun's rays. Jack still held the helmet in his hands. He reached over and screwed it down.

Almost immediately, Bogie gave a muted cry of frustration. The rending sound echoed in Jack's mind.

Gone!

Jack reached over quickly and took the helmet off. He grinned. "Not gone, Bogie. There's solars in the helmet . . . their job is to absorb the energy and channel it into the suit batteries. All you've got to do is learn how to tap into the circuitry. You've been doing it—I've got power drainage every time we go out, but what you're getting isn't solar energy. If that's what you need, there's no reason why you can't bypass the solars. We only need that if we're on extended field maneuvers. I'll work with you on the rewiring."

I can have the light.

"All you need. It'll just take a few days. Can you wait that long?"

His answer was a shout of fierce joy.

Amber waited until the sound of Jack's leaving had faded from the apartment and his warmth from the blankets before she got up. She would not sleep much more this night and there was no profit in tossing and turning. She dressed quickly, pulling on a dark blue jumpsuit and glove-soft leather boots. She had dreams of her own to pursue in the middle of the night. Raking a brush through her hair, she tied it back in a love knot and made a face at herself in the mirror. Soon, very soon, she'd show Jack what she could do. Then he would sooner leave his right arm behind than leave her.

Outside, the courtyards were half-illuminated by the security lights and she stayed in the shadows, working her way toward the training grounds. The closer she got, the harder her task got. New recruits swelled the facilities. Temporary dorms and lockers were being installed and Pepys had had a hundred acres of abandoned housing razed for a new obstacle course, just outside the wall of the old grounds.

Amber paused to catch her breath. The excitement of the deception set her pulse racing. It was a flaw in her, a fatal flaw, that she would always have to walk a tightrope, live on the edge, to have this feeling. Even loving Jack did not give it to her.

Excitement gave way to poignancy and she was standing there, hesitating, when a hand gripped her arm.

"Milady Amber. Out late, are you not?"

She looked up into the pasty white face of Vandover Baadluster. Her heart took a fluttering beat, then steadied.

"When I can't sleep, I walk."

"Understandable, but not wise," the Minister of War said as he steered her away from the shadowed outside walls. "The new recruits are many, and a rowdy bunch. I've been told rape is just as distasteful to a one-man whore as it is to a virtuous woman. I suggest you not make yourself a target."

His words took her breath away. She stood, momentarily speechless, feeling her nostrils flare in sudden hatred for the man. He sketched a bow. "Besides," he said, "we suspect sabotage. We've been monitoring activity and tonight have set a trap for the unwary Knight."

She kept her expression steady. "Sabotage?"

"There's been an intruder. He's been discreet and he knows the security systems well enough to bypass them, but there's no denying there's been unauthorized activity among the ranks. If we're very lucky, he's just an industrial spy gathering information on the armor for another manufacturer."

"And if you're not lucky?"

Baadluster pursed his thick lips. "Then we have a traitor on our hands. Commander Storm's latest reports show the Thraks have regressed to projectile weapons, a strategy unwarranted unless the enemy has made an extensive study of the armor."

A trap set for a traitor. Amber shivered as she realized she might have walked into it.

Vandover made a consoling noise at the back of his throat. "You have nothing to worry about, milady. But one would suggest a return to your apartment which is, undoubtedly, more secure."

She tilted her face slightly as she looked up at him. He knew that she knew that he meant he could not make any recordings off the security monitors. "Thank you, Minister Baadluster, for your concern."

"Not at all." He touched her again, a fleeting

gesture that stopped her in her tracks. The harsh dome of light accentuated his homely features even more, and his dark eyes were like burning embers. "You might reconsider the offer I made to you earlier. Commander Storm is in an awkward position, whether he acknowledges it or not. His friendship with St. Colin borders on treason itself and though we cannot associate him with the defection of Cadet Denaro, he does himself harm by thinking himself free of blame."

"Jack was not even on Malthen when Denaro went AWOL."

"No. But his induction of Denaro into the Knights borders on collusion. You are aware, are you not, that St. Colin had been ordered to turn the man over to Pepys for investigation of suspected treason? That the two of them instead buried the man as a recruit, knowing the emperor could not at the time afford the scandal such an investigation would cause. So that now, months later, Denaro has taken irreplaceable equipment and vanished. No, my soiled beauty. Your commander has not made wise choices in his career."

"Jack doesn't play your kind of politics!"

"No? Then what kind of politics does he play at? A Green Shirt perhaps? How do we know where he spent those seventeen years of his life?"

Anger made it difficult for her to breathe. She felt her eyes narrow. "Pepys has a fool for a Minister of War."

He stepped close to her. She could feel his heat as if it were an open flame. Her Bythian tattoos telegraphed danger to her, but she stood her ground.

"You have one chance," he told her, quietly but firmly. "And one chance only. And that chance is that Jack is as naive as he is brave. Tell me. Tell me of who he sees and what he does so that I may guide him in the months ahead, because, webbed lady—" His stare pierced her as if he could see the faint markings on her skin beneath her clothing. "—I am no fool and neither is Pepys, and you know that. Confide in me or Jack will be so tangled in the schemes of others that there will be no possibility either of you can survive."

She wished then, with all of her heart, that Hussiah had not taken from her the art of killing. If she had any way of shaping her thoughts into an arrow and aiming them into the core of Baadluster's being, she would do it. Him she would kill with even less conscience than Jack killed Thraks.

Baadluster read her expression and took a step back. "One day, milady, we'll meet again, and you will remember that I offered this opportunity to you, *and that you refused it.*"

"You give me nothing! I can't spy on Jack."

He bowed his head. "It is late. The grounds are secured. I suggest you return to your apartment. We have work to do here, and you are detaining us."

Amber turned on her heel and left as swiftly as she could without making it apparent she was fleeing him. She only had the satisfaction of knowing that Baadluster's trap would be empty tonight for it had been meant for her, and he himself had told her of it.

Later, in the cold bed, she curled up in the silken caftan she'd brought out of Bythia, and, feeling her skin crawl with mystic patterns, she cursed herself for having lost the ability to kill. Not only that, but as the patterns continued to fade, they took the last of her psychic talents with them. Soon she would have nothing left . . . nothing to bind her to Jack and Bogie. No weapon of her own to help them fight in their struggles to live. She had only her wiles left. And the clandestine training as a Dominion Knight.

Pepys was awake when Baadluster returned empty-handed. The emperor sat in his easy chair, sipping tea from a fine bone cup that was reputed to be over one thousand years old, and he did not refrain from a mocking smile even though Baadluster gave him a look indicating he wished, among other things, to smash that ancient cup.

"No quarry?"

"No. But we know there is trouble. Even Lassaday admits it, and Lassaday is Storm's man, as loyal a soldier as the commander has."

"There's no indication that the commander is involved."

"No."

"Good. Then let it be."

Baadluster glared at him. "Let it be? I have been reduced to catching spies and then you say, let it be?"

"The strike at Klaktut is far more important." Pepys put the teacup down and mopped his upper lip.

This brought a halt to Baadluster's ill-tempered pacing. The minister locked gazes with the emperor. "Then I can return to strategic planning."

"Of a certainty. After you place a call to Queen Tricatada."

Baadluster protested angrily, "We are winning, Pepys. You cannot throw it all away by telling the Queen we plan to hit one of her major nests!"

"No. No, I don't plan to tell her what we're doing." Pepys stood and smoothed down his clothes, preparing for a morning of judgment hearings. "With her embassies and consulates shut down, our network of information is greatly hampered. It appears that we both are under attack from a third party, and I'd like to know what she knows of that."

"A Thraks would never tell you."

"No." Pepys smiled. "Like anything else, Baadluster—it's what they don't say and how they don't say it that's really important. Go put in the call. When it's completed, come and get me from the chambers."

Vandover made a sardonic bow as Pepys left the room.

Chapter 27

The Rusty Bolt had changed little through the years of Jack's acquaintance with under-Malthen, except perhaps to get mangier. A sallow faced lump of a man smelling of *ratt* sidled through the privacy curtain and looked at Jack, the whites of his eyes gone yellow like a hard user with his liver about to give out.

Showing rotting teeth, the man said, "I'm supposed to say 'Ballard sent me.' " He put his hand palm up on the table and Jack pressed a hundred credit disk into it. The man looked at it, then pushed a small circuit card across the table. "That's for Amber. Ballard said she ordered it."

"Talk. I haven't a lot of time."

The man shrugged and his rotting teeth showed wider. "Neither have I, man. Ballard says you're supposed to hear about what happened to Washburn Industries."

"So tell me."

"Gone. Pulverized. Enemy incoming hit it, and internal explosives did the rest. I was supposed to be on shift, but I took a long lunch break . . . about two days earlier." The man shrugged.

"So if you weren't there, how do you know?"

"I wasn't there when it happened, man, but that doesn't mean I wasn't there. I got my scooter back in commission and reported back to work. Like, I was the first one to find the ashes. I got there even before the firemen. They had to come from half a continent away. Too hot otherwise."

Jack stared. The man had to be dead in his boots . . . and he knew it.

Another shrug. "Either this way or th' *ratt*. I prefer th' *ratt*."

"So would I."

The informant nodded.

"How did you get out? They must have cordoned off the area pretty damn quick."

"So fast I blinked and missed it. And then Washburn came in. Never saw him leave though. Heard he killed himself when they found his son's body in th' lower silos. His son's supposed to have been th' one let the shields down for the Thraks."

"Is that what you think?"

"No way. That kid was so straight, he was a real pain in the ass. Besides, I know better. I saw it."

"Saw?"

"That's right. It evidently hung around, scouted us before it left. I saw it planing over the Wide Windy . . . that's a desert area outside the defense state."

This was what had been hinted to Jack. He pushed a drawing over the table. "Like this?"

The sallow-faced man looked at it for a split second and shook his head.

Jack pulled another sheet from his short-jacket pocket. "Or this?"

Blackened nails tapped the second picture. "That's her." The man sniffled and rubbed at his nose. "Gotta go, all right?"

Jack nodded. The man stood. Jack hesitated and then pressed a second credit disk into his palm.

He looked at it. "Five hundred credits?"

"You earned it." That was enough money to buy enough *ratt* to O.D. The two men looked at each other levelly.

The second broke contact first, unable to meet the rainwater blue gaze holding him. "Thanks, man," he mumbled. "I mean it." He wove his way out of the Rusty Bolt and Jack watched him go.

The Thrakian ship he'd put aside immediately. The second drawing was a fairly accurate computer rendition of the unknown that had gotten Opus. So whatever had happened at Washburn Industries was known, only Jack hadn't been told about it. He was staging Operation Nest short of rifles and grenades, plagued with inexplicable back orders, and he wasn't going to be told the truth. Storm didn't have to worry about Baadluster or anyone else getting his hooks on the informer—he wasn't going to last any longer than it took him to get another load of *ratt*.

On the other hand, it was better than the lingering death that had been facing him.

Jack pushed his dirty glass aside, got up, and left the bar.

He traced the last of the tattooing over Amber's soft skin. She lay quietly under his touch, her eyes closed, not immediately responding to the news that he was leaving in the morning, news that no one had known for sure until an hour ago. Her pupils moved slightly beneath the transparent blue veining as she responded to his caress. *Even there*, he thought. *That snakeskin bastard had touched her even there*.

"How can you go, knowing that?" she asked, finally.

"I have to go. With Washburn dead, our backing in the Congress is very tentative. We have a 'probationary' war. It's the one thing I agree on with

Baadluster and Pepys. I have to show how effective we can be against the Thraks."

She arched her back as he drew his fingers down across her stomach, her loins and then her thighs. "You're being *very* effective right here and now," she murmured.

He slapped the flat of her stomach lightly. "You're upset."

"Of course, I am! Every time I take a deep breath, you're being taken away from me. And, dammit, Jack, you're making it harder to follow."

He smiled at her as he lowered his body over hers, pinning her to the bed, and she gasped a moment in pleasure, then thrashed her head to one side. "Don't you change the subject."

He began to move, very slowly, inside her. "I'm not," he said softly. "You are. I was talking sex."

He watched her bite her lip as he prolonged his movement.

"How can you go to war if you're not even sure who the real enemy *is?*"

He entered her again, deeply, and she took an intense breath. He kissed her. "I think," he said into her ear, biting her earlobe gently, "that this is a poor time to be discussing it. At the moment, I only care about who my *lover* is."

Amber sighed. He could feel the anger dissipate from the silken body cradling him. She wrapped her arms about his shoulders. "Who am I," she answered, "to disrupt peace negotiations?" And she pulled him closer.

Two weeks in hypnosleep with subliminal isometrics. No cold sleep this trip out. The engagement was too important. Cold sleep made them sluggish. Dull. Occasionally you'd find your best man was susceptible to cold sleep fever. No. Jack was taking no chances with any of his three ships this time. He was even going to allow himself to be put under after one last computer simulation. Operation Nest was too important to allow anything to interfere.

He ran the simulation through and sat, the illumination of the screen playing upon his face as he watched. Three thousand troops, though only five hundred of them were seasoned, but it was enough, and his Wings spearheaded the drops. Hit and run. A devastating blow to a major Warrior crèche. It worked. It was perfect. Jack sat back unhappily. Nothing in life was ever perfect.

Amber was the one with the psychic ability, but he'd never been one to discount the feelings he had from time to time. He couldn't put his finger on it. Maybe it was the unidentifieds that showed up from time to time, though he saw no way the assault on Klaktut could be tipped off. They would come out of hyperdrive, so close that a hair's miscalculation would mean disaster—turn the corner and they were *there*. The Thraks wouldn't even have a chance to react.

He sat back in the chair, searching through the meager memories Bogie had been able to give back to him. He found one and held on to it for a moment: his father, looking out the screened-in porch, while a field full of crops was being destroyed by clouds of hail. "It's like this, son," he'd said, and pulled Jack close. "You do all you can. Right fertilizers. Mineral balance. Natural herbicides. And then you plant and watch it grow. But sometimes, no matter how much good you do, something bad happens."

"What is it, Dad?"

"Flood maybe. Or brush fire. Or a plague of insects you can't possibly fend off. We call it an Act of God. Watch for it, Jack. It'll happen to you someday. All you can do is withstand it and get ready to start over."

An Act of God. Jack watched the computer simulation and wondered if it was too late to program one in and study the contingencies.

Unfortunately, there was no telling what kind of Act it would be.

Chapter 28

Jack stood wearily in the hallway. He'd not even been given a chance to bathe or get out of his armor. The stink of war and death hung palpably about him. Bogie throbbed against his shoulders and he thought, not for the first time, that soon there would not be room for the two of them inside the white armor. He carried his helmet in the crook of his left arm and his shoulder wound pulsed, a reminder that he had not completely healed. He looked down at the aide.

"Last time I was here, I spoke in appeal to a joint session of Congress. What's it called this time?"

The young man flicked a scornful glance at him, then looked back at the doorway for a signal. "It's called a Congressional Hearing," he said, briefly.

"Ah." Jack rocked back on his heels in fatigue. He dared not close his eyes. If he did, the nightmare might overwhelm him.

"Retreat! Retreat! Make your rendezvous point at all costs. Those Needlers are losing their asses coming in for you!" Jack cleared his throat, knowing his hoarseness made his commands bleed out over the com lines. Around him, the sky was rimmed with laser fire, an aurora borealis of war, and around him lay armor laden corpses that would never rise again.

A total rout. If he had not known better, he would think that the Thraks had known they were coming.

Three o'clock, boss.

Jack pivoted wearily and laid down a spray of fire. The tingling at his left wrist told him power was ebbing. Not expended yet, but he was at his last stand. It might not have been so disastrous with seasoned troops, he told himself. Perhaps.

A shuttle settled just out of his range, the land burned to obsidian glass, fused by previous landings.

"All right," Jack yelled. "Get on, quickly, that's it, let's *go!*" He watched the wave of soldiers making toward the shuttle, some running and others staggering, and a handful carrying comrades. He watched the horizon for a sign of incoming salvos, but the air was still and silent for now.

The shuttle filled, labored to a takeoff and was gone.

He took a deep breath. As long as he had power enough to fire and strength enough to stand, no one alive was going to be left behind. He no longer had any doubt that they had difficulty targeting him and when he returned, he would insist that norcite be glazed over every piece of armor in operation. If he returned.

Incoming, Bogie whispered in his mind.

"Hit the dirt, boys," Jack screamed.

The world splintered apart around him, but they missed the landing point, and another shuttle hesitantly hopped down.

He could hear Lassaday's guttural, "Hut, hut, let's move your asses or the Thraks will have 'em for you. Let's go!"

A glad noise shuddered through Jack. He had not known, until that moment, whether the sergeant was still alive. He got out, "You, too, sergeant, or I'll have your balls in a sling."

"Commander! That you, by god?"

"It is. And those were orders."

"Yessir!"

Jack braced himself. "How many more out there, sarge?"

"A hundred more, coming up the hillside. Let me stay out, commander . . . see if we can take some of . . . some of *them* with us. We've got room."

"No."

There was a flat silence on the com, then Lassaday said, "But, Jack . . . they're *human*."

"No. Not as far as they're concerned, Sarge. Now move it out!"

"Yessir." And this time, the belly of the shuttle muted the transmission and Jack knew the NCO had gone aboard the next to last shuttle out from this Thrakian hell.

It was not the sergeant's fault the new recruits had gone to pieces on their first mission.

Nor even Jack's.

No amount of war intelligence had mentioned or could have prepared them for the sight of Klaktut.

Jack had expected a sand planet, totally metamorphosed for the needs of the Warrior crèche. But Klaktut was not sand, except in those isolated nests. The rest of the planet was verdant, agraformed, domesticated. And humans were among the primary domesticated stock, facing the Knights dropped in for battle, staring as dumb-faced as any animal as the battle armor strode across their fields.

But that hadn't been the worst of it. As the fighting grew desperate and the Knights inexorably spiraled in to take out the major Warrior crèches, human flesh had formed the last ditch walls between the crèche and the invaders.

Jack could not blame the boys who'd signed on for honor and glory when they broke at the sight.

It filled his gorge also. He'd always been told the Thraks took no prisoners.

It redoubled his determination to get every Knight off Klaktut alive that it was within his power to do.

And, in the long run, only the retreat was a victory.

Jack thought, swaying with exhaustion as he waited in the corridors of Congress, that he would not even be allowed to savor that. Perhaps he should have allowed Lassaday to bring back one of *them* so that the inquiry he faced would have some idea of the horror of those days.

His stomach swam. He'd never made hyperdrive so fast, barely forty-eight hours after being docked with the shuttle. He'd slept the sleep of the dead in his armor. Luckier than some on board, who'd slept and not woken up . . . dying of their wounds, but at least not left behind to be buried in some alien soil.

Or worse.

It was naive of him, he reflected, to expect to be commended for his efforts. With Washburn dead, a major source of support for the probationary war was gone. Still, he'd beaten back the Thrakian attacks. It was only their initial invasion on the League's own turf that had gone sour.

The Congressional aide touched his armored sleeve. "It's time, commander."

He moved forward.

No applause this time. He heard dimly, as he moved forward, a muttering that followed him like a hungry and discontented mongrel, nipping at his heels. He moved to where another aide, a young lady who would not meet his eyes, indicated he should sit.

No podium. No telecast audience. As he sat and

looked across the chamber, he saw Pepys and Baadluster standing in the visitors' gallery, where they talked as if unaware he had entered.

A man stood. He had hair of silver and skin as dark as the void. When he stood, the room quieted.

"Tell us, commander, in your own words, what happened."

As he was still hoarse, Jack moved the mike sensors a little closer, and then he began to speak.

He told the truth. He did not play for sympathy or support. He thought, perhaps, that they ought to know that in war there would be winners and losers. But when he finished, when they had asked their myriad of questions, he realized that he was wrong.

It showed in their faces. They no more understood defeat than they had really understood his victory.

Jack swallowed painfully and hoped for an end to the questioning. He watched as Pepys took a seat on the dais.

"Thank you, Commander Storm. I yield the floor to Emperor Pepys of the Triad Throne, our noted ally and warlord."

Pepys stood. Jack was aware that there was movement to the rear of him, in the audience room doorway behind the dais, where he had originally waited months ago to make his appeal to the joint session. A cool breeze touched the back of his neck. His muscles stiffened. He winded a scent on the breeze, a smell of old enemies, and wished that he'd had time to take his armor off, or at least cleanse it of its stench.

"We can be thankful," Pepys said, "for Commander Storm's skillful handling of the retreat. We can be thankful, as well, for his quick assessment of the situation. As few lives were lost as possible. As for the invasion itself," and Pepys bowed his head,

"I will bear the hubris. It is mine and mine alone. And because it is, it is fitting that I am here today."

In a fog of exhaustion, Jack wondered what it was Pepys was leading up to. Why should he apologize for an offensive maneuver that could have, if successful, put a major dent in the Thrakian war effort?

"It is well, in these days of nearly instantaneous communication, that more sensible heads than mine prevail. While Commander Storm has been in transit to Columbia, a major decision has been discussed and reached. Congressmen and representatives, ladies and gentlemen. The past few days you have all seen and discussed the evidence that there is another aggressor in our space."

Jack lifted his head. *By god, he had told them!* Jack would have liked to have heard what was said, certain that he had not had all the evidence.

"I did not, therefore, refuse to discuss alternatives when first contacted by Queen Tricatada. I brought my reservations here and tabled them in these sacred halls where not only laws are made and upheld, but differences are met and melded. Because we kept open minds, we learned of the Ash-Farel, the ancient enemy of the Thraks, and the peril that faces us all."

The hair prickled at the nape of Jack's neck. He took a deep breath, and readied to turn in his chair as he heard footsteps behind him.

"Ladies and gentlemen. It is not only my wisdom but your own which has led us to this landmark moment. May I present our new allies and their representatives—Queen Tricatada, her warlord General Guthul who will become supreme commander of our allied forces, and the new second in command to Commander Storm, Admiral K'rok!"

As Jack staggered to his feet and stood, facing the Thrakian contingent, the huge Milot soldier stepped forward slightly and gathered him, armor and all, in an immense, furry, and smelly hug.

"I be glad to see you, Knight Jack," the Milot traitor grinned. "Now you be saluting General Guthul and I be saluting you!"

Chapter 29

The giant Milot dropped Jack back to the dais and stepped back, saluting smartly as he did so. The scent he had winded had not been his imagination and it threatened to overwhelm him now.

At Jack's back, the Congressional session had gotten to its feet, applauding. The sound was ironic to his ears; how many months ago had it been for him?

Behind K'rok, General Guthul stood, his mask horrific and dignified, and Jack had no doubt it was stylized with all the nuances of meaning a Thrakian war commander could arrange. Behind them, a lesser Thraks stood and Jack recognized the implants in the soft wattle of throat exposed by an inferior mask. An interpreter.

He then looked to the Thrakian queen. He'd never seen one before, nor any Thraks he could identify as female, though there must be many as the Thraks were incredibly prolific.

Did they even know the natural life span of a Thraks?

She stood, a brilliant and deep cobalt blue, irridescent wings coiled at her back, her body a pearshape meant for breeding. Her mask was streaked with color, although Jack could not tell if all the streaks were natural coloration or if some were cosmetic. Her height topped that of Guthul, making her a phenomenon even among Thraks.

She carried a scent, too, a dark and musky scent that stirred Jack for a moment until he realized he was responding to it. She stared at him, her faceted eyes like sapphire jewels, distinctly feminine—and totally alien. She trilled something and the interpreter stood forward.

"My queen says you have been a worthy adversary and now she hopes you will be an equally brilliant ally."

Jack inclined his head. He had been so worthy an adversary, he had scared the Thraks into suggesting alliance—and Pepys had been backhanded enough to accept! He closed his lips on any reply he might have made. He—all of them—had been betrayed. There was no answer he could think of to make to that. K'rok put an arm about him and drew him around to face the Congressional audience.

Quietly, in his ear, K'rok said, "My sorrows, Jack. This be a bad way to conquer an enemy."

Jack straightened in his armor. He put on a smile and answered back, out of the corner of his mouth, "I'm not done fighting yet."

Lassaday rubbed the dome of his bald head in frustration. "A week of alliance, ser, and them bugs have done everything but move into my bed! They've got more out of Pepys and the DC than if they'd beat the pants off us!"

Jack overlooked the parade grounds from the bridge, listening to his chief NCO vent his frustration. Lassaday was right. Not only were the Thraks back in the chief star lanes, and the inner planet trade lanes, but they were in the fleet and now Jack was expecting his first Thraks battalion to join the Knights. They were infiltrating with greater success than if they had conquered.

He didn't like it any better than Lassaday. Worse, it had been kept from public knowledge. Amber knew something troubled him, but had been unable to nag, wheedle, or even seduce it out of him. Pepys and the Dominion Congress planned to make a public announcement in another week, when all facets of the alliance had been sealed.

But Jack worried at it as if trying to get at the marrow. He knew of no fleet officers invited aboard the Thrakian vessels—the atmosphere and dietary demands "too complex" to allow that interchange. Thraks were more adaptable, they'd been told.

Nor had Jack had any of his officers assigned to League Warrior crèches. Again, humans were not compatible with Thrakian conditions. But he was expecting two dozen Thraks, hand-picked by Guthul himself, to arrive in less than forty-eight hours. Modified suits were to be molded to them and they were to be trained, if possible. When Jack thought of all the raw recruits and wounded Knights killed by dead man circuits to avoid just such an eventuality, his gut clenched.

Lassaday said, "Sir? Sir?"

"I'm sorry, Sarge, what was that?"

"I said, ser, that we've isolated that wing of the barracks like you told us."

Jack smiled at that. Amber had provided him with jammers, but she had nearly burst from the effort of trying to find out why. The Thraks would be unable to broadcast information unless they used official channels. He had no control over that, but he knew Pepys. The emperor might have sold out, but he had no intention of going around bare-ass naked in front of the Thraks. Pepys would be manipulating the official channels. Jack nodded. "We may have to have guests, but nothing says we have to make them welcome."

Lassaday saluted smartly and said, "I didn't hear that, ser!"

"On your way, sergeant."

Lassaday brushed past Amber and Colin on the way down. Sensing trouble from the purpose in the Walker's stride, Jack left the observation railing and went into the privacy booth.

Colin followed him in, Amber on his heels. She gave Jack a worried look and sat down in the corner to watch for intruders.

"To what do I owe this visit? Rawlins let you in again?" There was no point in telling Colin he'd breached some heavy security. The man had eyes and he'd probably seen for himself. If he hadn't, there was little doubt in Jack's mind that Amber had pointed it out to him. She sat now, with a faintly guilty look on her face, and he wondered if she'd disliked compromising him. He hoped so.

Colin sat down, folding his brilliant blue robes about him. Today, his miners' jumpsuit was a faded charcoal. To Jack it brought the grayness of Lasertown to mind. He had not thought of Lasertown much—it was as if the months of shanghai and enforced servitude had been pushed out of memory—but K'rok had brought it all back as if it had been yesterday. The Thraks had invaded the dead moon mining colony to take over the norcite mining operation as well as a Walker dig site. What he, Colin, and K'rok had seen embedded in the dead moon's surface before its destruction by Thrakian agents defied description to this day. Colin stayed silent, watching Jack's eyes, as though sharing in the same memories. He waited respectfully for another moment before speaking.

"We have a history together, you and I."

Jack smiled. "You must have some problem to start dredging all that up."

Colin smiled, too, a crooked expression that belied the age of a man edging past his prime. "It was a place to start."

"Why don't you start with what's bothering you?" Jack gazed out over the parade grounds. "My time here is short."

"What's going on? The base is locked down, and so is the city. I've been told by a few of my aides that the spaceport is all but impossible to get in or out of. Have we been beaten and nobody told us yet?"

Amber stirred. She put her chin up and pushed a wave of tawny blonde hair back off her shoulders. "He won't tell you. If he won't tell me, he won't tell you."

Jack wondered briefly why she hadn't used her psychic sensitivity to ferret out his secrets, but said to Colin, "No, but we might as well have been."

"I know some of it. I've been saying eulogies all week. The Knights took a beating. Almost half of them didn't come back."

Amber gasped. Jack looked at her. She hadn't known. He made a diffident gesture, not denying what Colin had said.

"What can you tell me?"

"You should be asking your old friend Pepys."

Colin snorted. "Pepys is as much an enemy as a friend. I had hoped never to say the same of you!"

"I can't tell you," Jack said, "officially." He made a movement that Amber understood. She got up and quickly checked the room's security screening. He waited until she was satisfied and sat back down.

"We didn't get beat in the war. We lost a battle, yes, badly, yes. But we didn't get beaten. We were sold out."

"What?"

Jack said bitterly, "It appears to be a trademark of Pepys. At any rate, we'd hurt the Thraks badly enough that they came to him with a suggestion of an alliance."

"An alliance?"

"Against the unknown aggressor."

As Amber made a noise of triumph, Colin appeared to deflate and sagged back in his seat. He put both hands to his face briefly, an eternal gesture of grief. It was touchingly effective.

Then he lowered his hands. "I should have known." He got to his feet and began to pace about the privacy booth. "I should have known."

"How could you? I didn't begin piecing bits together until after it had been done." And Jack told them about the disastrous drop on Klaktuk, and ended with the Thrakian League triumvirate's appearance before the Dominion Congress.

Amber had gone ashen. Colin stopped pacing, his tired face alert, as if he dared the years to slow him now.

"I never thought Pepys had that kind of nerve."

"He may not have any choice. You said we had history together. Well, so do K'rok and I, at Lasertown."

"He took over the mines. He used the Milot berserker to keep you laborers in line." That was Amber, her voice high and unsteady.

"More than that. He was as intensely interested in the Walker dig site as the Thraks were. He told me that, in his years as an officer after Milos had been conquered, he'd come to the notion that the Sand Wars began because a bigger, nastier enemy than the Thraks was pushing them out of their traditional breeding grounds. That they swept through our worlds because they were running from an enemy they couldn't beat. He was convinced an artifact from that enemy might be found on the moon."

"We found nothing," Colin said, "but the body of a beast."

"Maybe. Maybe not. K'rok disappeared while the site was being destroyed. I don't know what else he might have found or where he might have gone. I thought he might have been destroyed, too. But the Thraks gave their enemy a name: the Ash-Farel."

"So K'rok was right."

"I think so. He's been made my subordinate officer. He'll be my second in charge of the Dominion Knights."

Colin scratched his chin reflectively. "Do you trust this Milot?"

"Not as far as I can throw him which, even wearing a suit, won't be far. Since the Thraks have allied with us, they expect us to operate on the basis of 'an enemy of my friend is my enemy also.' "

"Convenient," Amber muttered.

"More than convenient. The attitude is the whole purpose of the alliance, I think. That, and the deep infiltration of the Triad and Dominion systems which they could never achieve before. When the wraps come off this alliance in a week, Colin—you'll think we've been invaded successfully."

"That bad?"

"Worse."

"Then I've come to the right man." Colin straightened. "You remember the report I showed you."

"Vaguely."

"I've got Denaro there starting the basics of a dig. We discussed it, and we discussed my fears regarding the operation. If we've allied with the Thraks, Jack, they've given no indication of it on the outer rim. We've been harassed to the point of open strafing. I came to ask you to send an independent detachment to cover my people before I have a slaughter on my hands."

Jack felt pain in his expression. "If you'd asked

me two weeks ago, I'd have had the authority. Now
General Guthul is over me. I'd never get orders
past him and Baadluster. How recent are your trans-
missions? Hostilities should have ceased."

"Oh, Jack." Amber sank down.

Colin shook his head. "I talked to Denaro last
night. The Thraks are bold and nasty, according to
him."

Jack spread his hands. "There's nothing I can
do."

Amber got to her feet and went to the door. She
paused at the portal and looked back over her shoulder. "The Jack Storm I knew wouldn't have let that
stop him."

He looked at her. The scorn on her beautiful face
pierced him. He felt it wrenching his gut somewhere just behind his navel. Hadn't he told himself
a variation of that ever since he'd left the dais on
Columbia without even an attempt to kill either
Tricatada or Guthul? He felt a spasm in his left
eyelid.

"There's more to it than you know, Amber."

"I know *you*," she bit off. "And I know that if
you have doubts over the Ash-Farel and the Thraks,
that they're well-founded. I have never seen you
hesitate to do the right thing, no matter how hard
or difficult it was. *Until now.*"

Colin put his hand on her elbow. "Amber, dear
heart—"

She shook him off. "Don't dear heart me! I'm
not your little street girl anymore! I'm a woman. I
sleep with him and I love him and goddamn it, I
can't even look him straight in the eye any more! So
don't tell me what to do. *Tell him.*" With a strangled sob, she bolted out the door of the privacy
booth.

Colin looked at Jack with a stricken expression.
"She didn't mean it."

Jack swallowed. It was difficult. He returned, "I think she did. And she's right. I don't have much time this afternoon because I'm waiting for a contingent of Thrakian warriors to come in. They'll be blended in with my Knights. I'm supposed to give them *armor*, for Chrissakes."

"I didn't know."

"No one does. I haven't even had the heart to tell the rest of my men yet. They died in droves on Klaktut. They saw things no one should ever have to see. And now I have to go and tell them that the enemy is now our ally." Jack broke off. His chest felt tight. He hadn't even worn his armor since they'd come back, unable to take the mental punishment Bogie had given him. Bogie felt that he'd surrendered on Columbia without even a fight.

But he'd told K'rok he wasn't finished. He just wasn't sure of the right time or place.

He looked at Colin and saw the Walker watching him. Watching him with a speechless pity etched on his handsome yet aged face. "Dammit, Colin, don't look at me like that!"

Colin shook his head. "Amber's right," he said, wonderingly, and made a move toward the door.

Jack said, "I could only send ten. And they'd have to leave tonight. No word, no warning."

Colin smiled. "I can pilot a corsair."

"What?"

He shrugged. "I'm a man of hidden talents."

Jack thought rapidly. A corsair was much faster than a needler—in and out of hyperspace—quicker because of its smallness. A thirty-man crew was its capacity. Ten or eleven of them, with armor and field packs, would equal that mass.

"And," Colin added smoothly, "I don't know about the alliance yet."

"No." Jack felt himself smiling in return. "You

don't. It would be difficult for me to withhold troop protection from you without telling you my reasoning."

"And," the Walker added, "you could go along to make sure diplomacy doesn't get out of hand."

Jack nodded. "Find a corsair and it's a deal."

"Good." Colin opened the portal. Amber stood beyond. She grinned. "When are we leaving?"

Chapter 30

To give her credit, she didn't look surprised when Jack answered, "There's no 'we' about it. You're staying here. We're taking a corsair. There's room enough for me and Colin and seven Knights."

She brushed her hair back from her face and said nothing as Jack pressed a button, then bellowed, "Lassaday! Get up here!" and turned back to her. "No arguments?"

She looked to Colin. "Even a saint needs a bodyguard."

The older man smiled wearily. "Ah, my dear. You've done a better job protecting this old husk in the past than I have—but I bow to Jack's decision. This is one trip it won't be easy getting back from."

"Since when has that ever stopped me?"

"Since now." Jack's eyes darkened and she stilled her tongue, knowing when she'd gone far enough with him.

Lassaday came panting onto the bridge. "Yes, sir?"

"What's the last word on our new recruits?"

"Th' bugs, ser, are in quarantine now. They'll be waitin' for pickup just after darkfall."

Colin said, "I'll go get ready."

Lassaday let him pass and looked at his commander with a quizzical expression.

"Can you get along without me for a few weeks?"

"With that stinking bear of a humanoid and those bugs?" Lassaday made a face as Jack looked at him, then said, "If I have to."

"Good. I need seven volunteers, a suicide mission, seasoned only—and men who can keep their mouths shut. And no one, such as yourself, vital to keeping a chain of command here at the center." Which, Jack reflected sadly, left out Lassaday, Travellini, and Rawlins.

"I'd give my right nut to go with you," Lassaday returned. He sighed. "When d'you want them?"

"We leave at dusk."

The sergeant crossed his bulky arms over his chest. "What's up, commander?"

"Our renegade Walker saint is about to embark on a mission which will seriously jeopardize our new alliance with the Thrakian League. Since I cannot reveal the treaty to him at this time, I have no choice but to accompany him in hopes of settling whatever grievances may occur without serious diplomatic breaches."

"Ah." Lassaday smiled widely. "I sincerely hope you get a chance to kick ass, ser."

"Me, too, Lassaday, me, too."

Jack looked the ground shuttle over. Colin sat next to him, muffled in a work jumper that neatly hid his Walker robes, which he had politely declined to remove in favor of being inconspicuous. Now, dressed as a port traffic director, he was in danger of being drafted to dock vehicles, but at least he was somewhat disguised.

The ground shuttle vibrated as seven Knights in full armor got aboard. Jack checked them out.

"Aaron."

"Sir!" His voice betrayed the tension his young face hid.

"Garner." No surprise there, the grizzled streetwise veteran hardly missed a chance to follow Jack into the tough spots. "Feeling fit?"

"Guaranteed, sir."

"Tinsdale."

"Sir."

"I asked for experienced men."

"I was a mercenary, sir. One of the few you missed when you took out General Gilgenbush's fortress satellite a few years back."

Surprise flooded Jack. Those were survival days when it was just him and Amber against the system. "Is this a grudge, cadet?"

"No, sir. I hate Thraks damn near as much as you do."

Jack had to live with his qualms. If Lassaday had singled out the man, Jack had to trust the sergeant.

"Maussaud."

"Sir."

No problem there. He'd gone to Bythia and back with Jack.

A lean Knight in deep blue armor sat. Jack didn't recognize the battle suit. He pointed. "Sound off, cadet."

"Skyler, sir." The voice was a trifle hollow.

"Experienced?"

"Lassaday sent me, sir."

Jack fought a smile. "All right then." He saw two gray suits move into the other bank of seats on the shuttle.

"Rodriguez, sir."

"And Patma."

Jack nodded to Colin. "There's our lucky seven."

The prelate returned a shaky smile. "Let's hope so."

And me you get as a bonus, Bogie remarked.

Jack looked down the back of the ground shuttle. "We're stealing a corsair. We're going in under the pretense of taking out the twenty-four Thrakian recruits who've been sent to us under the new alliance exchange program. That will get us in past security. What will get us out is keeping your cool and following my lead. Colin is unarmored. Protect him at all costs if any trouble breaks out. But I don't want any heroes. Understood?"

The affirmatives echoed. Jack put his helmet on. He sat down to drive.

WP security took a long look at Jack. Finally, he removed his helmet to look the man in the eye. The sentry was framed by needlers and corsairs at his back. Jack sorely wanted to walk over him and be on his way. "I was told quarantine was lifted."

The man shifted unhappily. "Yes, sir. You understand, commander, I have to be careful."

"I understand that you're holding us up. You've got the port screwed down and locked tight, but the longer you hold those Thraks bottled up here, the more risk you run that someone's going to see them. I got the impression we've been trying to avoid that." Jack leaned on what he knew of World Police procedure.

Unhappiness etched deep into the WP man's face. "You got that right, Commander Storm. And that one ton Milot is eating us out of the cafeteria. All right. Berth 41."

Jack eased back into the driver's seat and pulled the shuttle around the security post.

He waited until he was out of earshot before muttering, "Good. Berth 41 is out in no man's land."

Colin was scanning the printout Jonathan had given to him before leaving.

Jack looked over at it. "Where in the hell did he get that?"

The reverend looked up. "I don't think hell had a

thing to do with it. I don't know where Jonathan gets things like this. I just know he does." Colin tapped a plastisheet. "There's a corsair being reoutfitted in Berth 17. It's the best bet of five listed here. It's supposed to lift midday tomorrow."

"That means the crew is still out enjoying the sins and virtues of Malthen tonight. Sounds good." Jack checked the overhead map and steered toward Berth 17.

As he pulled toward the cradle where the slim silver form rested, a hairy black object lumbered in front of the shuttle. Jack hit the brakes, throwing Colin forward against the dash. His helmet went rolling on to the asphalt, and the form bent to retrieve it.

"Jack, my commander. I be thinking you'd never get here in time for dinner." K'rok grinned at them over the dash. Behind him, in the distance, a contingent of WP trotted, weapons up.

"Shit." Jack helped Colin up. "Make a run for it. They're after K'rok, but they'll stop anyone who looks suspicious. "Garner, the rest of you, let's go!"

The Milot paused. The whites of his eyes showed. "What be this?"

Jack took his helmet. He looked at his old foe and friend. "I don't think it would help you to know. We talked once, on Lasertown. I have the same doubts you do."

But K'rok nodded. "You are leaving?"

"I'm on escort duty, but I didn't have time to ask Guthul's permission."

"Nor did you intend to." The ursine form sighed heavily. "We have secrets, you and I. I have lived long under the Thraks. I have never been liking it."

Jack slapped K'rok's shoulder. "You run the Knights for me until I get back."

"I will. I be running a little interference for the Thraks, too." K'rok stepped back. He saluted.

But Jack was looking over the Milot's shoulder at the wing of WP guards which was now on the run. He slammed the Milot over even as laser fire pinged the ground shuttle's hood. K'rok hit the ground with a heavy thud and had the sense to lie still.

Jack put his helmet on as he ran.

Patma went down just outside the main lock. Jack vaulted his still form. He could see from the damage that he'd lost a man already. Even as he dove through the main lock, the corsair shuddered. Colin was powering up for launch. The lock closed on his heels as two of his men grabbed him and pulled him into the main corridor.

The irrevocable had begun. Ten days in hypnosleep, and then they would see what Colin's new world had to offer them.

The corsair slipped out of hyperspace and Colin sat back with a heavy sigh. "So far, so good."

"What are we looking for?"

Denaro's got coords pretty well set up. The norcite deposits are in the mountainous area I indicated to you earlier. And locals had superstitions about the regions."

"Locals?"

"Yes. None left. Colinada is a plague planet."

Jack sat down, feeling none too sharp after days of hypnosleep. "Colinada?"

"Denaro wanted to name it for me. I insisted it be feminine. A planet is a lot like a woman, I think. They all have hidden beauty and dangerous wiles."

There was a sharp movement in the cabin behind them where three of the Knights were up and about.

"What's this about a plague?"

"The locals were wiped out about forty years ago. The Dominion sent in their best anthropologists and xenobiologists, but the predominant mammals couldn't be saved. It's been quarantined ever since."

"And it was your bright idea to break the quarantine."

Colin rubbed the back of his neck before answering, "Actually, no. We became interested in it after the Thraks did. A few years after their survey, we made one of our own. Plague or not, after Lasertown and Bythia, I could hardly ignore it."

"Right." Jack slumped lower in the copilot's seat. A red panel went on. "Looks like I'd better get back in armor. And I want you in a deepsuit."

"When the time comes, I'll be ready."

Jack feel Colin's gaze as he left the control cabin. He barely had the suit sealed when he felt the first blow. The corsair rocked. Jack screwed his helmet on and ran forward.

Colin was getting hastily into a deepsuit. The instrument panel blinked, and Jack could see blips coming across a target grid.

"Shit."

"Amen," said Colin. "We're going to have trouble getting in."

Jack looked over the screens. "Not if you're any good at sewing."

"What?" The Walker stared at him in astonishment.

Jack tapped the target grid. "It's called 'Threading the Needle.' If you can do it, you'll get us past the Thraks."

Colin did a double take, then sat down. His hands shook slightly as he reached out for the controls, taking the corsair off automatic pilot. "This is a young man's game," he muttered. Jack stood behind him and finished sealing up the vacuum suit.

"You asked to be a player."

"So I did, heaven help me. Buckle down back there. This is going to be a little rough."

Colin was not normally given to understatement, but the corsair bucked and twisted. Jack swore and reached out to steady himself as the slender vehicle attempted to outrun and outmaneuver the immense Thrakian mother ships riding herd over Colinada's orbital approaches. He was uncertain whether the old mercenary offensive pattern would work . . . but it was better than no chance at all.

There was a high-pitched scream of metal and the ship shuddered violently. Colin thrust out, "Sweet Jesus, we've punched through!"

Jack twisted around.

"Damage?"

"In the tail section."

"Anybody back there?"

It was Garner's shaken voice that answered, "Not now. And the bulkhead's sealed off."

The five remaining Knights fell silent.

"Who'd we lose?"

"Tinsdale, sir."

Jack took a deep breath. An uneasiness lifted from his shoulders. He never wanted to lose a man, but he had not wanted to trust the ex-mercenary. "All right," he said.

The blue Knight got unsteadily to his feet, made his way across the corridor, and disappeared inside the toilet. A sound of retching followed his retreat.

The flight of the corsair smoothed considerably. Colin inhaled deeply. "I'm picking up Denaro's homing signal."

"Good. They're on our tail, reverend."

"What?"

Jack shook his head. "You didn't think it would be that easy, did you? And these are Talons. Keep it on manual and you can outrun them."

Colin mopped his forehead with the back of one hand, muttering, "And I thought I had faith."

Jack laughed. It was punctuated by an explosion and he had just enough time to grab his helmet.

Chapter 31

"All right, get your chutes on. We're going to take this just like a drop." Jack braced himself in the cockpit hatchway as the corsair shivered again.

Garner and Aaron had hold of Skyler's limp form between them as they dragged him into the corridor. Jack sized up the situation and decided they had it well in hand. Skyler's blue gauntlets twitched as he became semiconscious. "But, commander, this is—"

"No time to argue. We're breaking up. Get going!" Jack grabbed the two of them and steered them toward the belly of the hold.

Maussaud and Rodriguez needed no urging and fled past him. He reached out and stopped Colin in the passageway. "Where the hell do you think you're going? Get a chute on, you're dropping with us."

Colin smiled secretively. "We have some baggage on board we might want to take with us." He turned and trotted toward the forward hold.

This was no time to be touring the corsair, but Jack followed him. He stopped in the portal as a familiar sight met his eyes. "Holy shit. These fellas were gunrunners."

The Walker patted the casing of a mobile laser cannon. "Do you think you could hold onto one of these?"

Jack threw a chute at him. "You go first. I'll

follow." He bent and hefted the equipment. When the Talons came at them, he would have something slightly more effective than stones to throw at them. He caught up with the prelate. "Do you think Jonathan knew about this?"

Colin's voice was muffled as he stepped into the cargo hold, where Garner had opened up the bay doors. They were already so deep into the stratosphere that the ground below could be seen breaking through the cloud cover. "I wouldn't be surprised," he replied.

Garner and Aaron still held the unconscious blue Knight between them. "Commander, I think you should know—"

"Can you manage his chute between you?"

The two veterans nodded. Distracted, Garner looked up and sputtered, "What th' hell have you got there?"

Jack grinned. "Firepower. Altitude?"

Rodriguez was nearest the gauge. "Twenty thousand and dropping."

"How close?"

"Ten thousand should bring us closest to our original target area."

Aaron made a funny sound. Then he said, "How are we going to get off dirtside?"

"The Walkers have facilities here. They're just having a little trouble with the Thraks."

"Eighteen thousand."

The wind whistled into the open bay as the corsair plunged downward. Jack's armor grew cold. Bogie complained.

"There!" Colin pointed. An orange flare pierced the horizon. "Denaro's responding to my transmission."

"Fifteen thousand."

"Shit!" Garner broke in. His gauntlet pointed. Jack could see a brace of Talons outpacing them on each flank. Any man chuting down would be an easy target.

Jack put the laser cannon down. He reached into his equipment belt and pulled out a grenade. He keyed the firing sequence.

"Ten thousand."

"Go, go, go! I'll keep them busy."

Colin shuddered as Rodriguez and Maussaud pulled him out of the bay, their armor and his deepsuit arrowing into the high winds. Then Garner and Aaron went, dragging Skyler between them, who showed groggy signs of coming around.

Jack felt the chill inside the armor bite into his grin.

He tossed the grenade into the back of the hold, picked up the cannon, and jumped.

The corsair exploded into a fiery ball behind him, taking one Talon with it and sending the other into an out of control plunge. Jack wasted precious seconds freefalling to watch it go. Then, one-handed, he was very busy popping his chute and guiding it after the others. Much heavier than the others, he dropped like a rock. He was the first to see the third Talon sweeping in after them even as they approached the dissipating orange smoke of the flares. The Talon curled around them, and he could see the shots that took out Aaron and made Garner dance in the air like a broken puppet.

The warplane rolled in midair and swept around for a second run.

The ground came up fast. Jack braced himself and hit it running. He ripped off his chute so the ground winds couldn't carry him over. The rest of the chutes came tumbling down.

Rodriguez hit a cliff.

Then there was only Maussaud and Skyler ripping off their chutes and helping St. Colin to his feet. Jack felt his throat squeeze shut for a split second. Then he hefted the cannon and broke into a run to meet them.

Skyler's helmet had popped off and lay on the ground. The Knight hadn't bothered to replace it yet, too busy untangling Colin from his chute. The Walker's complexion had grayed, but he kept insisting, "I'm all right. I'm all right."

Amber didn't stop fussing over him until she had the chute off and could pat down the deepsuit for herself. The fierce ground wind of Colinada ripped at her long tawny hair, so Jack could not see the expression on her face as she turned when he joined them. The whine of the approaching ATV overrode his first words.

He didn't repeat them, but, instead, reached out and grabbed her in a fierce hug. She mumbled, "Garner and Aaron tried to tell you. I knocked myself out in the john. They must've put my helmet back on and dragged me to the bay. Shit, Jack. They didn't have a chance."

He curled his gauntlet and traced a gouge along her blue Flexalinked shoulder. "You didn't have much more of one." He swung on Colin. "Did you know about this?"

The prelate was hanging his helmet on his equipment belt. He looked up. "Cross my heart, I didn't," he said. With a devilish grin, he added, "I wouldn't be surprised if Jonathan did, though."

The ATV braked to a screeching halt in a hail of dust and gravel. Denaro stood up in full armor, broadcasting, "Here they come again!"

Jack panned the sky. He could hear the high-pitched whine of a Talon descending rapidly.

"Let's go!"

They hung onto the ATV wherever they could fit as Denaro ground the gears and put it back into motion. Colin said mildly, as they bucked across the wilderness, "How do you keep going?"

"We've gone underground. They strafe us daily, but we've got a fix on the site, your eminence. We may never get out of here, but we're going to see what it is they don't want us to."

"What about your ship?"

"Intact. But with them guarding the windows, it would be a suicide run to try to leave, sir."

Jack ground his teeth against a hard jolt, then said, "We'll have to see what we can do about that."

"What?"

He looked at Amber. "Lure the Talons in, damage them, then the mother ship will get mad enough to come close. I ought to be able to singe her a little with our contraband friend here."

Denaro looked back to see the cannon, then wrenched the wheel, narrowly avoiding a rather solid looking tree. Its lower branches whipped about the battle suits. Sparse forest gave way to outcropping, and Jack could see the sod-roofed underground installation. The ATV skidded to a halt.

Denaro reached for the cannon. "I'll take that."

In the flush of sunlight, Jack reached for the cannon, and Bogie stopped him.

Let him have it. The sentience wrapped around him, quelling the movements of his gauntlets.

Denaro looked at him, then took the cannon gently. "I'll get you the homing beacon."

Tell him it won't be necessary.

Jack could feel Bogie swelling along his shoulders. "What is it?"

It calls to me, boss. This is one of the memories I've been dreaming of. I know where it is.

The site on Lasertown had had its siren song, too, pulling unwary miners to their death trying to answer it. Jack hesitated.

Amber looked at them. "What is it?"

"Mutiny, I think." Jack swallowed. "Denaro, give me your armor."

"You can't ask him to make a stand without a suit!"

But the Walker militant was already stripping. He stepped out of the dark armor proudly, clad only in his trousers, and Jack was reminded of those moments on Harkness' freighter and of the young man who'd been undefeated even in that time of retreat.

Jack climbed out of his white armor. He sealed it back up and strewed the helmet on. "It's all yours, Bogie."

Maussaud scrambled back in shocked silence as the battle armor animated. Colin watched, his expression masked by the deepsuit helmet, as Jack's armor began to move. Its contortions were herky-jerky for a moment, then the suit walked off ten paces. It beckoned.

"God's balls," Denaro said, then flushed. "What have you got there?"

His elder pointedly ignored him. His helmet swung toward Jack. "Sentient computer run?"

"Not exactly. If we get through this, I'll try to explain it to you. Just take it that we need all the firepower we can get, and he's a big boy now." Jack stepped into Denaro's suit, the only armor big enough to accommodate him.

Amber unscrewed her helmet and popped out a small circuit board. "Synthesizer," she said as she palmed it. "So you wouldn't recognize my voice." She went to the opalescent battle suit, took off the helmet and installed the card. She talked for a few minutes and Jack wondered if she was explaining to Bogie how to utilize the circuitry. She screwed the helmet back and stepped away.

"Follow me," said Bogie within the armor. His voice was not the deep, grating voice Jack knew, but basso profundo, melodious—and joyful.

The Talon swooped over them.

"Get out of here," Denaro yelled, and dragged the cannon into position by the outcropping that hid the Walker installation. Maussaud hesitated, then said, "I'm staying here, commander."

Jack nodded. "All right."

They ran after Bogie.

It was like running after a child who'd just begun to walk. As they approached the hills, Bogie gained ability. He stopped only once, to spread his gauntlets as if drawing down the sun's rays to him.

"What's he doing?" Amber asked, her voice breathy as she tried to catch her breath.

"Refueling, I think."

Colin said nothing, but went to one knee, with his head bowed. Jack could hear him gasping over the com lines."

"This is no time to pray," Amber said, and tried to help him up.

The older man shook his head. "You've got power suits. I've got nothing. Forgive me, Amber, but I'm still an old man."

She looked at him in shock, then began to strip the vacuum suit off.

"What're you doing?"

She met Jack's stare. "It's no protection to him now! It's just weighing him down. And this way, we won't have to carry him as soon."

There were dull explosions in the background. As Jack pivoted, he saw the golden lance of the laser cannon's reply. The Talon veered off sharply.

Colin coughed. "It had better be worth it."

They looked over the horizon. They'd come up a steep incline of shale, and now looked out over a meadow lush with spring grasses and tiny yellow flowers. Bogie began to stagger down the slope, heading toward the mountain facing on the valley's far side.

"I'm here!" he cried out.

Jack reached for Colin's elbow and Amber took the other side as the air thundered over them. The three of them looked up. The Thraks were determined that this discovery not be made. If Denaro failed to hold the enemy, all of them would die here in this valley. They ran as the white armor ahead of them fetched up against a wind and rain exposed cliff, with eons of time written in its stratas.

Bogie scrabbled away at the sod and rock until he found a fissure, then tore at it with his gauntlets. The cliff face peeled away as though it had been chiseled to do so, in one slab which went to dust and pebbles at the battle armor's feet.

Amber caught her breath, but it was Colin who murmured, "Good God Almighty."

The white armor froze for a moment, its glove curved over the monstrosity exposed by the soft ground.

"What is it?"

"It's what we saw on Lasertown," Jack told Amber. "At the digging site, before it was destroyed."

Bogie's curved gauntlet fell downward in a gentle caress over the mummified being. A sound came over the suit mikes, a sound Jack had no other word for but *wail*, yet it was short and smothered.

"It called to him," Colin said. "Just like the dig site at Lasertown called to so many unfortunates. Even after death. Even these hundreds, maybe thousands of years later." He turned to look at Jack. "What is that inside your armor?"

"A gift from Milos."

A hissing intake of breath. "Berserker?"

"No . . . I don't know. I don't think so, but whatever it is, it's regenerating itself from a square of hide, a chamois, inside my armor. It's a small bit of flesh, but it thinks—and cares."

"And interacts with your circuitry."

"That, too."

"Alive," Colin murmured. "And aware, and called." After a slight hesitation, he moved forward to touch the mummified creature himself. Bogie's gauntlet went out as though to stop him, and then fell back.

It was saurian. No doubt of that . . . the skin retained its scaly pattern even through its crust of age and dirt. It looked upward, as though destruction had rained from the sky, catching it unawares. The head was broad, the eyes like a horse's . . . no sight directly to the front or rear, but well-set for vision otherwise. The teeth, bared in a death grimace, were sharp at the corners but well rounded otherwise. Colin touched them.

"Not carnivorous, at least, not strictly. These are for grinding, not tearing. Look at the hands."

For hands they were, not paws or toes, fully exposed as the find reared up.

"Bipedal?" Jack said and moved forward, as drawn by the beast as Bogie and Colin were. Amber stayed on point, watching the scene over one shoulder.

"It looks as if he was. And look at this." Colin reached for something wedged in the dirt, something held in the hand on the far side. It came loose easily from the beast's fingers.

"It's a nonbiodegradable polymer satchel."

Amber made a faint noise. Jack grinned. "It's a plastic bag," he told her.

She mouthed an indistinguishable curse.

Colin held it in his hands for a moment. Jack saw that they trembled. He looked up at Jack.

"Should I open it?"

"And have what's inside disintegrate when the air hits it?"

"Maybe. Maybe not." The Walker looked out over the hills, toward the reddening sky. "We may never get away from here to open it under better conditions."

Amber muttered, "Just seeing it may have to be good enough for you. Jack, I'm picking up blips on the long-range target."

"ID?"

"Not yet. We're out here in the open."

Bogie mobilized then. With movements almost too swift to follow, gauntlet fingers chiseled out the body and he lifted the fragile remains in his arms. "Boss, let's get out of here."

"You can't take that with you!"

"I feel him in my mindsong. I was meant to come here, to find him, to bring him . . . home. Jack—" and Bogie held out his arms, pleading.

The mummified form seemed to shift in the cradle of Flexalink sleeves. Jack sensed it and lunged forward too late. The mummy began to cave in upon itself, dust unto dust, ashes unto ashes, and rained through Bogie's helpless fingers as the sentience cried.

He did not stop until the mummy had finished disintegrating and was nothing more than particles upon the ground. Bogie stood still, his arms outstretched toward Jack.

"I'm sorry, Bogie. The exposure . . . it wasn't meant to be."

Amber said, *"Jack."*

Bogie turned his gauntlets over, emptying dust from his palms.

Then Jack added, "Your helmet cameras recorded the find. We'll have pictures, at least."

Then Bogie spoke, from the hollowness of the armor he inhabited. "At least," he echoed. He looked up. "Amber is right. We've been targeted."

Jack felt the rumbling then, a deep subsound that prickled the hairs on the back of his neck. A rumbling like the one that had awakened him in the

middle of the night when warships firestormed
Claron. Or the rumbling a soldier hears just before a
drop of enemy troops. By the time the sound became fully audible, it would be too late.

"Shit."

He grabbed Colin by the elbow. "It's time to
think about getting out of here."

Amber loped by them, her armor glinting in the
first blue rays of sunset. "Past time," she muttered.

Bogie shadowed Jack. "Boss, I'm getting three
blips. Two gunboats and a third, much larger ship."

The broken terrain made any speed difficult. He
kept a hand out to Colin's elbow as the older man
stumbled now and then, and a too bright flush
pinked the prelate's face. His thin fringe of chestnut
and gray hair ruffled in the wind, and he puffed a
little as he endeavored to keep up with Jack. But
the Walker kept a death grip on his plastic bag.

He could hear the sky's envelope giving way to
the gunships that were streaking in. Colin staggered
to a slow jog.

"Don't stop now."

"How far?"

"Far enough." Jack looked over the hillocks. He
said to Bogie, "Which ones are going to reach us
first?"

"The third ship, at this rate."

He stooped and looked up. "Then I think we're
going to be okay." He pointed as the Ash-Farel
swept over and the Talons disintegrated in its wake.
His shout of welcome was swallowed by the thunder
of its passage. He frowned then.

"How did you know?" Amber breathed

"I didn't," Jack answered her. "And I've changed
my mind. We may not live to tell the tale."

Chapter 32

He thumped Colin on the shoulder and grabbed Amber by the elbow. "Run for it. We need to get as far underground as possible."

"What is it?"

He took off his helmet and hung it from his equipment belt. Denaro's armor fit him well, but he didn't wish to meet Colin's gaze through the sunscreen darkened visor. "Curse me for a farming boy—Amber's right. I'm too thickheaded to play these games. We're just part of the bait in a trap."

Overhead, thunder rumbled, but the sky did not smell of rain. Soon, it would stink of battle. The three of them, tailed by a shambling Bogie, began to walk out of the valley.

"I don't understand," Colin said, between gulps of air.

Jack shook his head. Sweat had been trickling down his brow and now drops flew into the air. "I wondered why the Thraks kept you pinned down here instead of just blasting you off dirtside. This is a plague planet, after all—not too many people would even know you'd been here." He took Colin's elbow to ease the older man's efforts. "They were waiting to see who would show up."

"They wanted you."

Jack smiled wryly at Amber. "No . . . in fact,

they're probably disappointed I came in so quietly. I'm willing to bet they figured I'd come in force, warmonger that I am."

They paused on the crest boundary to the valley.

"What they wanted was a tremendous battle—what they wanted was to attract someone's notice."

"Whose?"

Jack pointed overhead as thunder drummed. "The Ash-Farel." A lightning strike obscured his next sentence, but it was not a natural phenomenon. With a curse, Jack grabbed both Colin and Amber and threw them down, protecting them with his body. He was aware of Bogie joining him, and then the heavens split open.

Afterward, he would curse himself for not leaving his helmet on—but his deafness was matched by Colin's as they shouted back and forth and tried to explain. Then, all he knew was that the sky went white-hot, and the air burst as the ships came streaking in over them.

It had been a trap, and a well-laid one. The golden ship of the Ash-Farel had little chance as the Thraks streaked in and crippled it. They harried it across the horizon and Jack watched sadly as the ships disappeared. The Thraks would not even give the Ash-Farel a mercy stroke.

Tears from the brilliance of the fight streaked Colin's dirty face as he lifted his chin to peer after them.

"Why," he said. "Why don't they finish them off?"

"They want it down," Jack said. "They want it down and cracked open like an egg."

"Why?"

Jack looked toward Amber. "The Thraks want to know what it is they're fighting. They're taking prisoners and gutting that ship for all the technology they can get their claws on."

"But—" her tawny hair swung about as she looked back in puzzlement. Bogie crawled back and lifted her to her feet.

"I think we'd better hurry," Jack said, his voice gone hoarse. "They bought us a little time. Let's hope it's enough." He sacrificed further explanations for speed as he called ahead. And when they got there Denaro had the dig corsair waiting in a launch silo.

The Walker holding of Farseeing was comfortable and homespun. They were welcomed as honored guests and soon forgotten in the fervor that surrounded Colin's presence. Amber found Jack quartered in the men's wing, packing to leave on the second day after their arrival.

"Rumor has it the Thraks have extended an apology to St. Colin for their grievous actions." She dropped down on his cot. "I still don't understand. The Thraks are our allies now, but you acted as if you thought the Ash-Farel were there to help us."

"Perhaps they were."

"But they've attacked Dominion colonies, too."

"I think they're attacking war efforts, whosoever they belong to."

She tilted her head. "Maybe. And so the Thraks found the norcite dig—"

"A site which has been known to attract Ash-Farel attention before—"

"And created a disturbance big enough to bring a warship in—"

"And sprang their trap. We, of course, got an apology. The Thraks are our allies, after all, and had no intention of harming us. We merely . . . got in the way while they were repulsing the enemy."

"They must have had this planned even before the treaty."

Jack nodded. "Having an alliance just made them do an extra little dance to explain themselves."

She shrugged. "And speaking of explanations, how do you plan to explain that?" Amber said, nodding her chin toward the fully animated Bogie.

"I don't."

She tossed her head, sending her tawny hair in ripples over her shoulders and down her back. She was dressed in borrowed clothing, the modest blouse and long, full skirt of the Walker women. The colors of the Blue Wheel sect suited her. "Come on, Jack. You can't just explain away fully automated, fully powered battle armor. Robots we've got, but sentient computer-grounded war machines, no. They've been banned. And you can't tell anyone the armor's inhabited. The xenobiologists will go crazy trying to dig him out, like he's some kind of oyster."

Jack raised an eyebrow and her torrent of words came to an abrupt halt as she realized why she had caught him packing. "Oh, no," she said. "Oh, no—not without me this time. You're not leaving me again!"

He grabbed her shoulders. "I have to, Amber. Where I'm going, you won't be able to follow. I can't take you and I don't want to have to worry about you."

Fear muddied her golden-brown eyes. "What are you going to do?"

"I'm going to desert. I'll be taking my suit and Bogie with me."

She went limp between his hands and only his strength kept her upright. He held her as though his very life depended on it. "You have to go back. You have to watch Pepys and Baadluster for me. And I have to go."

Baadluster scared her. "But why?"

"I think we're fighting the wrong enemy. And I have to know if I'm right, and if I am, I have to be able to bring back proof."

Bogie added, "And I must follow my mindsong." The synthesizer gave depth and sorrow to his basso voice.

Amber straightened. "What about Colin? He's never been more at risk."

"I know. And that's another reason I'm leaving you behind." He loosened his grip on her and ran the knuckle of his index finger along her jaw. "You'll have to fight the part of the war I can't."

She tilted her chin up as though it would stop the flow of tears brimming in her eyes. Baadluster would hound her, perhaps even imprison her, but she couldn't let Jack know. She would not be responsible for stopping him.

"I'll try," she answered, her voice barely above a whisper. "Where are you going?"

"That I don't know yet. It's better if you don't know, anyway."

She nodded. The tears splashed down in spite of her efforts. She raised a hand to dash them away. "Dammit. I've become a regular shower since I met you!"

He lifted her chin back to its customary insolent tilt. "No," he said softly. "You've become a beautiful woman."

A shiver ran through her, but she lifted her face away from his touch and glared at the white suit behind him. "You!" she called. "If you let anything happen to him, I'll rip you out of there and throw you in the deep freeze!"

Bogie just laughed, a deep rumbling sound. "Yes, ma'am," he said and saluted.

"How will I know how you are? How will you contact me?"

Jack looked at her. "That's up to you. You've kept your power shuttered ever since Bythia . . . but it's the only way we'll be able to keep in touch. You're going to have to reach out for me and hope you find me."

"Telepathically? Not over those distances." Her tremors reached her throat and spasmed her muscles, threatening to shut away all sound. Hussiah had not only taken away her ability to kill, he'd taken away her ability to reach out to Jack. "I can't—" Her voice failed her, as she'd feared.

He saw the doubt in her eyes. "Then you'll have to trust me, Amber. You'll have to trust me that no matter where I am or what happens to me, I'll come back to you."

She denied him, shaking her head.

He nodded then, and reached out, pulling her roughly to his chest where she could hear the thumping of his heart. "We have to believe it," he promised. "I'm going to fight this war and I'm going to win, and then I'm going to come back to you for good. Nothing is going to stop me. Nothing."

DAW

NEW DIMENSIONS IN MILITARY SF

Charles Ingrid
THE SAND WARS

He was a soldier fighting against both mankind's alien foe and the evil at the heart of the human Dominion Empire, trapped in an alien-altered suit of armor which, if worn too long, could transform him into a sand warrior—a no-longer human berserker.

☐ SOLAR KILL (Book 1)   (UE2209—$3.50)
☐ LASERTOWN BLUES (Book 2)   (UE2260—$3.50)
☐ CELESTIAL HIT LIST (Book 3)   (UE2306—$3.50)
☐ ALIEN SALUTE (Book 4)   (UE2329—$3.95)

W. Michael Gear
THE SPIDER TRILOGY

The Prophets of the lost colony planet called World could see the many pathways of the future, and when the conquering Patrol Ships of the galaxy-spanning Directorate arrived, they found the warriors of World ready, armed and waiting.

☐ THE WARRIORS OF SPIDER (Book 1)   (UE2287—$3.95)
☐ THE WAY OF SPIDER (Book 2)   (UE2318—$3.95)

John Steakley
☐ **ARMOR**

Impervious body armor had been devised for the commando forces who were to be dropped onto the poisonous surface of A-9, the home world of mankind's most implacable enemy. But what of the man inside the armor? This tale of cosmic combat will stand against the best of Gordon Dickson or Poul Anderson.

                               (UE2368—$4.50)

DAW

DAW Presents the Fantastic Realms of
JO CLAYTON

DAW

C.J. CHERRYH
THE ALLIANCE-UNION UNIVERSE

The Company Wars
- [ ] DOWNBELOW STATION — (UE2227—$3.95)

The Era of Rapprochement
- [ ] SERPENT'S REACH — (UE2088—$3.50)
- [ ] FORTY THOUSAND IN GEHENNA — (UE1952—$3.50)
- [ ] MERCHANTER'S LUCK — (UE2139—$3.50)

The Chanur Novels
- [ ] THE PRIDE OF CHANUR — (UE2292—$3.95)
- [ ] CHANUR'S VENTURE — (UE2293—$3.95)
- [ ] THE KIF STRIKE BACK — (UE2184—$3.50)
- [ ] CHANUR'S HOMECOMING — (UE2177—$3.95)

The Mri Wars
- [ ] THE FADED SUN: KESRITH — (UE1960—$3.50)
- [ ] THE FADED SUN: SHON'JIR — (UE1889—$2.95)
- [ ] THE FADED SUN: KUTATH — (UE2133—$2.95)

Merovingen Nights (Mri Wars Period)
- [ ] ANGEL WITH THE SWORD — (UE2143—$3.50)

Merovingen Nights—Anthologies
- [ ] FESTIVAL MOON (#1) — (UE2192—$3.50)
- [ ] FEVER SEASON (#2) — (UE2224—$3.50)
- [ ] TROUBLED WATERS (#3) — (UE2271—$3.50)
- [ ] SMUGGLER'S GOLD (#4) — (UE2299—$3.50)

The Age of Exploration
- [ ] CUCKOO'S EGG — (UE2371—$4.50)
- [ ] VOYAGER IN NIGHT — (UE2107—$2.95)
- [ ] PORT ETERNITY — (UE2206—$2.95)

The Hanan Rebellion
- [ ] BROTHERS OF EARTH — (UE2209—$3.95)
- [ ] HUNTER OF WORLDS — (UE2217—$2.95)

NEW AMERICAN LIBRARY
P.O. Box 999, Bergenfield, New Jersey 07621
Please send me the DAW BOOKS I have checked above. I am enclosing $_____
(check or money order—no currency or C.O.D.'s). Please include the list price plus
$1.00 per order to cover handling costs. Prices and numbers are subject to change
without notice. (Prices slightly higher in Canada.)

Name _____

Address _____

City _____ State _____ Zip _____
Please allow 4-6 weeks for delivery.